BITE OF BETRAYAL

BLOOD OATH
BOOK TWO

R.L. CAULDER

WHITE RABBIT PUBLISHING

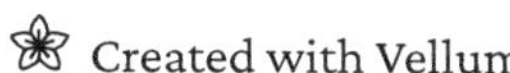 Created with Vellum

CHAPTER ONE
DRAKE

She was here.

My mate.

My Queen.

What should have felt like the most profound moment in my life—one punctuated with an overwhelming feeling of gratitude—was not shaping up the way I'd always pictured it to be.

I'd finally found my true mate, and yet...she was attempting to kill me by viciously trying to dig both her sword and dagger into my neck, while soaking my shirt with tears.

"Fated mates can never kill each other, Alina," I breathed out, confusion over her question and demeanor bleeding into my tone.

Initially, I'd felt like the luckiest vampire in the world to have finally found my Queen. It hadn't even phased me when Estrid announced that she was a Van Helsing, although the irony hadn't escaped me that a slayer was my fated mate.

Her dagger clattered to the ground beside us, all the fight seeming to seep out of her as her body relaxed on top of mine. A shaking sob wracked her body, and defeat curled her shoulders inward in a way that I felt profoundly in my gut. Brushing my thumb across her cheek, I forced down the growl burbling in my throat from spilling over my lips, swallowing the emotion I felt at the sight of tears falling from her eyes. I should be the one to ensure she never feels the need to stain her cheeks with such emotion, yet I couldn't help the sinking sense of dread that I was the one who put them there.

"Alina?" I questioned softly, not wanting to alarm her but desperate to understand and console her. It was unbearable seeing her in such pain and not knowing why or how to fix it.

What had I done to cause her such grief? It wasn't mere sadness I saw lurking in her bright crimson eyes. No, there was a deep, burning hatred...for me.

"Alina." Her name fell from my lips with a

ragged breath as I grappled with the grief and happiness rolling through me in confusing waves. "Please tell me—".

My plea cut off as her face morphed into a deep scowl once more and she drew back her hand. While I could have easily stopped her fist from cracking against my cheek, I decided to let her get one good shot in. Perhaps if I allowed her to assuage her thirst for violence, she would calm down enough to see reason.

Through the inky haze of confusion, something deeper swirled within me—Alina's tenacity and fire were alluring, calling to the deepest parts of me as the Fates showed me the Queen they had gifted me. She was not a timid woman, and I was so thankful for that. With my title and power came thousands of vampires throwing themselves at my feet with the promise of fulfilling all of my wants and desires. The simpering behavior disgusted me to my core, and I'd prayed to the Fates to offer me a mate who would challenge me and make every day an adventure.

I suppose they'd granted my wishes. I just hadn't expected our first adventure to be...her attempt at murdering me. It would seem I should have been careful about what I'd wished for.

Feigning my head snapping to the side as her fist

connected, I hoped it looked believable to make her feel proud of herself. I pulled back as much as possible while upholding the ruse, wanting to soften the blow to her precious hand. If I'd stayed still, the impact would have certainly crushed all of her bones.

"Fuck you," she seethed down at me, baring her small fangs in an adorable attempt to look menacing.

Now was *not* the right time to mention how cute I found her baby fangs to be, not while I was trying my damnedest not to grind my cock up into the soft curves pressing against me. I'd been alive for a long time, and while I didn't know everything, I didn't doubt that she would attempt to cut my favorite appendage off if I gave into my baser urges.

While I appreciated her sensual body, I'd been too enraptured by her large doe eyes and plush lips to focus on anything else until she'd been lying atop me. From the moment I'd entered the room and her lips parted with a deep inhale, all I could think about was how fucking great they'd feel wrapped around my cock.

In due time.

"Darling," I murmured, straightening my head

to glance up at her once more. Her chest heaved with her uneven breathing, and I could feel her heart beating erratically with each ragged inhale she took, pressing her chest closer to mine. "Can we please halt the violence to talk about this?"

After all of these years spent facing the world alone, wondering why I'd never been blessed by the Fates with a mate, my heart had practically jumped out of my chest the moment I laid eyes on Alina. The bond would have to be confirmed by exchanging blood, but my soul knew. She was mine, and I was hers. Forever.

Given her state of shock, I assumed she had sensed who I was to her, just like I had when I saw her. I'd thought she was playing hard to get by not acknowledging the simmering connection after the room had emptied. Before I'd had the chance to bring it up, she'd launched herself at me with a blood-bound weapon she'd conjured, so perhaps not.

Inhaling sharply, her eyes widened as she shouted, "Stop the violence?! This is a fucking joke from the universe that *you* are the one saying that to me, right?"

Rather than responding, I tracked the way her

shoulder bunched in the moment before she pulled her fist back once more. As she let it fly toward my face, I darted my hand out with ease and stopped her. Wrapping my hand around her petite one, I raised a brow at her. A scowl marred her face with her determination, her arm shaking as she tried to push against me.

"No more," I said, voice tight as my patience began to run thin.

This was nothing more than child's play. While I found myself enjoying her spunk, there were far more important issues rising between us that needed to be addressed. Her frenzied emotions were concerning, and I needed to understand where it was all stemming from.

She'd sworn vengeance for the slaughter of her family, yet I was unaware of an attack on the Van Helsings. I'd start there, if nothing more than to get her to stop attacking me like a vicious, feral creature.

Her free hand darted to grab the dagger resting near my head, but I grabbed her waist and flipped her beneath me in a flash, easily cocooning her smaller frame. Grabbing the hilt of the dagger, I tossed it into the far side of the room, waiting to hear it thunk into the wall before I turned my attention back to my infuriated mate.

Alina now knew that she couldn't kill me, but based on what I'd seen thus far, I wouldn't put it past her to attempt to hurt me in various other ways with that pesky little weapon.

"Alina!" I growled as she gnashed her teeth and bucked her body wildly, trying to throw me off of her. Grabbing both of her wrists in one hand, I held them above her head with ease, using my hips to pin her down. With my free hand, I grabbed her chin to draw her focus to my face. "It is my duty as your mate to ensure your safety and happiness. I can't do that if you won't talk to me or explain what has happened!"

Finally, her body stilled, but my relief was short-lived. Tears sprung into her eyes, throwing me completely off with her drastically changing moods as she muttered, sarcasm dripping from her tone, "Explain what has happened? You orchestrated the murder of my entire family, ordering me to be turned into the very creature I swore to protect the world against."

Despite the bite of sarcasm in her voice, she spoke softly, and vulnerability shone in her eyes as they faded into a stunning deep blue. As the red left her irises, the way she stared up at me, hopeless and bereft of joy, I felt fucking broken. She believed every single word she uttered though none of them were true.

Her tongue darted out to lick her lips, wetting them before she huffed out a lifeless laugh and shook her head the best that she could with my grip on her chin. Vitriol dripped from her tone as she continued, "And on top of that shit sundae, I can't even complete my blood oath to get vengeance for their deaths by killing you because *apparently you're my fucking mate.*"

For the first time in my long life, I was left speechless, staring down at her as turmoil tore my gut apart. How was I supposed to convince her of the truth of the situation, when every fiber of her being screamed with the conviction of her words?

She wasn't fighting me anymore, body completely still as she stared at me, hopelessness filling her eyes as she sagged, a lone tear streaking down her cheek to soak into her silver hair. Her words were hardly a whisper as she closed her eyes, quietly admitting, "If I can't kill you, there's no point in living. Kill me."

I'd never experienced such profound grief as I did the moment the request fell from her lips.

My hand splayed over her chin, fanning across

her cheek as my voice grew gruff with my own heartache. "Please, don't ever say such a thing," I pleaded, voice cracking as my eyes grew damp, a feat that I didn't think my body capable of doing any longer. "I have waited a millennium to find you, Alina. Even if I was able to, I could never bring myself to harm you. You are the most precious thing in the world to me now."

Her throat bobbed, jaw tightening as her eyes popped open, burning with fire once more. "You've already hurt me. I suffer every day with the memory of seeing my family members dismembered and strewn about our manor. Each time I close my eyes, I'm tormented by the way my mother pleaded with me to kill her, so she wasn't turned by the venom coursing through her veins..." she trailed off before taking a shaky breath. "And even worse, I hear the cries of my best friend and see the look of fear in her eyes as I bled her dry after being turned."

Burning rage blazed through me as I racked my brain, attempting to figure out who could have done this to her. Whoever it was, I was going to rip their entrails from their body before forcing them back down their throats in the public square of my city for all to see. Once my vengeance was wrought, no one would ever dare make a move against my mate again.

Staring down at her, I opened my mouth to respond, struggling to find the proper words to convey both my own despair for her as well as the desire to help her get her vengeance. My body shook with blinding rage, and I struggled to control myself. I wasn't there to help her when she needed me most. I wanted to paint all of Sanguis red until I found the one guilty of doing this to her.

A tear fell from my eye, rolling down my cheek before dropping off my jaw and onto her.

The smallest intake of breath escaped her at the liquid splattering against her cheek and for the first time since meeting her, confusion clouded her eyes as her brows pinched together.

I found myself just as perplexed as her, that a tear had fallen from my eye amidst the volatile and violent thoughts I found myself having.

"I...I didn't—" I started to explain but was cut off as the doors to the room were flung open. My breath caught in my throat as I turned, surprised that anyone would interfere with my orders to leave us alone.

A new pair of blood-red eyes stared at me as a snarl curled his lip up.

How fucking dare he interrupt this moment.

This piece of shit had written his death warrant earlier when he bristled as I kissed my mate's hand. That slight curl of his lip had given away his feelings for her, and while I could have perhaps gotten over it with time, this intrusion had sealed his fate.

It hadn't escaped me that Andrei had a similar reaction, but he was merely a child who would kiss my fucking shoes to get a spot on the board. He wouldn't interfere once it was known that Alina and I were mates.

Lincoln, though? He'd been jaded and aggressive ever since he showed up on my doorstep after his parents were slaughtered while trying to live a normal life in Ordinarius. While I wasn't callous or without empathy, I wasn't sure what he'd reasonably expected me to do. I couldn't resurrect the dead, and they'd chosen to leave the protection I could offer them in our world.

"Lincoln, no!" Alina screamed as I pushed myself from her, jumping to intercept him before he tried to plow into my side. Lincoln was braced with his shoulder and head tucked, ready for impact.

I'd waited far too long to find my mate. I wouldn't let a single fucking person come between us now that I had her.

Lincoln was far from a fledgling, but he was still powerless against me as I used all my agility and strength to dart to the side at the last minute. Twisting, I grabbed him around the waist, using my momentum to spin once before launching him through the air. The sound of the wall cracking and caving in around his body with the impact was an immediate source of enjoyment.

A satisfied huff of air came from me as I turned to focus back on Alina, but my delight was short-lived as I watched her dart toward him. Sincere concern for his well-being was painted all over her face. Horror bled into her wide eyes, her mouth dropping open as she took in what I'd done.

What was this? Did she have feelings for him?

A feral growl bubbled out of me at the thought. Perhaps they'd started a relationship prior to knowing I was her mate, but I wouldn't fucking share her with anyone now that I was here. To show her I wasn't without mercy, I'd allow him to live if he respected our boundaries moving forward.

With horror, I watched as she used her sharp nail to cut into her wrist before shoving the flow of blood against Lincoln's parted lips. "Drink," she pleaded.

All I saw was red at the sight of her sharing her

blood with someone other than me. It was an act reserved for mates only. My legs ate up the distance between us in a split second as his mouth latched onto her and drank in earnest.

I reached for her, and her head snapped toward me, tracking my movements with alarming accuracy for one of her age. Her eyes burned bright red once more. "Stop!" she screamed, baring her fangs as she moved to cover him with her body, using herself as a shield. "Don't you dare fucking touch him."

My breathing turned ragged with my fury, but I reminded myself that she hadn't grown up in our world. She didn't know our customs and how disrespectful sharing herself with him in this way was to me, her mate.

"You cannot share blood with him," I rasped, feeling like needles were pricking every inch of my skin as I watched him drink from her vein. "Such an act is reserved for true mates only, Alina."

Those beautiful lips split into a sinister smile as she narrowed her eyes at me. She bared her teeth as she spat, "He is my mate. We have the marks to prove it."

No.

She had to be lying. She was mine. I knew it. Fate knew it—preventing her from killing me.

My stomach lurched at her words, but what made me damn near fall to my knees was her turning her head and pulling her long hair off her neck, exposing the single black blood drop marking her tan skin.

How could this be?

CHAPTER TWO
ALINA

Throwing the fact that Dracula wasn't my only mate in his face filled me with a sick sense of satisfaction. Already, he thought he fucking owned me, showering me with flowery words of affection that he had no business bestowing upon me.

I wasn't sure yet what game he was playing, acting like he was oblivious to the slaughter of my family. I detested that the tear he'd forced from his eye had softened my resolve for the tiniest of moments. I hated myself for even that split second of doubt that crept into my mind at his simple act.

How fucking pathetic was I? Standing before me was the monster I'd sworn to kill, and the second his tears fell, empathy blossomed in my chest. I was weak, once again letting my emotions rule my actions and my mind.

Would I ever learn?

Huffing a self-deprecating laugh, I shook my head in disappointment as I allowed my hair to fall back down, covering my mark. I turned, ensuring I always kept a wary eye on Dracula.

For all I knew, he'd known I was his mate this whole time and *that's* why he'd killed my family. Disgust churned in my gut with the thought that he'd ordered me to be turned, so I would be forced into the eternal hell of immortality with him. With no family to turn to, knowing that slayers would hunt me down, he was forcing me into a position to have no one else to turn to. My trauma played into his hand perfectly.

The veins in Dracula's forearms bulged as he curled his hands into fists, and my eyes tracked to the rolled sleeves of his shirt. A flicker of delight rolled through me as I watched his fist clenched tightly at his side while a wild, untamed look of fury rolled through his black eyes.

It was astounding how much emotion bled through those bottomless pits for eyes.

"No, he isn't," he hissed at me, fangs longer than any I'd seen before. "You are *mine*."

When he'd first appeared, he'd exuded the picture-perfect look of a well-dressed man who had his fucking life together...and then I'd blown that up. He stood before me now, nostrils flaring with deep, shaky breaths, and his previously slicked back hair falling into small pieces hanging into his eyes.

My center coiled, desire rolling through me, as Lincoln drank from me. I should have been disgusted by how much I loved it, but right now, my ill-timed arousal was the least of my damn concerns. Though, I was absolutely going to blame the endorphins from Lincoln's fangs for making me hyper-aware of the enticing allure that rolled from Dracula in waves, making my legs squeeze together in search of friction.

A tiny voice popped into my mind, reminding me of the attraction that had punched me in the gut when I laid on top of him and tried to shove a blade through his neck. Lincoln's fangs hadn't been in me then.

Struggling to process what the fuck was happening, I fell back into my familiar snark, retorting, "You can keep telling yourself that, but your denial doesn't make it less true."

A low groan escaped Lincoln before his fangs retracted from my wrist and he shoved off the floor.

Hurtling to my feet, I wrapped a hand on his arm, nerves wracking my body as I glanced at the literal hole in the wall. A cool breeze drifted into the room now that Lincoln's body no longer blocked it.

There was a laundry list of things to work through between me and Lincoln, but the moment his body had melded into the wall like he was supposed to fit there, my brain had snapped back to attention.

Until that very moment, I had been lost to my despair, swimming in a consciousness full of dejection and worthlessness. All I could think of was how I'd failed my family, friends, and all slayers. It felt like I couldn't do a single thing right. So there was nothing I wanted more in that moment, than for someone to take it all away from me. Ending it would have been the best gift anyone could have given to me.

Blissful nothingness...

I was tired—*so, so fucking tired*—of trying to keep my grief and memories at bay every second of the day. The only thing that had kept me going was the desire to better myself and earn a position near Dracula that would allow me the chance to fulfill my blood oath.

Without it, what did I have?

But Lincoln's cry of pain had been the answer, even if I wasn't ready to admit it to myself. There was still something to fight for, to protect. For now, that was enough. Pure instinct had roused me from my emptiness, alarms blaring in my head when Lincoln's grunt of pain had met my ears.

Lincoln licked the remnants of my blood from his lips, stepping forward to stand chest to chest with Dracula, who refused to take his eyes off me. Prodding his finger into the chest of the deadliest vampire in existence, Lincoln leaned in, tilting his head back to look up into the massive man's eyes in pure defiance.

"She. Is. Mine," he growled, shoving his finger further into Dracula's chest to emphasize each word, but no matter what he did, he couldn't draw Dracula's focus.

His steely gaze seemed to be reserved for me, and only me.

His stare was intense and slightly unnerving, sending a chill down my spine as he looked at me with passion burning in his eyes that I didn't understand. I was ready for him to drop the fucking act because with each passing moment, I felt my jaw clenching tighter. His emotions practically bled from him, floating through the air with the sole purpose of suffocating me.

"Alina," he rumbled in that sultry fucking voice of his that probably made everyone around him simultaneously orgasm. "If you do not get this imbecile away from me, I'm going to rip his fucking spine out through his throat."

The threat should *not* have been attractive in the slightest, yet I found my mouth opening and closing. Okay, apparently we were just quickly burying that momentary lapse in judgment before speeding right on by it.

"Uh," I breathed out in confusion, eyes flicking back and forth between the two of them.

Dragging my bottom lip into my mouth, I bit down with the intention of nibbling on it. But I forgot about my fucking fangs that refused to go away with all these damn emotions and hunger bubbling through me like an overheating cauldron.

Lincoln's head snapped in my direction as Dracula inhaled sharply, his eyes darting to my lips, hunger swirling in the depths of his black orbs.

"Shit," I muttered, flicking my tongue out to try to staunch the flow of blood.

I knew the knick would heal quickly, after all, the skin on my wrist having sealed itself seconds after Lincoln had retracted his fangs. But my knees went weak as I watched Dracula's tongue dart out to lick his top lip. My brain felt like it was putty, but I couldn't let myself forget one thing: if he ingested my blood, all he had to do was force his blood into my mouth to seal the bond that he claimed we had.

That could *not* happen, no matter what.

"Lincoln, can you please step back?" I asked breathlessly, balling my shaking hands into fists at my side to try to steady them.

This situation wasn't ideal, to say the least.

I wasn't convinced that Dracula was my mate, but my inability to kill him, coupled with the soul-deep pain I'd felt at the idea of doing so…it forced me to consider the possibility. If I tried to suppress the idea of the bond being true, all I'd be doing is digging a new hole to bury my problem in. As it was, I already had a cemetery's worth of issues that I'd accumulated, and this wasn't a problem I could afford to ignore.

I had to figure out if there was truth to his words, and if so, how to circumvent the rules of mate bonds. If I couldn't kill him, perhaps I could pay someone to do it for me. Reasonably, I knew it would take a fuck ton of time to accumulate the wealth that a bounty like that would cost me. I'm sure I wouldn't be the first to request it, and if no one had been successful in the past, I'd have to ensure I employed an assassin of the highest caliber.

Just as Lincoln's foot lifted to do as I asked, Dracula had to go and open his fucking pretty mouth, pulling me from my mad thoughts. With a simpering smile, he taunted Lincoln, "Good boy."

Holy hell. Did he really just say that?

A scream of frustration tore from my throat as their bodies blurred a split-second later, fighting once more as Lincoln brought him to the ground.

What the fuck was I supposed to do with them? My fear for Lincoln's well-being was currently being smothered in its infancy by my annoyance at their pissing match.

The only relief I had was that Dracula seemed to be holding himself back in the fight now. I was at least able to track their movements, which was a relief. I felt like I'd barely blinked between seeing Lincoln coming through the doors earlier and seeing him splattered partially through the wall.

Was he...was he holding back to not upset me by hurting Lincoln again? My face screwed up, eyes narrowing as I considered the thought. That couldn't be right.

The longer I watched them, though, the more

obvious it became. Instead of landing as many blows as he could, it seemed Dracula was spending more time evading and staying on the defensive more than anything. Though, despite Dracula holding back, Lincoln got in maybe three hits for every ten Dracula could have landed.

If you'd told me two weeks ago, when I'd been whining about being forced into a marriage with a slayer, that I'd end up here in my current predicament…I would have never believed you. I'd always longed for someone who would push me and not roll over at the briefest display of my strong personality. But never had I thought my desire would be granted in the form of bloodsuckers as my fated mates. Like really, I would have looked like an evil witch as I cackled hysterically if you'd shown me the image of my current reality.

My mind flickered back to how Andrei had acted with Dracula's arrival, puzzling over the way he'd walked out of the room without a lick of his usual fire when he'd been dismissed. Looking toward the doors, I found myself wondering if he was still waiting in the hall. If he was, he would have heard everything going on in here.

While I was still frustrated with his shitty reaction to the mate mark on my neck, I couldn't forget the way he'd made me feel while I was tucked against his chest that night. For one brief moment, it felt like it wasn't just me against the world anymore. He'd made me feel safe and...happy.

The thought of losing the opportunity to explore what was burgeoning between Andrei and me was like a knife twisting in my gut. While I was willing to try to work out my issues with Lincoln, it didn't mean that Andrei suddenly meant nothing to me. Quite the opposite, actually. The thought of having to cut off our connection before we'd even been able to explore it was nauseating.

I knew he felt something for me, or he wouldn't have had such an intense reaction to the mark and fought with Lincoln this morning. But if he knew about Dracula, what would he do now?

Suddenly, the ability to care about the fight in front of me seeped from my body. I was too...tired for this. I was tired of not understanding what the hell was happening in my life and the way my emotions still seemed to rule me. The only thought I could force through my mind was my need to see if Andrei was still outside and talk to him about everything.

And then after that? I would go back to my dorm and curl up in a fucking ball while I sorted out the events of this morning and all the complications that came along with them.

Pinpricks of frustration left me feeling on edge as I glanced between the door and the seemingly never-ending fight before me.

"I'm leaving," I muttered, not caring if either of them heard me.

I hoped they wouldn't, so I wouldn't have to deal with this bullshit right now. Now that I wasn't *really* terrified of Dracula killing Lincoln, there was no reason for me to stay and watch them uselessly beat the shit out of each other.

As suspected, they were so wrapped up in their fight for dominance, they didn't falter at my words. I ran my tongue along my teeth and let out a heavy sigh, shoulders sagging as I turned away from them.

A cold feeling of emptiness washed over me as I walked through the door and found Andrei slumped against the floor, head hanging down.

There wasn't a question. He'd definitely heard everything.

"Andrei," I started as I took a step toward him, but I stopped myself. I mean, what could I say? That I was sorry?

There was nothing I could do to change Fate. She seemed to be a fickle bitch with a hard-on to destroy my life. If there was anything I was sorry about, it was that I couldn't shake my feelings for him despite knowing they were wrong for so many reasons. My mind began to try to argue the reasons why it was wrong every time they ran through my mind.

He was a bloodsucker—*but so was I.*

He occupied the top spot on the rankings of students that I had wanted to be at—*but wasn't that pointless now?*

He'd been a fucking douchebag since the moment I ran into him at the academic building and had an ego that was big enough to occupy this entire sector of the academy. Was that just a front, though?

As his head lifted, peering at me with those light green eyes of his, he looked so fucking lost. My bottom lip wobbled with barely restrained emotion. Why was I so goddamned *in my feelings* today? I'd hardly ever cried in my life as a slayer. I didn't do emotions. Hell, I didn't do physical affection.

Yet everything in my life had been flipped upside down, and I found myself wondering if I even knew myself at all anymore.

"Is there any chance?" he asked softly, eyes scanning my face for answers that I didn't have.

Taking a deep breath, I slid my back against the wall to sit next to him as a crash sounded from the training room, letting me know that the fight was still in full swing. Tucking my knees up, I leaned against him, resting my head against his shoulder.

There were so many damn questions swirling through my brain, and I uttered the only words I knew to be true.

"I don't know up from down right now, Andrei."

CHAPTER THREE
ALINA

Extending his hand, he pointed up. "That's up," he whispered before swiveling his wrist the other direction, "and that's down."

I couldn't help the small laugh that bubbled up from me. "Thanks—that's very helpful, you fuck."

His answering chuckle pulled the corner of my lips up into a small smile. Somehow, he always managed to do that to me, even without trying. I felt warmth flowing through my chest in response. I wasn't sure if Lincoln had stormed into the room with Dracula because of what he could hear from the other side of the doors, or if it was because of what he'd felt from our bond. What I did know was that I didn't want to hurt him with my thoughts about Andrei, so I made sure that I had my mental barricade up now.

The moment of levity soured as silence stretched between us once more.

If there was one thing I could always count on with Andrei, it was that he would make me laugh, no matter the situation. He might be a prick to everyone else, but I couldn't help but feel like he was *my* jerk. I knew I shouldn't feel that way, that I had no right to claim him, but the thought of him making another woman laugh made my stomach churn with acid.

Maya's face popped into my mind, and I barely restrained the growl that fought to burst from me at the thought of her pawing all over him.

A part of me wished we could stay like this, with all the unspoken things left unsaid between us. I didn't want to confirm that I had two mates. I didn't want to admit that it felt wrong to continue with whatever this was between us. I didn't want to admit that I still wanted to explore this and work through our issues.

Gently, he lowered his head until it rested lightly on top of mine as he pulled my hand into his lap, threading our fingers together. "Don't worry, I know the answer to my question," he murmured, running his thumb across my knuckles lightly. "I just couldn't bring myself to walk away yet."

I didn't want him to walk away from me.

My eyes burned. I wanted to bash my head into the wall behind me to try to make my body focus on physical pain instead of the emotional turmoil that had woken up and chosen violence with me this morning.

"I've always thought that you were a queen in your own right, but I never thought it would be as the Queen on Dracula's board," he admitted with a huff, and my heart squeezed at this tender side of him I didn't often see. He was just particular about who he let see that side of him, and once again, I found myself feeling like we were two sides of the same coin. "I've respected the hell out of you since our first encounter, and my respect only grew with each passing moment. I let myself think that maybe I'd found my match," he breathed out quietly, squeezing my hand with the admission.

Fuck. His honesty would be my absolute undoing.

"I wanted to protect you from the world, despite knowing you had everything you needed within you to protect yourself," he tacked on before bringing my hand up to press a light kiss to it.

My chest squeezed, and I slammed my eyes shut, feeling like he was nearing the end of what he needed to get off his chest before he walked away for good.

"Can you promise me one thing, new girl?"

My throat tightened with emotion at the nickname that had felt like such a dig before but had since become a pet name I loved from him.

Despite trying my damnedest, my voice wobbled with emotion as I croaked out, "What's that?"

He took a deep, even breath, and I lifted with the heavy movement of his shoulders before he deflated and sagged on the exhale. When he spoke again, there was a bite to his words, like he was already locking away the gentle side of himself.

"Promise me that you won't let either of them dim your shine. Because *fuck*, Alina," he groaned, "you burn so fucking brightly."

I couldn't help the gasp that tore from me as he said almost the exact words my grandma had imparted onto me. At the sound of my surprise, he pulled me up with him as he stood, holding me against him as I struggled to pull it together.

My hand tightened into his shirt, as I whispered, "I promise."

I felt his lips brush against the top of my head

before he pulled back and brushed the few tears that had managed to escape from my cheeks. He smiled at me, but it was so clearly forced by the way it never reached his eyes and his lips thinned. "My father is on Dracula's board, so I can't risk drawing his ire by being close to you anymore. It could jeopardize everything I've worked for the past three years to be on top."

That explained why his entire demeanor had changed once he entered the room.

His lips thinned, and his eyes pinched like he was in pain as he admitted, "My father isn't a kind man, Alina. If it wasn't for the threat of him looming over me, I wouldn't be forcing myself to walk away from you right now. I can't risk losing that spot."

My pity-party ended abruptly as I soaked in this new information. His father sounded like an absolute nightmare, but suddenly, the way Andrei acted made so much more sense. It wasn't simply that he wanted to be at the top of the leaderboard—he had to be in order to prove to his father he was on top. Dracula mentioned he was at DIA to look at the talent because of the praise Andrei's dad had given the Academy. His father was grooming Andrei to either take his spot on his board or to have him on the board with him.

Andrei's life was chosen for him, dictated by what was expected of him by his parents. That was a fate I knew all too well.

I wanted to tell him to tell his dad to fuck off if that wasn't what he wanted to do. He deserved to live his life however he saw fit, but who was I to give that advice? I hadn't been strong enough to go against the grain with my own family before the decision had been made for me.

Taking a deep breath, I accepted that this was his choice to make. It would be far too selfish of me to ask him to not to walk away from me. Not only did I have a hell of a lot to figure out with Lincoln, but I also had a shitstorm lingering over me with this supposed bond to Dracula as well. It wasn't fair of me to drag him further into my life, especially when it could jeopardize his future or put him in a position to draw his father's wrath.

"Okay," I whispered softly as I gazed up at him, hating that I had to accept this but knowing it was only fair.

I had to let him go.

Taking a step back, I waited for him to walk away, but he didn't. We stood there, staring at each other with uncertainty wafting in the air between us as if waiting for one of us to be strong enough to actually leave. His green eyes drifted over my face, searching for something. Was he waiting for me to tell him to stay? To tell him to fight for this?

The selfish side of me wanted to give him exactly that, but for once I needed to stop thinking about my needs.

Shoving all my emotions down, I let my face go blank as I steeled my back, making the decision to leave before watching him walking away from me broke me further. Maybe if I made the choice first, it would be easier for him to move on as well.

I could sit here and tell him everything I felt for him and about our situation, but all that would do was torture us both.

With one last, lingering glance his way, I whispered, "Bye, Andrei."

I couldn't allow myself to see or hear his reaction, so I put on a burst of speed, refusing to stop until my hand landed on the door to the dorm house. Yanking it open with a bit too much force, I tried to let my mind go blank as I took a sharp right turn into the cafeteria.

"Oh, there she is!" Maya's voice called out in a singsong, cheerful tone. The octave alone made it feel like someone was shoving shards of glass in my ears.

Doing my best to ignore her, knowing she truly wasn't worth my time or energy, I closed my eyes and took a shaky, calming breath. She was trying me at the worst possible time, and while she'd riled me in the past with trivial things, I didn't *actually* get pleasure out of beating up someone who was helpless in combat. Honestly, it kinda took all the fun out of it.

At this point, hitting her was like kicking a defenseless, starved puppy.

Don't let her rile you, Alina. She isn't worth it.

"Having an issue finding something to eat?" she taunted, snapping me out of the mantra that was the only thing keeping her face intact this morning.

My eyes zeroed in on the bags that she had in her lap, noting the deeper shade of the blood. Rage coiled in my gut at the sight of the darker-tinted animal blood. No one else drank it besides me that I knew of, and since the bags didn't need to be refreshed as often as the human blood, they didn't tend to stay as fresh.

A trash can had been pulled up between her dangling legs, and she smiled gleefully as she turned a bag upside down and emptied it. She tossed the empty bag onto the floor, and I sucked in a sharp breath at the sight of how many she'd emptied already. They littered the floor around her, droplets of the darker blood splattering the normally spotless tile.

This fucking bitch had taken my supply overnight to purposefully put on a display this morning.

Why couldn't she just leave me the hell alone? It couldn't possibly feel good having me constantly toss her around like a rag doll, and I knew for a fucking fact that her ego was damaged even more with each fight. So why keep testing me like this?

Glancing around the room, I took note of how everyone gathered seemed to shake their heads at the antics before quickly returning to their conversations. The only person left hanging around Maya was Milina. My, how the mighty had fallen. It seemed everyone else was as tired of this merry-go-round between Maya and I as I was. Perhaps if the outcome ever changed, they'd feel invested again. But I didn't plan on letting that happen.

Letting out a deep sigh, I walked toward her as she continued to empty the blood bags, maintaining eye contact with me the entire time. "Seriously, Maya? Don't you have better things to do with your life than continue to provide me with situations in which to prove to everyone else in our class that you are beneath me?"

Right on cue, her gorgeous face screwed up into an expression of ugly rage as she spat, "The only person I'm beneath is Andrei, and that's by choice. Every. Single. Night."

If I hadn't just had the second-most emotionally draining moment of my life, I would have retorted that all she was doing was proving my point of her loving to be a pillow princess, but I just didn't have it in me.

All her words served to do was dump ice over the tiny fire of anger she had stoked within me. I had tried to grasp onto it like a lifeline to avoid everything else I was enduring, but it seemed like life was hell-bent on forcing me to face my emotions today. *Fucking bitch.*

"You know what, Maya?" I said, shrugging my shoulders at her in indifference and fighting off the urge to dive after the remaining blood bags in her lap. "Enjoy wasting both the blood *and* your time."

Turning on my heel to go upstairs, I decided to let her think she'd won this battle. All I wanted to do was try to force myself to go to sleep, yearning for a brief reprieve from my reality. Before, I would have welcomed the fight between us, but with hunger overwhelming me, I didn't think anyone could prevent me from killing her if a bloodhaze and bloodlust overcame me at the same time.

I didn't know all the rules of the Academy, but I would bet my life that killing a fellow student wouldn't just get me detention. I'd be expelled, and while I didn't necessarily know what the point of being at this academy any longer was, DIA was all I had.

What a fucking depressing thought.

Resigned to take the loss, I started up the stairs before Maya let out a screech, sounding disturbingly like a banshee. "You will not keep winning this, you bitch! You don't get to just walk away from me."

"Already did," I tossed over my shoulder, rolling my eyes at how she thought I was still winning by walking away. Though I suppose not letting her rile me was winning in a way.

But why did she insist on fighting me?

Then it hit me.

She wanted to get me into trouble. Me starting the fights was likely the only way to ensure I was expelled in her mind. She wanted me out of her way so she could reign over all our peers with Andrei at her side once more.

The thing was, that power she thought she

wielded before I arrived? It never really existed. It was a figment of her fucking imagination, and I honestly felt bad for her now that I realized how pathetic her life was. She didn't have what it took to get to the top of the leaderboard with her academics or fighting ability, so this was the shit she resorted to.

Sleeping around and getting rid of anyone who threatened the precarious grip she had on her standing here.

Her shoes slapping against the floor told me she was coming, but as I spun to defend myself, Lincoln appeared between us. My body sagged with the relief of seeing him in one piece, albeit somewhat disheveled. Despite feeling with certainty that Dracula wouldn't kill him now that I'd made my position clear as Lincoln's mate, my brain had apparently still been worried about his well-being.

If Dracula wanted to continue his charade of caring for me, though, I'd use it to my advantage. At least until I found an alternate solution for my plan.

Two could play the game, and I'd ensure I was the victor. Afterall, the Queen was the most powerful piece on a chess board.

Throwing his hand out toward Maya, he barked, "Ms. Federman, from where I stand, you're inciting a fight while also wasting school resources. Disposing of blood, really? Detention, now."

I didn't think there were many things in life that could have made me feel even the teensiest bit better after this shit-tastic morning, but fuck me, Lincoln had just managed to find one of them.

The way her mouth dropped open in shock before she spluttered, "But...no! I can't have a mark on my report!" was nearly a toe-curling level of enjoyment.

Flicking my fingers at her, I batted my eyes and said, "Run along."

"Alina," Lincoln growled in warning, but his tone didn't stop me from waving at her as she spun on her heel to head out the door.

"Bye now!" I called after her cheerfully.

Who knew that, when I wasn't on the receiving end of it, that letting administration dole out justice could feel so good? Funny that.

As soon as she was out of sight, Lincoln whirled to grab me by the bicep, half dragging me up the stairs. "What is it with the two of you?"

I ignored his question in favor of asking my own as we rounded the stairs to head to the fourth floor where the professors stayed. "Your play date is over so soon? But you two looked like you were getting along so well!" I gasped with mock-horror.

In a second, he had us inside of his room. My back was pressed flat against the wall and his hand was wrapped around my throat in a way I didn't even know I was craving right now.

Oh my god. *Yes.*

"This isn't a fucking joke, Alina," he hissed as he brought his nose within a hair's breadth of mine, the challenge in his eyes daring me to fight back.

I had nothing left in the tank for that, though. The spoons were gone. The cup was empty. All I wanted was for him to help me forget about everything else and turn my focus on what I *knew* we had between us: passion.

I had wondered what I had to live for, and I was quickly realizing that this live wire of a relationship with him was the answer. I needed him. That much wasn't a question at all. While I knew I should work through our shit like adults, I just couldn't handle the overload of information I needed to process right now.

Something in my expression must have made my need for distraction abundantly clear. The tension in his body faded as his hand loosened around my neck.

Quickly, I reached up to grab his hand and keep it there, hoping to convey what I needed with my next words. Just like the other night, I said, "I'm asking you to make me forget about the rest of the world while it's just you and me in these four walls."

His throat bobbed as he swallowed hard, his hazel eyes swirling with indecision.

"Please," I begged, needing to feel grounded with the wildly changing emotions storming through me.

There was one thing I was very sure of in my life right now, and that was how fucking badly I still wanted him. He was mine, body and soul.

A breath puffed from his lips before his fingers tightened on the sides of my throat, constricting my air flow slightly. "Okay, Princess."

CHAPTER FOUR
ALINA

The smallest sigh escaped through my lips with the realization that he wasn't going to fight me on this. Him calling me Princess was his way of signaling that we were entering territory that I felt comfortable exploring.

I needed it now more than ever.

While I'd thoroughly enjoyed the little show I put on in the window for him and the mutual masturbation that took place in our separate rooms afterwards—and even dreamed about the way he made me choke on his cock until tears streamed from my eyes before feasting on my pussy in the training room—those times felt like the tiniest sample of what we had to offer each other in the grand scheme of things.

If those moments were delectable, how explosive would it be when we stopped with our little games of foreplay?

Sexual tension hung between us like a thick blanket of fog, and somehow I knew that he was going to awaken my body in a way I'd never experienced before.

He'd already managed to penetrate my heart, despite my best efforts to not allow him to worm his way into that traitorous organ. But now it was time for my preferred method of penetration. Sure, I knew this wasn't the best way to cope, but I didn't care. Right here, right now, this was a step toward furthering our relationship in a way that I desperately needed from him.

His lips traced along the shell of my ear lightly, making me shiver as my eyes fluttered closed.

"But if we're going to do this, you're going to do exactly what I say, Princess," he murmured, his deep voice grumbling through his chest and against mine, hardening my nipples. "There are a few things I need from you first, though."

"Mhm," I hummed in quick agreement as my back arched, desperate to press against him and be as close as possible to his warmth. My brows pinched together in frustration when a gap grew between us, all the heat from his body gone except for the hand around my throat.

Popping my eyes open to glare at him with every intention of asking him *what the fuck* he thought he was doing, but I slammed my mouth shut as I studied him instead.

My mouth dried as I stared at his handsome face. While I loved the put-together version of Lincoln that he portrayed to his students, there was something so fucking enticing about his current disheveled state.

His wavy hair was messy, with several pieces hanging over his forehead and just barely obscuring the tops of his eyes as he gazed down at me. Dried blood stained the corner of his mouth, and I wasn't sure if it was mine or his, but my tongue itched to dart out and lick him clean.

"Do you understand?" he asked in a gravelly tone that had me nodding my head instantly, ready to agree to anything he asked.

His sharp jaw was clenched tightly, and his eyes narrowed before he offered me a devilish smirk that seemed to dare me to object. He could have told me to swear that the sky was filled with turtles, and I would have relentlessly defended that fact to anyone who dared argue that it was in fact not.

His head tilted slightly, granting me a view of his slightly swollen eye. Noticing a few busted blood vessels in it, I couldn't help but wonder if he'd managed to get any good blows in on Dracula. If I went down the path of thinking about the shitbag, all it would lead me to was the persistent need to figure out where the fucker was now. It was a compulsion, needing to know when and where to be prepared to face him again. That was the very last thing I wanted to care about right now.

Everything was fine if he wasn't near me. At least for now.

Lincoln's gaze ran the length of my body, hunger swirling in the reflection of his eyes as he growled out, "Say it," before locking gazes with me once more. "Tell me you're going to do every damn thing I say, Princess. Tell me exactly *who* is in control now. I know my hand isn't wrapped around your neck tightly enough to stop that smart mouth from running—*yet*."

My nostrils flared gently at his demand, something deep within me bristling at what he wanted me to admit.

Tell me exactly who is in control now.

My body was more than willing to submit to his every whim and desire, but there was still a part of my brain that wanted to tell him to shove it where the sun doesn't shine. Why did I yearn for this fight for dominance with him, despite knowing deep down that the outcome I really wanted was for him to take that control from me?

Maybe that was it—I didn't want to hand him the keys to the castle. I wanted him to take them, each time, not just the first time we were intimate. I was a more than willing participant, but there was just something about an extreme loss of control that I wanted with him.

My fangs lengthened, aching painfully in my gums as my body came alive, itching for that fight.

He loved that I was a spitfire, always willing to go head-to-head with him. Yet he'd also made it clear how much he got off on silencing me and doing what he wanted with my body.

Staring up at him from beneath my lashes, I fluttered them in an act of innocence.

There was something intoxicating about knowing I could give him the power he craved. It felt like euphoria each time I finally caved. Did it make us a fucked-up pair? Some might say yes, but if this was what made us feel satisfied, I wasn't going to knock it.

His lips curved into a wicked smile that

promised the fight I wanted as he asked, "Or do I need to hold a knife to your neck and make more of your pretty crimson blood stain your skin to get you to obey?"

Even the reminder of the cold steel pressing against my neck had my clit throbbing in want. I blinked slowly at him, inhaling deeply through my nose and loving the way his eyes tracked my heaving chest.

"Weren't you the one who told me the hard way was so much more fun, *Sir*?" I sassed back as I raised a brow toward my hairline, feeling my voice strain slightly around his tightening grip.

I wasn't going to make it as easy as standing still and letting him lift a knife to my throat this time, though.

Using the space between us, I quickly pulled my knee up and kicked out with my boot, throwing him from me and sending him flying into his door. A loud crack echoed—signaling that he'd splintered the wood—drawing a smirk to my lip.

A deep laugh rumbled from him as he pushed himself up, reaching up to brush the hair out of his eyes as he stood to his full height once more.

"Are you *sure* this is how you want this?" he

asked, eyes searching my face for an answer as I popped my hip and placed my hand on it.

A laugh spilled from my lips. "What? Can you not handle it?"

For a moment he didn't answer, seemingly pondering the question. Rubbing his hand over the scruff of his beard, he clicked his tongue once before asking a question that froze me for half a second.

"Tell me one thing before this begins, Princess. Are you a virgin?"

I couldn't help but let my head rear back in shock as my brows pulled up. "A virgin?" I parroted back.

He simply nodded and crossed his arms across his chest, biceps flexing with the movement.

I let my words drip with sarcasm as I asked, "Why, is it going to ruin your ego to know you don't get the honor of breaking the sacred seal of my pussy?"

My eyes rolled at the thought of him being annoyed by that. I'd never understand why men gave a shit if we were virgins or not—it's not like most guys were out there saving themselves for their 'one true love.' So why did they expect us to?

When I decided I wanted to lose my virginity, I hadn't even told the slayer that he was my first. I wouldn't give him the satisfaction of knowing that. He'd been like a five-pump chump anyway, so his ego really didn't need to be stroked.

Also, with practice comes skill, so wasn't it a good thing to have someone who knew what they were doing?

Lincoln's jaw ticked once, but that was the only sign I got before he was on me. As he reached for my throat, I dodged to the side, but he was quick to wrap a hand around my arm, preventing me from darting away. His chest collided with my back as he yanked me into him—hard.

My breath whooshed out of me on impact, leaving me gasping as he snaked an arm around my waist, anchoring me to him. As his free hand trailed up my thigh and to my blazer, I felt the cool air running along my skin as he unbuttoned the jacket, leaving my bra exposed.

Tipping my head to the side as his scruff scratched along my neck, his lips found my ear once more as he nipped lightly and wrapped his hand around my throat.

My breathing was ragged but came to a halt entirely as his fingers pressed in harder. With a low growl, he bit out, "I don't care that you've fucked someone before me, Princess, as long as you know that my cock will be the only one sinking into your wet cunt from now on."

Fuck. Yep, that did it for me.

Rubbing my legs together, I tried to swallow around the grip he had on me but found that I couldn't. The adrenaline and endorphins releasing from the lack of breath left me feeling like I had a fuzzy high. It was pure bliss, and I could feel the fight bleeding out of me as my body relaxed, floating through this euphoria.

"Now that that's cleared up," he murmured before releasing my neck just as black dots began to litter my vision. He loosened his grip around my waist but didn't drop his arm as he continued, "I still have a few things I need from you first. Are you going to be a good girl for me now?"

Sucking in a gasping breath as oxygen began to flow to my brain once more, I swallowed hard and blinked rapidly.

"Yes," I croaked out, turning around in his grip. His dark gaze swept down to the swell of my breasts being pushed up by my black, lacy bra. Trailing my sharp nails up his chest before flattening my palms against the hard muscle there, I let my voice drop to a seductive purr as I answered, "You're in control, *Sir.*"

Why had I given in? Because I wanted more of *that*. Whatever that was he had just given me was the exact weightlessness my conscious yearned for.

All of my heartache over walking away from Andrei was suspended in those moments.

My desire to fall to my knees and scream to the sky while asking what I did to deserve the sick fate of being Dracula's mate was gone.

The constantly revolving door of shit I'd been desperately keeping at bay had halted.

He'd given me the most precious gift he ever could in that moment: peace.

Leaning down, the warmth of his lips pressed against my forehead. My stomach fluttered in anticipation before he uttered words against my skin that made my toes curl, "That's my good girl."

If I had been a cat, I'd be curled up in his lap, contentedly purring as he stroked me.

"The first thing I need you to do is strip for me, Princess," he ordered gruffly before backing up to give me space.

I was quick to oblige, letting my blazer fall off my shoulders and into a heap on the floor before quickly unbuttoning my jeans. My eyes tracked his movements as he walked backward toward his bed, stripping his shirt off quickly and letting out a soft growl as it caught around his neck. It was as if he was pissed at the material for obstructing his view of me standing before him in my bra and thong.

There was something both powerful and graceful in the way his muscles bunched and moved doing the simplest things. My mouth watered at the sight of his exquisitely toned body. His broad shoulders bulged as he settled back, crossing his arms behind his head as he leaned against the espresso-colored headboard, showing off his lean and perfectly carved abdomen.

Heat speared through me, and it felt like I was back in the window with him gazing up at me all over again.

Taking slow, measured steps toward him, I trailed my hand across my collar bone, my pinky skimming along the swell of my breast, before slipping one strap off my shoulder. Tugging my bottom lip between my teeth, I let my fangs knick my skin on purpose as I reached back to unclasp my bra.

The warm copper liquid filled my mouth, though I allowed some to trickle down my chin and splatter onto my breasts as my bra fell to the floor. Stopping at the foot of the bed, I smirked in victory as he brought his hands down and fisted his cock, pulling it from his athletic shorts.

"You're so damn beautiful, Princess," he breathed out as his eye followed the two thin lines of blood dripping over my breast and continuing a path toward my stomach.

Hooking my nails under the sides of my thong, I gave them a quick flick, shredding the material and tossing it to the ground. He groaned deeply, and his head smacked lightly against the headboard as his eyes rolled back.

Already, I was soaked and felt needy for him. My body was coiled so tightly with desire that the simplest flick of a touch against my clit would have me exploding. I dropped a knee on the bed, hands falling against the plush comforter as he smirked.

"The second thing I need is for those lips to be wrapped around my cock," he murmured, eyes half-lidded with lust as I began to crawl toward him on the bed.

As I moved to settle over his legs, he shook his head once. "No, Princess. By my side, here," he commanded, pointing to his left before patting the bed.

Raising a brow, I regarded him with curiosity for a short moment before deciding I didn't care what he had in mind as long as it brought me pleasure. I crawled next to his side, sitting back on my calves when my knees touched his hips, and reached for his cock before taking over stroking. Our eyes caught for a moment, electricity practically crackling through the air around us.

His hand snapped out, dragging my head toward his as he met me in a frenzied clash of lips and fangs. Increasing my pace on his cock, I opened my mouth to invite him in, scraping my fangs along his tongue as he pushed in. My body felt like it was being lit up from the inside as his blood trickled into my mouth.

His hand moved from the back of my head to wrap around my neck from behind, dragging me away from his mouth and toward his cock as he groaned, "Take me into your throat, Princess. All the way back like I taught you."

As the thick tip of his cock passed through my lips, I quickly retracted my fangs before relaxing my throat the way I'd needed to before to accommodate his girth. There was nothing slow or teasing about this moment as his hand gathered my hair, pulling on it tight enough to leave a bite of pleasurable pain smarting my scalp. My eyes bulged as I struggled to take him in.

"Swallow, Princess," he commanded as his free hand worked its way around my side, plunging two fingers into my pussy.

The sudden feeling had me gasping, and he took the opportunity to shove his hips up, forcing his cock further down my throat. I swallowed on instinct. His fingers began to plunge in and out of me at a quick pace as he moved his hips in the same rhythm.

Tears pooled in my eyes, streaming down my cheeks seconds later as he thoroughly fucked my mouth.

I loved everything about it, moaning around his cock as his fingers curled and fluttered against the spot inside of me that was quickly dragging me toward the edge of an orgasm. As I clenched around his fingers, he growled, "Are you going to come on my fingers, Princess?"

I wasn't sure exactly how I was supposed to respond, but a moment later, his hand holding my hair dropped to find my nose. Pinching my nostrils closed, he shoved deep down my throat and stilled. I flailed for a moment, confused by the abrupt motion and lack of oxygen until that same hazy feeling from earlier overcame me once more.

Shit. This man would be my undoing.

Giving into the moment, I stopped struggling and relaxed into it, earning praise from him as he increased the pace of his fingers. "Such a good girl for me. I need you to come on my fingers, Princess. Now."

The sharp demand in his tone, coupled with the endorphins flooding through me had my pussy pulsating with the most intense orgasm I'd ever experienced.

I completely shattered in his hands, and even as he pulled my head off his cock, allowing me to take in a deep, gasping breath of air, he continued to stroke me, extending the waves of pleasure crashing through me for longer than I knew was possible.

My face was streaked with tears, and as our eyes met, he lifted his hand to brush away a few strands of hair sticking to my face. Cupping my cheek, his thumb brushed against my bottom lip as I took in another deep breath to try to calm my racing pulse.

All I heard was the whooshing of blood in my ears as he pulled his fingers from my pussy and lifted them to his mouth.

Was he...

The question in my mind met a quick, brutal end as he stuck them into his mouth and swirled his tongue along each finger, cleaning them completely of the remnants of my orgasm.

My hearing returned as he dropped his hand and grinned at me, fangs on full display. "Exquisite."

I didn't have words for how incredible my body felt, and as he swept us to our feet, I didn't question him as he positioned us in front of his curtain, my back to his chest once more. All I knew was that I wanted to finally feel the hard cock digging into my back inside of me.

Swiveling my hips and pushing onto my tiptoes to try to get access to his cock, he chuckled as he quickly snapped the curtain open. "You wanted to put on a show the other night, so let's put on a fucking show, Princess."

My mouth popped open in shock at the sight of my fellow classmates' backs as they left the building to head to classes. As I gaped at the possibility of one of them turning to see us, his hand came to wrap around the back of my neck, pressing my face against the window gently.

I couldn't stop myself from crying out as he shoved his cock inside of me with one long thrust of his hips. "Fuck! Lincoln!"

This. This was everything.

"Yes, Princess," he growled as he stilled for a second, likely trying to let me accommodate his impressive size. He began to drag his hips out before thrusting back into me quickly. A moan fell from my lips as my eyes fluttered closed.

"Remember what I said earlier. This pussy is mine now."

As his hips began to gain momentum, he snapped, "Open your eyes. Look at all those people who could look up here at any moment and see your breasts bouncing as I fuck your wet cunt."

Doing as he requested, my cheeks flushed with heat as I watched them going about their day, totally unaware that I was stories above them getting my brains fucked out. I couldn't help but clench around his cock at the thought of getting caught, making him hiss in pleasure.

As Lincoln's fingers tightened on the sides of my throat, I felt his free hand come around my waist before delving between my legs. "Shit!" I cried out as his fingers fluttered across my clit, sending shooting sparks of pleasure through my core.

"That's it, Princess," he praised, increasing the pressure like a fucking reward that I was all too happy to claim. "Squeeze my fucking cock."

I hated that that's exactly what I did as soon as he demanded it, but fuck me, it was so blatantly clear that I wasn't in control of my body anymore. He truly was in control in every single way, and I couldn't get enough of it. I would *never* get enough of it. He was everything I needed.

My breathing grew ragged as he increased the pressure to exactly where I needed it to be, demanding once more, "Come for me, Princess. I want to feel you wrapped around me as my cock pounds into you. I want you to scream so fucking loud that the students hear you."

Crying out as my orgasm hurtled toward me once more, he growled, "I want them to know you're mine."

Stars exploded behind my eyes as I yelled his name and collapsed against the window. He stilled a moment later before pulling out. Hot spurts landed over my ass, and if I wasn't riding such a high right now, I would have smacked him in the face for coming on me like a piece of furniture.

With barely any heat to my words, I mumbled, "You better clean that up."

His chuckling response made my lips curl up into a smile, warmth flooding my heart and body as he tossed out, "Yes, ma'am," before the sound of his feet carrying him toward the bathroom met my ears.

Thankfully, all the students had cleared the area, so I didn't feel rushed to cover up or close the curtain.

My eyes snagged on the edge of the tree line, and

what I saw had the corner of my lip pulling up into a sinister smirk.

The blood red eyes staring up at me shocked me but felt like a victory in the same breath. Who knew the owner of those eyes could feel enough rage at his age to succumb to the bloodhaze just like any one of us.

Bringing my hand up, I gave my fingers a little waggle of greeting before yanking the curtain shut.

I might not be able to kill Dracula yet, but I would gladly settle for pissing him the fuck off for now.

CHAPTER FIVE
LINCOLN

I shook my head lightly, chuckling to myself at the way she instantly snapped back into my spitfire the second I pulled my cock from her. *That's my girl.*

Snatching a hand towel from the bathroom, I made quick work of wetting a small portion of it to clean her off. It had taken everything in me to not come in her pussy. Fates, I'd wanted to thoroughly mark her as mine and force her to put her thong back on to keep it nestled into her for as long as possible. It had nothing to do with the thought of getting her pregnant but everything to do with marking her as mine.

With the fucked-up childhood I'd had, I'd never pictured myself as a father, but it was a stark reminder of all the things that we did need to talk about. If she wanted kids, I honestly wasn't sure that I'd be able to give that to her.

I couldn't deny how fucking perfect she was for me, though, and the longer I was around her, the thought of not being able to give her everything she wanted was...it just wasn't something I even wanted to admit to myself as a possibility. Despite thinking Fate had some twisted, fucked up sense of humor for giving me a slayer as a mate at first, Alina had managed to completely flip what I thought I knew on its head.

Now the fucked-up twist was that *Dracula* claimed her as his mate as well.

"You might have gotten to her first, Lincoln, but I'll make sure she ends up at my side in the end."

Those parting words from him had played through my mind on a loop, like a fucked-up mantra, as I followed the trail of her scent once I realized she wasn't in the room with us any longer. Knowing that she hadn't fed and feeling how fucking emotionally raw she was, I'd felt like the biggest jackass in the world for getting lost in a fight with him rather than focusing on her. The blood-haze had completely obscured all logic.

Turning on my heel, I caught a devious little

smirk on her face as she pulled the curtain shut and spun around. As I stared at her slender frame, I couldn't help but picture the way she'd been trapped beneath Dracula the way a lover would be when I'd stormed in. Anger coiled tight and heavy in my gut.

I'd never let him trap her again.

Clearing my throat as the anger threatened to bubble up through my chest once more, I forced a soft smile to my face, not wanting to concern her. The last thing I needed was her thinking I was angry with her after we'd shared such an intimate moment.

"What's got you looking like that?" I mused, wondering what diabolical plan her mind could have come up within seconds of coming on my cock.

"Oh, nothing," she sighed out breathily, turning around to stick her ass out for me to clean off. My cock twitched, ready to go another round at the sight of my cum dripping over her ass and down her legs. "Just enjoying the way my body is practically purring in contentment now, Sir."

Dragging the wet cloth over her skin, I growled as she wiggled her ass enticingly. Smacking it playfully, I growled and demanded, "Stand still."

"*And* I saw the look of fury on Dracula's face

from where he stood on the edge of the woods outside of the building at the very end."

Her words were like a bucket of ice flowing over me, drowning the serotonin that had been coursing through me still.

Just the thought of *him* seeing her naked in that window...I wanted to throw my fist through the damn wall like a fledgling that couldn't handle their emotions. Never in my life had I felt as out of control as I had today.

Closing my eyes, I inhaled deeply, letting the breath blow out slowly before opening my eyes again.

I'd pull his eyes from his head, but even that didn't feel like enough. I didn't want him to have the memory of her face in the throes of passion playing in his head as he likely went back to his castle and jerked off to it. Sick old fuck. The only solace I had was that he got to see exactly how satisfied I made *my* mate.

Our power struggle and eventual roles when she gave up control wasn't something that could be duplicated. It was just the way we burned for each other, and I knew in my soul that he couldn't give her what I could.

Continuing to clean her off, I tried to make

casual conversation, though I couldn't hide the bitterness in my tone. "He said he'd be back to talk to you tomorrow."

While I didn't want her anywhere near him, I was still man enough to recognize that I couldn't control her. She was a wild, untamed woman, and I'd never try to be the one to break her. Her take-no-shit attitude was what I adored the most about her, despite it also being the reason she pissed me off the most. Still, I wouldn't change it. There would never be a day that her smart mouth didn't make my cock and hand twitch with the need to take away her need to sass me.

I only mentioned his words about coming back because I needed to know how she felt about him... about the possibility of his words being true. I could infer how she felt about him simply from what I'd felt and seen, but it didn't mean I knew everything.

At that, she straightened, and for what felt like an excruciating amount of time, only our breathing filled the space. I didn't want to push her into talking to me, but I didn't want her to feel like she had to go through this alone anymore.

While Dracula was the highest power in Sanguis, he didn't own all of Praeditus. If she felt unsafe here at DIA now because of him, I wouldn't stcp until I found a place she could call home in peace. All she had to do was say the word, and I'd take her away from here. Without thought.

She'd done well to keep her mental shield up since I'd practiced with her, but there was a moment that it had crumbled to the ground when she was with him. I could feel the extent of pain that he'd pulled out of her.

I'd felt such an overwhelming sense of agony and hopelessness flowing through our bond that it nearly brought me to my knees with its weight. I'd pushed off the wall with the intention of flying through the doors, stumbling when two words floated from her mind to my own. *Kill me.*

It was like trudging through quicksand, over-coming the waves of grief enough to keep putting one foot in front of the other until I'd finally snapped myself out of it and centered my mind.

I knew I was risking a hell of a lot by walking through those doors and interrupting Dracula, but in that moment, I knew I was willing to put down my life for her. It hadn't even been a question, just an instinct to protect my girl.

She finally turned and looked up at me, painting a pathetic little smile on her face that did nothing to disguise the despair pooling in her eyes.

"Alina—" I started, bringing my hands up to rest gently on her arms, wanting to pull her into me, but she held out a hand, stopping me.

Taking in a deep breath, she exhaled slowly before letting the smile drop away. Her voice wobbled slightly before gaining a bit more confidence, "I'm okay, I think I just need to take a shower and eat. It's hard to settle my moods when I feel so on edge with hunger—or hanger, if you will."

Liar.

Her attempt at a joke at the end was such a clear sign she was bullshitting me. I was the king of deflecting shit I didn't want to talk about.

I knew she was probably hungry, but I'd seen her at the height of her bloodlust as a newly turned vampire the first morning she'd been here. Even then, she had some of the best control over her emotions I'd ever seen in a fledgling.

Searching her face, I waited for any flicker of a clue that she was going to say anything further but found none. Her jaw was tight, like she was forcing her mouth to stay shut on purpose.

If she wasn't ready to talk about it, I wouldn't be a dick and try to force her. I'd already proven to her that I was a massive asshole and unworthy of placing her heart in my hands—I wasn't going to go out of my way to make that any more obvious.

I knew I wouldn't be able to become a changed man over night, but fuck, I had to try something. I wasn't walking away from her ever again, even if she pissed me off which was an inevitability at this point. Neither of us was ever going to stop challenging the other, but the difference now was that it wasn't coming from a place of malice on my part. I just thoroughly fucking loved ruffling her feathers.

Dropping my hands to my side, I turned to find my clothes and give her space. "Okay, why don't you get in the shower, and I'll run down and see if there were any bags spared from your nemesis' dumb fucking plan."

She blew out a small puff of air before muttering under her breath, "Fucking cocksucker."

There she was. That was my spitfire.

I needed to call Estrid quickly anyway and let her know that I wouldn't be in until my second class of the day. I'd never called in before, so I was hoping like hell she wouldn't chew my ass out for it.

I pulled my clothes on before grabbing my phone from where it sat on the dresser. I waited to hear the shower turn on before heading out the door. Dragging the phone to my ear after dialing Estrid, I waited two rings before she picked up.

I set a languid pace down the stairs to the first floor, laughing as her perky voice asked, "How'd it go with Drake? Isn't it incredible that he made an appearance here at our Academy to test the students? I mean, I can't—"

Cutting her off, I decided to just rip the bandage off. "We got in a fist fight, and there's a massive hole in the wall that needs to be patched. I'm back in my room cleaning up, so I'll need coverage this period."

The silence that met my statement was deafening.

I made it all the way to the first floor before she spoke again. "Does this have to do with Ms. Van Helsing?"

I guess there was *one* more bandage to rip off.

Moseying over to the heap of empty bags on the cafeteria floor, I cleared my throat before responding. "She's my mate, Estrid."

A gleeful laugh floated through the phone. "Oh, that's so wonderful, Linc—"

Make that a *third* bandage to rip off.

"And so is Dracula."

Her voice reached a level of screeching that I didn't know was possible, forcing me to pull the phone away from my ear as she yelled, "What the fuck, Lincoln! How is this possible?"

My eyes scanned the room as I considered her question. Honestly? I had no fucking idea how it was possible, and I didn't know how to even begin addressing it. Letting out a breath as I spotted three bags still full in a chair tucked under the table, I tried to change the subject. "We need a new supply of animal blood today. Ms. Federman thought it would be amusing to empty them all to force Alina to drink human blood, it seems."

She spluttered on the other end. "Fates, I always know there's going to be a commotion when I bring students in that I was guided to, but this is—" She cut off abruptly before exhaling a harsh breath. "*Shit*...I have to call Drake to ensure he's not pulling funding."

I rolled my eyes at the reminder that he wasn't entirely a fucked-up bastard. After all, he did end up donating a sizable amount of money annually to the academy that funds a few sectors, not just the vampire sector alone.

"I highly doubt he'll do that," I retorted as I made my way back upstairs. "I have to go, Estrid. I'll be in for my second class today. Thanks."

She continued to talk, but I clicked off the line,

having done my part to fill her in on what little she needed to know to keep her off my ass for missing class and excusing Alina's absence as well.

Pushing the door open, I couldn't help but think of how great it felt to have my Spitfire in my space like this. I'd always been a man of solitude, using my room as my refuge, but I was finding that sharing it with her felt right.

A small hiccupping sob carried through the air, pausing me in mid-step as I passed through the threshold. She was crying.

Shit.

I knew she wasn't okay, but dammit, what was I supposed to do now? She'd made it clear minutes ago that she didn't want to talk about it.

Indecision wrenched my gut as I considered whether to leave her in peace or try to offer my support. I wasn't good at this part. I knew I wanted to be there for her, but I didn't know what to say to help her. Part of me felt like I'd just fuck it up and end up pissing her off.

Would I just bother her with my presence? Maybe she wanted to be alone.

The decision was made for me when her crying reached new heights, with her gasping for breaths between every gut-wrenching sob. I'd risk pissing her off if it meant her knowing that I was going to be here for her now, through anything.

Before I could even think twice about it, I tossed the blood onto the bed and sped to the shower. Gently opening the steamed-up glass door, I found her standing in the corner with her glistening back to me as the water sprayed over her.

My own throat tightened with emotion, my heart feeling like it was being ripped to shreds with each passing moment. How had I ever walked away from her before?

Not giving a shit about being in my clothes still, I entered the shower and shut the door behind me gently. They were soaked through within moments as I walked toward her. Reaching out to run my fingers over her shoulder, I held my breath, waiting for her to scream at me for interrupting her in such a vulnerable moment. But when she didn't stop me, I slowly pulled her away from the wall, turning her toward me as I did.

"I'm here, and I'm not going anywhere this time," I whispered, knowing she'd still hear me over the water spraying loudly between us.

My wet hair fell into my eyes as I waited for her to let me in. Her body shook as her head hung down, her silver hair falling around her face like a security blanket.

All I could do was wait to see if she wanted to let me in.

The moment her head lifted and she looked me in the eyes as her bottom lip wobbled, I was a fucking goner. I would drop to my knees and beg for her forgiveness for *ever* adding to the list of reasons she'd ever shed a tear.

I exhaled in relief as she stepped into me, wrapping her arms around my waist as she continued to cry. Holding her to me, I shifted us until I was able to slide down the wall with her in my arms. Situating her on my lap, her head drifted to the nook between my head and shoulder, her hands fisting my shirt in her grasps.

Dropping a kiss to the top of her head before settling mine on top of hers, I gave her a gentle squeeze before murmuring, "It's going to be okay. I'll make sure of it."

I knew I couldn't fix everything for her, but I hoped she'd give me the opportunity to prove that I'd help her burn the world down around us until there was nothing left if that's what it took.

CHAPTER SIX
ALINA

I didn't know how long Lincoln held me in the shower, but when he finally picked me up and turned off the water, the tears had long since passed and I was shivering almost uncontrollably. After wrapping me in a towel, he carried me to the bed where a few bags of blood lay before gently setting me down.

"Drink those," he ordered softly, pointing at the bags. "I need to get out of these wet clothes. Do you need anything?"

I shook my head 'no'. I felt numb as I sat there and simply watched him, but the one feeling worming its way up through the ice around my heart and body was how safe I felt with him now.

Holding back my huff of disappointment at not

being able to watch him as he closed the bathroom door to change, I looked around at the room. His impressive liquor collection drew my eye for a moment, making me question whether I should pour myself a glass of whiskey.

Maybe liquor wasn't such a good idea for someone who was barely holding onto their sanity as is.

I let out a sigh and did as he requested, burrowing into the pillows at the top of the bed and sucking down the bags he'd found for me. The pang of hunger dulled to a low discomfort. The few bags weren't enough to satiate me completely, but I was thankful nonetheless for what he'd been able to find. If he had come back with bags of human blood as my only option...I don't know what I would have done. I was apparently already at my limit of shit that I could bury in such a short span of time.

The moment I heard the door close behind him, the dam had burst. I thought I could bury it with the pleasure we'd shared, but for some reason when Lincoln uttered the reminder that Dracula would be back to talk to me tomorrow...everything from the morning came rushing back to me. There was nothing I could do to stop it this time.

Did I truly think that he'd disappear forever into

his bat cave or what the fuck ever after our altercation this morning? Absolutely not. Did I want to hope that my attempt at killing him and openly admitting that I knew what he did would keep him at bay for at least a few days so I could ignore my reality a little longer? Yes.

Tossing the empty bags onto the nightstand, I flopped onto my back and stretched out like a starfish, staring up at the ceiling.

What the fuck was I going to do now? I'd relentlessly focused on my one goal since my life had gone to hell. My thirst for vengeance had been my lifeline, and I'd clung to it when the murky waters of my consciousness got too rough.

The bathroom door clicked open, but I kept my gaze up, not knowing what to say to Lincoln. He'd shocked the hell out of me by silently sitting with me and not prodding me, instead letting me know he was there and that everything would be okay.

Was this even the same man who had sneered at me with such venomous disgust during our first meeting, telling me how awful slayers were and that I wasn't going to last a week here? It was mind-blowing to think about where we were now in comparison, but there was still a part of me that was hesitant to place my faith in him...in us. As much as I wanted him, I had to be honest with myself and realize that I really didn't know who he was at his core. He'd shown me equally awful and wonderful sides of himself in such a short time, but which was the real him?

I heard the telltale pop of a bottle being opened before he asked, "Want anything, Spitfire?"

My toes curled as a dumb smile tugged my lips up at the use of the nickname.

Never the easy way, Spitfire.

"Nah," I answered, shocked by how despondent I sounded to my own ears.

It matched exactly how I felt inside though...just *blah*. It was as if all my emotions had gone down the shower drain with my tears.

"Who do you think you are, the queen of all of Praeditus?" he asked with mock annoyance in his tone as he approached the bed. "Move your ass over, or I'll move it for you."

The jab drew a small chuckle from me as I shuffled over to the left side of the bed, giving him room to slide in next to me. My body dipped toward him as the mattress sank down a bit with his arrival. He quickly settled himself, pulling me to lay my head on his lap, soaking in his warmth as he sat up against the headboard.

My body tensed at the intimacy of the moment as he ran his free hand through the wet strands of my hair. This felt too good to be true. My stomach clenched with apprehension as everything in my body urged me to run. I was getting too fucking attached to him, and eventually he'd let me down. He was a bloodsucker, after all.

Just before I was about to bolt for my own room, his voice halted me. "Do you want to know why I had such a visceral reaction to you that first morning in Estrid's office?"

My head jerked back slightly as I glanced up at him, confusion swirling through my head in a hazy fog. This wasn't the topic of conversation I expected from him. Everything in me assumed there was only so long he would let me keep my thoughts to myself in our quiet reprieve.

I couldn't help the smart-ass comment that left my mouth, slightly stunned by him offering up personal information at his own behest. "Do I need oxygen to breathe?"

Tugging strands of my hair, he let out a beautiful, genuine laugh as his eyes glittered with amusement. "You're such a little shit."

I wasn't sure if I'd ever seen him so...carefree,

and that made my own heart feel lighter than it had in days.

Smirking at him, I lowered my head back down to get comfy, feeling like it was a little too much to maintain eye contact as he let me into his personal life.

"Yeah, but I'm your little shit," I retorted, nuzzling into him. "Or so the Fates have said."

Shocked by my own open admission, I froze up completely. I didn't dare even breathe or blink as I waited for his response.

Fuck, fuck, fuck. Why did I say that? We were so *not* on that level yet.

Did I even truly feel that way?

Thankfully, he didn't make it awkward. His hand moved back to a soft, stroking motion as he mused, "Yeah, you are."

My body slowly relaxed once more as his glass clinked above me. I heard him swallow before he let out a heavy sigh. "So, I'm sure you were surprised to hear Drake—or Dracula—refer to Andrei and me in such a casual way." I hummed my agreement before he continued. "The reason is because both of our dad's worked for him. I grew up in his court of insiders, until my parents decided that it was too dangerous to stay. My father was a Knight on his board, tasked with being the first line of defense around Dracula."

That lined up with the information I'd heard from Andrei, but it also sort of explained the weird tiff they seemed to have from day one. Undoubtedly, it had only increased with my involvement with both of them, but I'd never forget the look of hatred when Lincoln had threatened to give Andrei detention the morning I'd run into him. He'd dangled his dad finding out about him having that on his record…

Shit. My eyes widened as some of the pieces clicked together. Lincoln had to know exactly what a piece of shit Andrei's dad was if he grew up in that group of people.

I tried my damn best to keep my mouth shut despite the dozens of questions running rampant in my brain. He'd shown me patience and kindness with his willingness to let me keep my thoughts and secrets to myself until I was willing to share them, and I'd do my best to return that.

Finally he continued, though I almost wished he hadn't. My heart broke as he gruffly whispered, "My parents were killed by slayers when I was just a young boy. We'd escaped to Ordinarius to live amongst the humans in peace."

His drink clanked once more, and suddenly I wished I'd taken him up on the offer to have my own. This was much heavier shit than I expected.

It was illegal for any supernatural being to live in Ordinarius. If they'd been reported, it would have been the duty of slayers to bring them back to Sanguis. But if his parents had fought them, slayers were allowed to kill them by law.

The way he'd practically spat in my face at the mention of who I was made so much damn sense now.

"Linc," I breathed out, pushing myself up to lean against the headboard next to him. He was staring straight ahead at the wall on the far side of the room, but I didn't need him to look me in the eyes to see the pain that was rolling from him in waves. It was a grief I knew all too well. "I'm so sorry."

His head swept to look me in the eyes as he admitted, "Yeah, we shouldn't have been in Ordinarius, but my parents risked it for me, Alina. They didn't want me to grow up around the violence and political warfare that came with Dracula's board, but it isn't a job you can just walk away from. They would have been hunted down in Praeditus for all the secrets my dad knew. Ordinarius was the *only* option."

Not too long ago, I wouldn't have blinked twice at his story. It was a black and white scenario for slayers. Don't break the law, and we won't have to enforce it. But now...now all I felt was shame at thinking life was ever that simple for anyone.

Going back to Praeditus wasn't an option for their family, so of course they'd fought to stay. All they'd wanted was to live peacefully with their son in a safe environment. They'd risked so damn much to even try.

"I came home to find them dead. I managed to find my way back to the portal we'd used that connected to his castle, thinking I could find help," he admitted with a single, dry laugh. Shaking his head, he looked up at the ceiling as he added, "I don't know what I thought they could do to help. I just didn't want to admit my parents were gone."

My throat clogged, and I nodded my under-standing as I pictured Lincoln as a little boy, finding his parents dead. It was a scene I could picture all too vividly from my own experience. It was the kind of gut-wrenching horror that would stick with you for the rest of your life. There was nothing you could do to get those images out of your memory.

We truly were two sides of the same coin, forged in the pits of the hell that was our past.

"We were happy there for a month before they found us," he admitted, a tight smile pressing over his lips as he reached up toward my face. His thumb brushed against my cheek, coming away wet with tears. "I'll always hold onto those bright memories, but I've never been able to let go of my hatred of all slayers, nor for Dracula and his board members."

Clearing my throat, I asked, "What did they do when you returned to the castle?"

Inhaling deeply, he let out a shaky breath as his head tipped back to look at the ceiling. "The guards scoffed in my face, telling me my parents got what they deserved for deserting our kind. I became a ward of the government. They sent me to combat school and provided me with a cot in an orphanage alongside other unfortunate children who either lost their parents or were turned by vampires with nowhere to go. That's all I knew until I was approached by Estrid after coming of age. I've been here ever since, happily staying far away from all that Sanguis represents to me."

I stared at him, realizing I was finally seeing Lincoln for the first time. All his jagged, broken edges were on display for me to see, and I'd never been more drawn to him than I was now. His vulnerability and willingness to share such a core part of his life was admirable.

His phone blared from the side of the bed, startling both of us from our little bubble of heartache and honesty.

I knew our conversation was over the second a mask of calm confidence took over his face as he snapped the phone to his ear and barked out, "What, Victoria?"

I almost smacked him on the shoulder for talking to her like that. I knew they were close friends, but damn.

Her voice floated through the air as he pulled the phone away to glance at the screen. "I have appointments to attend, Lincoln! You said you'd be in for your second class, so get your ass over here."

Honestly, I'd completely forgotten that classes were even going on right now and that he was supposed to be teaching them. Everything had fallen to the side as soon as we'd entered this room.

"Shit," he hissed, lips thinning as he lifted it back to his ear. "Sorry, Vic. I didn't realize it was that late already. I'll be over in a few minutes, but just so you know, Alina won't be in for your session today, and I don't want to hear shit about it."

My brows lifted toward my hairline as he hung

up on her and pressed a kiss to my forehead before jumping out of bed. Tossing the phone onto his nightstand and depositing the empty glass next to it, he rushed to his wardrobe.

Calling over his shoulder as he pulled out a crisp, white dress shirt, he asked, "Do you want to come with me? Estrid already knows you won't be going to any classes today, but if you don't want to be alone, you can come sit in the room and watch."

"I'm okay. Thanks, though," I responded, still reeling a bit from everything he'd just shared with me. "I'll just head back to my room for the rest of the night. I owe you big time for getting me out of therapy."

"I can think of a few ways you can pay me back," he quipped in a sultry, deep tone, making my mind flip back to just how incredible our time together had been, despite the surrounding issues.

Chuckling at his words, I lifted the covers off and reached up with both arms, stretching side to side. He turned around at my movement, and as he pulled on black dress pants, he offered, "You can stay here if you want. Up to you," before tucking his shirt in and grabbing a belt.

I paused at his words, shocked by his offer. Thinking it over quickly as I looked around, I found that it felt odd to think about staying here without him. I wasn't quite ready to combine our spaces like that. Going back to my room and having time to myself sounded...good.

For the first time since coming to the academy, I wasn't horrified at the idea of being alone with my thoughts. I wasn't looking to pick a fight to keep that fire within me burning any longer as a distraction. It was an odd realization.

"Thanks, but I'm going to head back to my room and study a bit," I answered, slipping off the bed to find my clothes. I pulled them on quickly, shoving my shredded underwear into my pocket. I wasn't leaving them behind for him to claim like some trophy. Who knows, maybe he'd be that weird guy who carried them around and sniffed them.

He zipped around quickly before meeting me at the door and offering a folded note to me. "Victoria gave this to me to pass along to you from someone named Alexandra."

Today just continued to be full of surprises, but I found myself eager to see what the note had to say. I couldn't deny that I'd been bummed to not find her and her friend Alora at the party the other night. Who knows, maybe the entire night would have turned out differently if I had.

With a promise to find him if I needed him, we headed our separate directions, and I opened the note to read as I made my way slowly down to the third level.

Alina,

I'm not sure if you showed up to the party Monday night, but I promise I'm not an asshole who ditched you on purpose. I was looking for you at the beginning, but some shit happened with the headmistress and myself that took me away from the party.

It's a lot to explain, and right now Victoria is watching me as I write this during our session, so I don't want to take too long. She told me Lincoln will get this message to you for me, so if you're reading this, LINCOLN, stop reading this personal message. (But thanks for stepping in when Professor Helen tried to attack me. That earns you cool points.)

If you don't have anything going on Sunday, meet me at the library. I'll be there all day researching. I'd love to catch up on how your first week went. Plus, I don't know if they told you that all sectors are allowed to go to the library in my area. It's a ghost town, though, so we should have plenty of privacy.

Give me one more chance, and I promise I won't disappear!

xX Alexandra

P.S. I thought I was going to get sent back to the naughty bin today. Hope you're faring better than me and staying out of trouble.

A cackle erupted from me at her continuing to use the term naughty bin and the fact that she'd potentially been sent back already. Here I thought I was going to rub off on her, but she was getting into more trouble than me.

I'd have to ask Lincoln if he read the note and what the comment about defending her from a professor was all about. My hackles rose at the idea of someone trying to attack her. I wished I could say that I was appalled to hear that a professor of the academy had done that, but I knew all too well that prejudices transcended responsibilities of some people here.

Cracking my door open, I tossed the note onto my desk before changing into something more comfortable. I slid into my chair to read the note once more and smiled at her determination to be friends.

I could really use some of those right now.

CHAPTER SEVEN
ALINA

Blearily rubbing my eyes, I stifled a yawn before my body went through the routine I was becoming accustomed to here: do a little upper body stretch, stumble to the bathroom, and then let the heat from the shower revive me like a demon desperate for the warmth of the flames from hell.

After I was slightly revived from the shower, I tugged on the black, high-waisted skirt and tucked in the white, long sleeve blouse under the waistband. I glanced longingly at my dirty leathers in the corner. I needed to clean them as soon as possible but looking at myself in the floor length mirror in the corner, I uttered words I'd never dare let anyone else hear in reference to academy clothing.

"Not too shabby," I admitted, nodding my head in appreciation for the whole naughty schoolgirl look it gave me.

While I knew I was supposed to wear the blazer on top of my plain top to display the emblem of the school, I refused to comply entirely. It wasn't like I'd gotten in trouble for not being in line with the dress code yet, anyway. The only reason I was even giving this skirt a chance was because it wasn't that god-awful black and red plaid one I'd seen a few of my peers wearing. That shit would stay in my wardrobe forever to collect cobwebs.

Grabbing socks, I quickly pulled them and my boots on before sweeping a comb through my hair. Thankfully, my skin, swollen all day yesterday from what felt like a never-ending torrent of tears, was normal now. Unfortunately, I now had dark bags under my eyes, giving away the fact that I'd struggled to find peaceful sleep last night.

After going cross-eyed from studying, I'd laid in bed tossing and turning as I thought of what today would bring with Dracula. I didn't know what the hell to think if he followed through on showing up to talk to me today. Thinking about how it would feel to have to be around Andrei in classes now that we'd agreed to call an end to whatever we'd had going on certainly hadn't helped my insomnia either.

I wasn't looking forward to any of it, to say the least.

The only bright spot of my night had been the delivery of a mini-fridge full of animal blood to my room. Estrid sent a note along with it, saying that she would ensure all her students' needs were cared for and to let her know if I needed anything else.

Color me shocked at the special treatment, but I wouldn't bite the hand that fed me or whatever the fuck the saying was.

Splashing some water onto my face to try to help brighten me up, I grabbed the hand towel to dry off before pinching my cheeks to try to bring a hint of color to my gaunt face. Crossing to the small fridge near my bed now, I drained a few bags before depositing them in the trash can.

One of the major perks of this new set up was being able to completely avoid the always-packed cafeteria. Glancing at the alarm clock on my night-stand, I let a breath out, knowing I couldn't hide in here forever and needed to head over to Praeditus 101.

Looking at the mirror in the corner once more, I straightened my shoulders and tilted my chin up.

"You are Alina Van Helsing. You can handle whatever today throws at you. One foot in front of the other. Day by day."

Even if I didn't feel it now, I'd continue to remind myself of that. It was one of the first tricks they taught us as young slayers in training who lacked the confidence to fight—if you said your affirmations out loud often enough, eventually your mind would begin to internalize and believe them. While the slayer affirmations were more along the lines of: *You will become a great slayer, you will make your House proud,* I found it helpful to apply the basic principle to my needs now.

Commotion and high-pitched squeals pulled my attention toward my window, interrupting my little pep talk. Drawing back the curtain, my brows slammed together at the absurdity before me. Hundreds—no, thousands—of black roses littered the ground outside, making up the shape of a heart.

Letting out a fake gag at the ridiculous display of affection, I yanked the curtain shut before heading down the stairs. I honestly couldn't understand why anyone would want to be the center of attention like that. I mean really, was all of that for the intended recipient or was it to make the person who'd set up this nauseating display seem a great person to everyone else watching?

The small victory for me was that it would at least distract all the students and I could make my way to class in peace. No doubt Maya would be on a warpath after getting detention, and I was severely lacking gas in the tank to deal with her right now.

Pushing the doors open, I kept my head down, preparing to put on a burst of speed to get by the crowd gathered around the heart of roses.

"Alina," a deep, rumbling voice called out, halting me mid-step.

No. Not now. Not so soon.

My throat dried—all the scenarios I'd practiced in my head flying out the window as his familiar scent washed over me. I hated that it made me feel like I was being wrapped in a soft and warm cashmere blanket at a bonfire, the woodsy scent mixing with an undertone of vanilla. The scent itself should have been soothing with how pleasant it was, but all it did was make my body lock up as shivers ran down my spine.

I felt like prey that was being stalked by a predator, and there was nowhere to run.

The second his large hand wrapped around my shoulder, my shock wore off, quickly replaced with the fury that I thought had dove off a cliff and died within me. I was wrong. So, so fucking wrong.

Welcome home, my old friend. Kind of you to show your face again.

Whirling around, I smacked his hand away from me, and my nostrils flared as I glared up at him. "Do not touch me. What gave you the impression that I would ever fucking welcome that?"

Once again, he was dressed impeccably, wearing a three-piece all-black ensemble that matched his eyes, hair, and very soul, it would seem.

"First and foremost, because you're my mate," he retorted, a look of incredulous shock on his face at the venom dripping from my tone.

Gasps went up around us, and I fought to keep my eyes on him, not wanting to see who heard him. It's not like it mattered, anyway. Whoever wasn't here would hear about it through the grapevine by the end of the day. It was the kind of juicy detail that was too good not to share.

Great, just what I wanted to be known as now: Dracula's mate. Before now, everyone seemed content to let me do my thing other than Maya, but now I'd probably have a group of adoring fans wanting to use me to get close to him.

Taking a step closer to me, he tilted his head

down, towering over me with his height. I refused to back up. He knew what I thought of him after everything I'd spewed to his face yesterday. What was the point of cowering now?

You are Alina Van Helsing. You can handle whatever today throws at you.

"And two, because I simply wanted you to see the gift I brought this morning, but you seemed hellbent on walking out of the building without looking around."

My jaw went slack, mouth popping open as my eyes finally bounced to the monstrosity of roses behind him and the gathered crowd of whispering students.

"That's...for me?" I asked, spluttering in shock as I returned my focus to him. I couldn't help but let out a laugh before crossing my arms at my chest. "Are you fucking joking?"

His brows pinched together as he looked back at the rose sculpture and then back to me. "You don't like it?"

Running my tongue along my teeth, I closed my eyes briefly as I tried to find the right words to convey how much I didn't fucking like it.

Snapping them open, I let a huff of amusement escape me as I uncrossed one hand to press my finger into his chest, stepping further into his space. It didn't escape me the way his lips parted, the tip of his tongue darting out to wet them as he watched me with an unnerving focus once again.

"I don't like it, at all," I announced loudly for everyone to hear. "Not only do I think it's ridiculously cliché, but it also just proves that you don't know me at all. So much for being my *fated mate*, I guess."

I was prepared to spew a hell of a lot more about how the only gift I could ever want from him was his head on a plate, but he cut me off, grabbing my arms tightly as an energy filled him that I could only describe as impassioned. "You won't give me a chance to get to know you, Alina!" he seethed, eyes wide as his chest heaved. "You won't let me explain a single fucking thing about how everything you said to me yesterday is utter bullshit."

I let my fangs snap out at that, baring them at him.

"You're too wrapped up in your own pity party to see that maybe, just maybe, you played directly into someone's hand, believing the shit they spoon fed you."

How fucking dare he.

Shoving against his chest, I screamed when he

didn't budge an inch. "Fuck you!" Letting my hand fly out, it cracked against his cheek. My palm burned, tingling like a motherfucker at the strength I'd put behind the blow.

A cold glint entered his dead eyes as he smirked. "Any day, darling. We have forever, after all."

My chest heaved as anger rolled through me. We stayed there in a stand-off, neither refusing to look away first, breathing each other's air with our nearness. Electricity crackled between us, like two opposing storm fronts colliding. Minutes ticked by. Or maybe it was seconds. Or possibly even eternities before he broke the silence.

Dracula narrowed his eyes as he offered, "I have one other gift for you, and I have a feeling you'll like this one, darling."

My mouth opened to tell him that there wasn't a single thing in this world he could give to me that I would accept, but he turned sharply and called out, "Maya Federman! Step forward."

Color me fucking curious at where this was going, though. I snapped my mouth shut and watched as she pushed through the throng of students with her head held high like she was about to accept a fucking award.

"Yes, sir?" she asked innocently, batting her eyes

up at him.

"Such a fucking kiss ass," I muttered beneath my breath, rolling my eyes at how fucking predictable she was.

The polite, good girl mask slipped as she glared at me, making me smile at her and wiggle my fingers in a taunting wave.

"Don't look at her! Don't even fucking *think* about my mate ever again," Dracula snapped loudly, making her jump slightly as finally, a hint of fear entered her eyes. "Go to your room and pack your fucking bags. Your admission to this academy has been revoked."

What. The. Fuck.

"You can't order that!" she screamed as tears pooled in her eyes, looking around frantically as if someone was going to come out of the woodwork and stand up for her. "You don't run this school!"

I wished I could say there was something satisfying about absolutely no one stepping forward to defend her as she began to sob in earnest, but there wasn't. I never truly wanted her to suffer, at least not after I realized she wasn't a true threat to me. I just wanted to be left the fuck alone.

Dracula tutted, holding his finger in the air to silence her. "I might not run this school, but I do run

Sanguis, and your father was none too happy to hear about the issues you've been giving my mate here at the academy. He's agreed with me that it's in your best interest to return home."

Everything I'd learned from Andrei and Lincoln about the way everyone feared Dracula and his board came rushing back to me. I wasn't sure if he'd gone to threaten her father himself or if he sent one of his lackeys, but whatever he thought he was doing right now to impress me...It wasn't working.

I didn't need anyone to fight my battle for me, and she truly was nothing more than a pesky nuisance at the end of the day.

"Leave her alone," I said, keeping my voice strong and sure. I stood my ground, refusing to be affected as Dracula turned around and tilted his head at me, letting his eyes run the length of me for a moment.

"No," he answered simply before turning back to her and pointing at the door. "Go pack, now. I'll be personally escorting you through the portal to return home."

My face heated with anger at his dismissive attitude, and I stomped over to him as Maya headed inside, shoulders sagging as she drug her feet.

"Go to class, everyone," he commanded in a

sharp tone that brokered no room for argument. He turned to face me fully as the crowd dispersed, lifting a brow and holding his hands up. "What did I do wrong now, darling? I know you love an opportunity to find anything wrong with me to cement those false truths swirling around in that mind of yours."

He wasn't wrong about me loving to find more things wrong with him, and luckily he was making that task all too easy.

For a second in the combat room, when that tear had fallen from his eye and splashed onto my face, I'd really questioned if I knew the full truth. He'd seemed so damn heartbroken and grief stricken at my attempt to kill him and the truths I'd spat at him.

Each time he pulled a stunt like this, though, I found it all too easy to double down on my truth.

"Do you think you're my knight in shining armor or some shit?" I asked with disgust. "All you proved to me is that you're a bully that shoves his weight around to get what he wants."

His hand snaked out to grip my chin tightly as he melded our chests together. "That's fine, darling. I'm okay with being the villain in your story if it means ensuring you're safe," he whispered, making my heart twist. "If you think it's wrong of me to use the power I've amassed to protect you, then I truly don't want to be right, darling. I'm not going to stop."

I gritted my teeth as he brought his lips within an inch of my own, breathing over my face as he added, "I'm just getting started."

Anger and confusion swarmed within my stomach, making me feel sick. There he went again.

Why did he continue to try so hard to seem like he gave a shit about me? What the fuck was his goal here? I wasn't some valuable pawn to use on his board.

"I'm more than capable of fighting my own battles," I answered, ripping my chin from his grip as I took a step back. "I won't forgive, and I won't forget, no matter the lengths you'll go to try to brainwash me into believing whatever *this* is."

"We'll see about that darling," he called out as I turned to head to class. "All I have is time to prove you wrong."

Holding my slender middle finger up, I waved it in the air toward him as my parting goodbye.

He wanted time to prove me wrong, and I wanted time to find a solution to killing him.

I guess we'd see who achieved their goal first.

CHAPTER EIGHT
ALINA

The whispers were incessant around me.

Do you think she's really his mate?

There's no way he'll keep her around. She's not good enough.

My jaw clenched so tightly as I walked through the halls that I feared my teeth would crack from the force.

She probably slept with him to even get into the academy to begin with.

Yeah, right. He fucking *wishes* I'd sleep with him.

Staring at the clock above the board, my boot tapped against the tiled floor impatiently as I prayed to the Fates for Professor Levia to hurry up and get the lesson started so these vultures would have something else to focus on.

I could have set them straight about the truth, but it would be a waste of my breath. All they'd do was twist my words and play telephone until suddenly they were telling people I admitted to taking Dracula's cock up my ass or something.

I wouldn't lose sleep over what these losers thought of me, anyway. They'd never be of concern unless they put themselves directly in my path of wrath. Although I knew I had Lincoln on my side now, that didn't mean the other Professors would suddenly think of me as exempt from detention, so I needed to hold in my annoyance.

If a moment presented itself outside of the watchful eyes of the academy's staff, then maybe I'd be singing a different tune. I couldn't afford to be kicked out of the school right now, not with everything else in my life literally in shambles.

A familiar face walked into the room and all but sucked the oxygen from it. My breath caught in my throat as our eyes clashed. I had been curious where he'd been this morning after not seeing him amongst the crowd outside or in the class when I'd arrived.

A small part of me had panicked thinking maybe Dracula had ordered him to go home as well.

"Hey, Alina," he mumbled as he slid into the

desk next to mine before facing toward the front of the room once more.

Just like that.

Clearing my throat, I croaked out, "Hey," before focusing my attention on the pen in my hand as I tapped it against my notebook.

Sneaking a peak out of the corner of my eye, I saw him staring lifelessly at the board.

It was like watching a shell of who I knew Andrei to be. The way I craved for him to call me *new girl* with some heat to his tone was unreal. More than anything, though, I wanted to see him not looking so damn defeated.

Where was the arrogant, self-proclaimed king of the school who had seemingly lived to butt heads with me? I wanted him back, even if all we would ever be was platonic.

She's such a slut. She's sleeping with Dracula and Andrei.

In the span of me blinking, Andrei was up and out of his desk with his hand wrapped around the throat of the man who I'd come to learn was the one and only Jared. The fucker who'd ripped me off Maya and thrown me into the wall.

I hadn't forgotten about the payback I owed him, but as I watched Andrei smash him into the wall, blood quickly streaming down the white brick, I considered maybe calling it even.

There he was. That was the dangerous and explosive side of Andrei that made my core heat with need. If Dracula wanted to be my knight in shining armor, he could certainly start by taking notes from Andrei.

"Don't ever fucking call her that ever again," Andrei hissed darkly before threading his fingers into Jared's blonde man bun and using it as leverage to pull his head back before slamming it back into the wall again.

A resounding crack sounded before bits of brick crumbled to the ground and a cloud of dust swept around them.

Turning in my seat to enjoy the show, a wicked smile took over my face as Jared tried to throw a few weak punches at Andrei's ribs to get him off. The man was like a stone wall of muscle though, unmovable and dangerous.

My eyes widened as I watched Andrei drag Jared by the hair behind him, moaning in pain and leaving a trail of blood in their wake. No one was whispering anymore, and the silence was like music to my ears.

Desks and chairs squeaked against the floor as he forced a pathway toward me before tossing Jared at my feet. Placing the bottom of his boot on top of Jared's face, he pressed down as he smiled at me. "Apologize to the lady."

Maybe I was a little bit of a hypocrite but watching him stand up for me against disrespect that was happening right in front of me was...Fuck, there was no other way to put it than that I was all kinds of hot and bothered by the display.

The difference between what Dracula had done and what Andrei had done was stark. Dracula had quite possibly ruined Maya's chance at a good future, painting a target on her and her entire family's back for crossing *Dracula's mate*. Andrei simply showed he wasn't going to tolerate disrespect by knocking Jared around a bit right in front of me. I could have stopped him if that's what I wanted, and I know he would have stopped with a single word. But Jared's wounds would heal, probably a lot faster than his ego would, and he'd go on with his life with hopefully a little more tact and humility.

I'd like to think of it as a friendly life lesson.

"S...sorry, Alina," Jared stuttered before coughing and spitting a mouthful of blood onto the floor.

Professor Levia chose that moment to enter the room, coming to a halt and throwing her hands up. "What in the world? Alina, go to the Headmistress' office! Clean this mess up, students. If you're going to start it, you're going to fix it."

My head fell back as a groan slipped through my lips. Why was I being sent to see Estrid when I hadn't lifted a damn finger or said anything? Lincoln would have praised me for being a good girl if he'd been here.

I guess we're going tit for tat with our visits to the naughty bin, Alexandra.

As I pushed to my feet, awkwardly stepping over Jared's body, Andrei's hand snapped out to halt me. That damn smirk that I'd missed so much tilted a corner of his mouth up, as he offered, "Sorry, new girl."

My own smile toyed at my lips as I let out a small chuckle. "You owe me, fucker."

And just like that, it was like we'd breathed life back into our...friendship.

Fuck me for not being able to stop smiling like an idiot about it the whole way over to the administration building. What I realized during the short walk, though, was that it had breathed some of my own fire back into me too. Suppressing my feelings for Andrei had felt like burying a piece of myself, and it seemed, from my view at least, that it had hit him in the same way.

I needed to talk to Lincoln about this, because it felt wrong to hold onto it in secret now. It would probably hurt to hear, but I didn't want to ruin what little trust we'd managed to build between us by holding back. It felt like I was living a lie by simply not admitting the truth to him, and I didn't want to live like that.

Heading up the steps to the third level, I hesitated at Estrid's door.

"Come in, Alina!" she called from the other side just as I lifted my knuckles to knock against it.

Letting myself in, I peeked around the door and winced at her beaming smile.

Why did I feel like all I did was disappoint her after she took such a big risk on me? Honestly, I was a bigger risk than she even knew. She had unknowingly offered to train a fledgling vampire who had the sole intention of killing a leader of a sector in Praeditus.

Sweeping her hand out, she chirped, "Please, have a seat."

Settling into the leather chair in front of her, I decided to just lay it out there for her. "Estrid, look, I was sent here because of a fight that broke out in class, but I was merely a bystander this time. I swear. Please don't kick me out," I ended with a plea. "This place is all I have right now."

What I wasn't expecting was her laughter as she shook her head and responded, "Alina, that isn't why you were sent here. I asked Professor Levia to send you to me when I saw her in the lounge this morning. But I will say I'm proud of you for not being directly involved in the fight this time. Baby steps, am I right?"

All I could manage was to blink at her. Was she... joking around with me?

"I wanted to see how you were doing with everything going on right now," she continued, either not noticing my state of stupor or ignoring it entirely. "I hope to have a fresh supply of blood stocked in the cafeteria for you by tomorrow morning if all goes to plan. Is what you have in the mini fridge enough to get you through?"

While I'd always had a sense that Estrid was a very kind and supportive woman, this felt like overkill, even for her. My eyes narrowed slightly as I asked, "Where did the fridge and blood come from? It was very kind. I'm curious if I'm able to keep it or if I need to give it back tomorrow once the new supply comes in."

She didn't even miss a beat. "A generous, anonymous donor of the Academy."

Lifting a brow, I asked, "Does this donor have a name? I'd like to thank them for their most kind gift. It was quite thoughtful."

I had a sinking feeling in my stomach that I knew the answer to that, but I needed it to not be true. I didn't want to give him an iota of gratitude, even if the personal supply of animal blood and a way to keep it fresh might be the one thing he got fucking right in the gift giving department.

It showed that he didn't dismiss my inability to drink human blood and found a way to ensure my needs truly were met. What I did have an issue with, however, was him getting information on me from others. Fated mate or not, he was still my enemy, and it didn't sit right with me that he suddenly had more intel on me than I did him.

Crossing her hands and setting them atop the desk in front of her, her throat bobbed before she seemed to force a smile to her face as she admitted, "Drake did after we spoke yesterday about the issues you've faced here."

My lips pursed at her admission. Of fucking course it was him. Damnit.

"Estrid, I'm very thankful for the opportunity

you've given me by bringing me here," I started as I forced myself to take calming breaths. It wouldn't be right of me to take my frustration out on the wrong person, because hey, I was trying to work on myself, "But that was my private information that he is not privy to."

Confusion drew her eyebrows together as she cocked her head and asked, "Is he not your mate? I was under the impression that he was based upon his word and Lincoln's."

My head fell into my palms as I let out a groan. "Lincoln told you?"

"Well…" she began, trailing off for a moment, "Yes. He also told me he was your mate as well, though. Those are things I do need to be aware of as they transcend our own rules at the academy about no professor-student relationships."

While I understood the need for Lincoln to tell her about *our* bond, I wasn't sure why he'd ever acknowledge the shit between Dracula and me. Clearly I wasn't accepting it.

Estrid prattled on, an air of defensiveness in her tone this time, though. "He is also one of the biggest donors to our academy, helping us run without collecting tuition from students, so his generosity isn't out of the norm. He wanted to ensure your needs were met, Alina. He delivered it himself and asked me to get it to you. He did request that I *not* tell you where it came from, so, if you could refrain from letting him know I told you, that would be most appreciated."

I was going to go ahead and ignore the mention of his donation to the school because I wasn't ready to credit him with such a kind gesture. For all I knew, it was just a generous act to make him look good to the public.

But in the same breath, he'd requested I not be told he provided the fridge and blood...Perhaps he wasn't as dense as I made him out to be. If I'd known, I probably would have refused to drink it out of pure spite. After his gifts today, the only reason I could think of for him not wanting credit for this one, was to ensure I actually accepted it.

I hated to admit that maybe he knew me just a little bit better than I wanted him to.

"Are you doing okay, Alina? Truly, I know that I can't relate to what you have going on, but I'm here as an unbiased ear if you need it."

Before finding out that she'd talked about my struggles with Dracula, I might have taken her up on that. I couldn't deny that having someone to talk to that wasn't Lincoln, Andrei, or Drake sounded incredibly enticing. But now? I didn't feel I could trust that my words wouldn't be relayed.

The lack of privacy I felt right now was something I'd never thought would happen here.

I hadn't even had a week to sit with all this shit going on in my life, yet other people already knew. Estrid, the students in my class, and hell, I was sure it was spreading all throughout Sanguis if Dracula had his way.

My blood chilled at the last thought.

Lifting my head from my hands, I swallowed a lump of dread in my throat as I asked, "Estrid, is my...bond to Dracula public knowledge?"

I hated even referring to it as our bond, but I was at a loss for what else to call it.

Finally, the smile from her face fell, like she understood where I was going with this. "I can't say for certain that everyone knows, but he's certainly not hiding it, Alina. He's elated to have found you and isn't afraid for anyone to know that it's you, even with your origins as a slayer."

All the blood drained from my face at what that meant. It would be the most highly talked about gossip of Sanguis, and it would most certainly get back to the slayers. They'd have no context of the situation and who knew what else was being said alongside the information.

Grief swirled within my chest at the bite of betrayal that would make them feel, hearing my name attached to the king of vampires...Right after my House was wiped out by them. I'd already brought dishonor upon my name for allowing myself to be turned and killing Skye, but this was like pouring acid in a gaping wound.

I told Jade what had happened, and that Dracula was to blame for this, but I had no way of knowing if she told anyone else that after I left our territory.

"Estrid, do you know what's been going on in the slayer territory since you found me?" I dared to ask. "I know that they are outside of the typical Praeditus jurisdiction, despite being a part of Sanguis, but I need to know if they're okay."

Pushing from her chair, her heels clicked against the wooden floor as she crossed to sit in the chair next to me. I had to force myself to leave my arm on the side of mine as she reached out to squeeze it gently.

"The only information I have is what Drake told me, which wasn't much," she offered with a rueful smile. "But Alina, I'm so sorry about what you endured. He told me that your family was killed, and I'm assuming it was the same night I found you."

Was nothing allowed to be private in my life anymore?

My lips pursed as I nodded in confirmation. "Yes, it was."

"From what I know, the Devaroux House is in charge now, but to the extent of how that is going, I'm unsure."

My shoulders sagged in relief. That was Jade's family. I knew they would uphold the mantle of leadership and honor with grace. They would ensure that everyone was okay and would rebuild with fervor, until the slayers recovered from the heinous attack. I knew that in my heart.

"He's on a warpath, Alina. I've never heard of something like this happening in Sanguis in my lifetime."

My head jerked, unable to hide my alarm as I demanded, "Who? Who is on a warpath? What is going on?"

She blinked rapidly before cocking her head at me. "He didn't tell you? Drake has publicly announced that he wants the head of whoever attacked you and your family. There's a formal investigation as well as a massive reward for anyone who has information."

I could barely process her words. Why would he openly say he wants to seek retribution against the vampires who killed slayers? It went against everything they stood for. If anything, this would make him appear weak to his own people.

What the fuck is your angle?

CHAPTER NINE
ALINA

Surprisingly, Diplomacy class allowed me to detach from the questions cycling through my brain. I was able to focus on the mock-meeting Professor Trillio put together for today's lesson. We were split into opposing sides, consisting of one diplomat each to represent their designated sector. All sectors and scenarios were drawn from a hat, so there was no predisposed luck on anyone's side.

I'd gotten quite a thrill from it, happy to have been the defending diplomat of Hell, with Milina as my rival, representing Sanguis. The scenario had been the vampires' desire to be classified as demons, earning them a territory in hell.

Milina's only argument was that demons were

classified as monsters, and vampires were monsters in the eyes of everyone in Ordinarius and Praeditus. That they deserved to live in a realm that welcomed their tendencies.

Recalling the history of Hell, I'd easily argued the true classification of a "demon" was those who were descendants of the original six Houses as well as the hybrids that came from them. Queen Ama had wanted to unite the hybrids and pure lines of all creatures already in Hell by giving them all one name. Thus came the birth of saying Hell was full of demons as a generic statement, despite all the subclasses of demons consisting of fallen angels, wraiths, dark elves, hellhounds, succubus, incubus, reapers, and all hybrids. Therefore vampires would never be classified as demons and did not have the right to request a territory of land in Hell.

My technical point earned me the victory, which had given me a boost of confidence in myself that I hadn't quite realized I needed until I was back in my room, changing into clothes for my mentor training.

Smiling on my bed as I drained my third bag of blood before tossing them in my overflowing trash can, I realized I was proud of myself. Sadly, I couldn't remember the last time I'd truly felt that way.

It was easy to get caught up in feeling like I was failing in every aspect of my life, mostly due to my emotions making things not feel as black and white as they would have prior to my admission here. I'd always been my toughest critic, having such high expectations placed on my shoulders with the knowledge that I would one day govern the slayers.

In some ways, I still hadn't come to terms with the fact that leading the slayers was no longer my destiny, and that the only expectations upon me were the ones I placed upon myself. In part, it felt like I was betraying the earlier version of me, but eventually, I needed to make peace with knowing that version of me was dead and never coming back.

Grabbing a hair tie from my counter, I threw my hair into a bun before changing into leggings and a tank top from my wardrobe before heading toward the combat classroom. I was looking forward to my training session with Lincoln, knowing it would continue to help ground my moods.

I enjoyed combat and enhancing my skills, and now that we've found a healthier way to enjoy our struggle for control, I was hoping I'd be able to check my ego at the door and actually learn from him now.

Running the distance to the room, I smirked at

the thought, knowing I'd never be able to fully check my ego with Linc. Pushing his buttons was honestly becoming one of my favorite hobbies.

"Hey, Spitfire," he called in greeting, jogging over to me and wiping sweat from his brow with the back of his hand.

He bent down to plant a quick kiss on my lips, and I welcomed it before reaching out to swat his ass playfully. He let out a playful growl before gnashing his teeth at me. "Be careful. Don't start something you can't finish."

Enjoying this easy banter between us, I decided to let it go that he mentioned Dracula and I's bond to Estrid. At the end of the day, she would have found out without him explicitly telling her anyway. I had way more shit on my plate to be frustrated about than that.

Purposefully eyeing him like a piece of meat, I sassed, "I think we can both agree that I'm capable of finishing you off."

Letting out a huff, he nodded. "I suppose you're right. *For once.*"

Gasping dramatically, I held my hand to my chest as I padded over to the mat to begin stretching to warm up my body.

"Listen, Spitfire," he started awkwardly as he

walked toward me, rubbing the back of his head as his gaze flickered around, looking at anything other than me. "There's something I've been meaning to talk to you about."

Please don't let this be anything personal or emotional. While I thoroughly appreciated the gigantic leaps we were taking to fix our issues and get to know one another on a deeper level, I desperately needed a moment to fall into the comfort that training brought me.

I just wanted to let it all flit away for a moment of time. All day long, new information was thrown at me left and right to process, and I personally thought I'd been handling it like a champ. I deserved a reward for that, right?

"The night of the party was before I'd taught you to control your mental barrier," he admitted with a bit of a bite to his words. "And well...What's going on between you and Andrei?"

Fuck.

My chest tightened. Had I not held my mental barrier in place today when I decided earlier to tell him how I felt about Andrei? It seemed like crazy timing to decide that and have him bring this up.

Extending my legs into a v shape, I bent over until I could bang my head against the mat lightly.

How could I tell him what I needed to, without hurting his feelings?

The conflicting feelings I had for Andrei still felt too raw to talk about, and honestly, they still felt really fucking wrong on my part too. I was doing my best to stay true to Lincoln and focus on us, but Andrei was still there in the back of my mind. And despite my best efforts, my damn stomach had still fluttered at our very brief interaction in class earlier today.

He sighed heavily seconds before the mat shifted in front of me. Lifting my head to stare at him, I found his lips tight as he cocked his head at me. "Trust me, I'd rather not have to have this conversation either, but I can't deny that what I felt from you that night regarding him has stayed in the back of my mind ever since. I was an absolute piece of shit for walking away from you then, and I blamed myself for driving you into his arms. But the feelings and thoughts I picked up on from you when you were with him...they were real."

I found myself nodding along as he continued, fighting the urge to slam my head back against the mat again. Everything he said was technically correct, which did absolutely nothing to assuage my guilt. "Yesterday morning after I'd pulled my head from my ass and realized you'd left the room, I ran into him in the hallway. He was just standing there and staring at the doors leading out of the building like a fucking zombie. But you know what he did when he noticed I was there?" he asked in a huff, shaking his head like he was still in disbelief. "He told me that I'd better protect you against Dracula and learn to treat you right. Before I could even respond, he simply walked away. He didn't bother sticking around for an argument or fight."

My lips parted with a small gasp. "He did?"

Lincoln simply nodded as he stared down at the mat, but after a moment, his lips thinned. "He truly cares about you, as much as I fucking hate to admit that, Spitfire," he whispered before lifting his eyes to mine. "I know I can be a selfish fuck, and when it comes to you, I don't want to share you. I want to be enough for you, but I'm man enough to admit that I've fucked up multiple times and given you ample reasons to want someone else."

Knowing that it was my turn to share, I reached out to grab his hand, loving the way it engulfed mine. "I'm so happy with the progress we've made, Linc. But yeah...I did develop feelings for him, and they haven't gone away, despite me feeling like an absolute piece of shit for it."

His gaze shifted downward at my admission, and his shoulders slumped forward as he winced.

"We agreed to go our separate ways yesterday morning, but I want to be completely honest with you moving forward. The truth is that I'm really struggling with letting go of him. It feels wrong, and I'm so sorry for that. I can't help how my heart feels, though."

I waited for him to tell me I was a piece of shit as the tense, silent moment stretched between us. His thumb brushed across the top of my hand, and my heart squeezed. I hated not being able to hear what was going on in his head for once.

The last thing I wanted was for him to walk away from us, but he deserved to know the truth and make a decision that he felt was right for him, just like I did.

"I want to kill him," he whispered, keeping his eye on where his finger traced circles on my skin. "I want to kill anyone who looks at you for longer than necessary. I want you to myself, Alina. But I know it isn't fair to expect that of you just because Fate says we're true mates"

I was absolutely gobsmacked by his logic, but his words soothed my soul, taking away the sting of the conflict I'd been feeling about the situation.

The knowledge that we were fated mates was a huge pressure that weighed down upon me—I didn't want to spit in the face of a gift that so many people yearned for. But he was right, I hadn't even known him for a full week yet and we'd been through hell with the ups and downs ever since we first met.

Maybe I wasn't crazy for what I felt. I just never expected Lincoln to be the one to help me realize that. There were so many facets to this man that I was just beginning to see, and each one made me feel like maybe Fate did something right for once.

"But I've never been afraid of a bit of competition," he tossed out as his signature cocky smirk spread over his face, instantly lightening the energy between us. "I'll prove to you that I can be a man worthy of *all* of your heart."

I stared at him in awe. A second later, I launched myself at him, knocking him onto his back as I melded my lips to his. "You're incredible," I breathed, nipping his lip playfully.

As his arm circled around my waist, anchoring me on top of him, his free hand came up to cup my cheek in his palm. "I know that we're from two different worlds, with generations of hatred fueling the gap between us, but I've never felt as seen and understood as I do with you, Spitfire. I'll never stop fighting for that."

I literally had no words for him. I had never been the best at relaying my emotions, despite working on that recently, but his cock pressing up into my clit was distracting the hell out of me, my brain firing on the absolute wrong wavelengths for this conversation. I felt at peace for now, but I knew at this point, only time would tell how things would fall between us.

Letting out a breathy sigh as he rolled his hips up into me, I asked, "Aren't we supposed to be training, *Sir*?"

With a quick spin, he had me pinned beneath him, trailing his scruff along my neck in the way I loved. "I'll make a deal with you. If you can disarm me with your weapon today, I'll owe you a favor of any kind."

Arching a single brow at him, I found myself wondering what the catch was. "And if you win?"

His lips trailed kisses along my jaw as he whispered, "I've already won with you."

Oh, fuck me. He was such a smooth talker.

"Deal, now get off me so I can whoop your ass in an embarrassingly short amount of time, old man," I sassed, using my strength to push him to the side, speeding to my feet and bouncing around in excitement.

Adrenaline coursed through me at the thought of being able to use Devorare more. I needed to make it a priority to bond with her more and find the connection that was supposed to exist between slayers and their soul weapons.

Getting to beat Lincoln in a fight and being owed a favor was just the cherry on top of what was sure to be a kickass sundae.

After he selected a simple longsword from the rack of weapons in the room, we stood across from each other in a white circle that marked the boundaries of how far we were allowed to move in the fight.

Pointing his weapon at my chest, he said, "Don't be shy, now. Call your sword out. I'll go easy on her."

Slicing into my palm, anticipation and nerves twined together through my stomach as I closed my eyes and connected to that piece of my chest that always lit up when I called to her.

Devorare.

Feeling the tether between us snap into place, I smiled as I felt the familiar hilt fill my hand. Opening my eyes, I loosened my wrist and swung her around a bit, enjoying the perfect weight and balance of her in my hand. Even though I'd yet to connect to her completely, she still felt like an extension of my body every time I held her. That had to count for something, right?

Without waiting for me to signal I was ready, he launched himself at me, but I was quick to dart to the side and bring her up to block his attack. Our metal clanged together, echoing through the room as we exchanged blows. We dodged and blocked as we circled around each other, neither of us finding the advantage to push the other further.

I felt so damn alive in these moments. I missed it so much, but a realization hit me as I thought of not being able to focus my life solely on combat anymore.

How many vampires would I have killed if I had continued on that path?

Would they have been deserving of the punishments and the death sentences we doled out?

Or would any of them have been families like Lincoln's, going against the laws to protect themselves and try to find peace?

Who would I lift Devorare against in battle now? Slayers? Vampires?

I let my thoughts intrude on the fight, giving away the smallest opening as I faltered in my step toward him, which could have been a blow of victory. Instead, he advanced on me in my small second of hesitation, dropping his sword to the ground as he swept my legs out from under me, dropping me onto my ass.

Shit.

My tailbone rattled with the impact, and I heaved a deep sigh as I stared at the ceiling. Hazel eyes obscured my field of vision as he stared down at me. "Where did your mind go at the end? I could tell you weren't fully focused on the fight anymore."

My chest expanded as I drew in a deep, full-chested breath before slowly blowing it out and sitting up. Pulling Devorare's blade into my lap, I ran my fingers along the cold metal as I considered my words. "I was thinking about who I would have used my sword against if my life hadn't ended up this way. I'd like to think that I would have only lifted her toward those who truly deserved it, but the longer I'm away from that life and hear stories from the opposing side, I can't help but have doubts about whether that would have actually been the case. Things were so black and white just a week ago, and now I feel like I'm living my life in this murky greyscale."

Plopping down next to me, he bumped his

shoulder into my own. I leaned against him, relishing in the comfort he offered me as he asked, "What's her name?"

I appreciated his ability to know when to not pry and simply listen instead. If he'd tried to ask anything about my life as a slayer or my musing of whether I would have possibly been the bad guy in a scenario, I wouldn't have known what to say.

But this I was happy to talk about. She was truly the last tie I had to my heritage, and there was nothing anyone could do to take her from me until I died.

"Devorare—it means devour," I answered, smiling at my reflection in her gleaming blade. "She chose me in our coming-of-age ceremony. Not every slayer is gifted a weapon. The weapons must find us worthy, but you know what's special about her?" I mused, glancing over at him. "She's the only soul weapon with no record of her existence prior to choosing me. Every other weapon has a book detailing their lives and all those who have wielded them."

Lincoln pursed his lips as he mulled over that information for a moment. "The first wielder, huh?"

Which would have been a pretty cool thing to

claim if I felt like I could truly say I wielded her, but there was something missing still.

Letting go of her hilt, I watched as she faded away, quietly admitting, "I still can't connect to her properly, though. It's said every wielder can hear their weapon like another soul speaking to them. Supposedly, it allows the wielder to hone into the true power of their weapon when they find the synchronicity of the two souls."

"You're both the first of your kind," he murmured. "Don't force it. It'll happen."

My brow knit together as I swung my gaze to him, echoing his words. "First of our kind..."

Shrugging his shoulders, he leaned back on his hands. "What if she was only ever meant for a Van Helsing vampire? That could be why there's no record of her existence. It's just a thought, though."

His words implied that everything was fated if she was destined to be mine before I was even turned. Was it possible? I mean, I was the first Van Helsing to have to live with being turned...

A week ago, I would have told you Fate could get fucked and that we all had the ability to decide our future. This week, I wasn't so sure anymore. The loss of control I felt with the possibility of accepting that our futures were predetermined didn't sit right with me, but hell, who was I to say definitively how the world worked? I wasn't a god or goddess.

Being the first in my line to live a life like this had felt like a curse shackled and bound to my soul, but maybe it was something else entirely.

CHAPTER TEN
ANDREI

My fists tightened so hard that my nails dug into the fleshy part of my palms, cutting them open as I tried to control myself. The sting of pain grounded me enough to make myself sit the fuck down on the edge of my bed after pacing in front of my door for what felt like hours.

I knew that nothing good waited for me at the end of the path I seemed hellbent on taking with Alina. At least not regarding my father's retribution. I constantly reminded myself of what his wrath could be like, but my willpower crumbled too easily whenever I was around her. I'd tried to keep myself out of common areas because of it, but I couldn't avoid her in classes.

A part of me was thankful that I couldn't, though. She'd filled my veins with a fire that made me feel alive, and without it, I realized how monotonous and empty my life had been before her. I didn't want to go back to that version of me.

The version that was living each day to satisfy my father.

She'd given me the briefest taste of what life could be like outside of his control, and I felt like an addict, needing another dose of it after depriving myself for just one fucking day.

How was I supposed to stay away from her?

"Fuck!" I screamed, shooting from the bed and smashing my fist into the wall across from me. My knuckles cracked open, stinging as plaster dug into the wounds, but I left it planted there as I took in deep, ragged breaths. It seemed that I couldn't stop destroying walls today.

"Great, just fucking great," I muttered, shaking my head as I pulled my hand free, watching small pieces of plaster crumbling to cover my desk. My skin felt like it was crawling, and I knew I'd need to clean this up now before I could do anything else. Control was a necessity, and my space was something that only *I* could affect. I kept it meticulous, always neat and clean, to keep me from spinning out.

The same didn't apply for anyone else's space, though. I would have told Professor Levia to suck my cock if she even considered telling me to clean up a mess I'd made. A week ago, that's exactly what I would have done, knowing there was nothing her or any of the staff here could do to touch me. My father's protection extended to this academy, and I sure as hell had used it to my advantage. Even Lincoln's threats to tell my father if I stepped out of line felt empty, though he was the only one with a direct connection to the board. He knew exactly how fucking brutal those motherfuckers were, so his threats always felt personal, knowing exactly what it would lead to.

Crossing to the bathroom, I rinsed out the wound before it had a chance to heal with that shit saturating it.

My ears strained then, feeling exceptionally tuned into anything that came to Alina. I just barely heard her laugh, but it was enough to draw me to my door, cracking it open to see what she was doing.

Call me a stalker, but I'd take whatever I could get when it came to her right now.

"I think I just want to be alone tonight," she

muttered as I caught a view of Lincoln and her heading up the stairs to her level above mine. His arm was tossed over her shoulder, showing his claim on her to anyone who was looking. My jaw clenched tightly, teeth grinding together with fury.

Had he upset her?

I'd seen a different side of him yesterday morning, though, when he was worried about Alina's safety. That had actually softened me to the asshole. Smirking as I thought of how she had a way of changing people around her for the better, including myself, I let her sad blue eyes fill my mind.

I warned him to protect her and take care of her, but from what I'd seen so far, she didn't seem happy. I didn't want to think about how he was treating her, or I wouldn't have any untouched walls left in my room. Because even if he was treating her like the absolute gem she was, it gutted me to think of how I should be the one showering her with affection instead.

"Rain check?" she asked, seeming to force a jovial tone to her words as she flashed him a smile.

"Sure, Spitfire," he murmured before pressing a kiss to her forehead as they rounded the staircase out of my view.

So, she'd be all alone in her room. Pity that.

Something in my heart urged me to go to her. To see if she was truly doing okay, even if it was just as her friend. I'd heard the whispers of what happened with Dracula in front of the dorm building this morning, and while I was shocked to my core at his display of affection, I was grateful he'd sent Maya home.

I didn't believe in hurting women, but she'd been wearing my patience so fucking thin with her lingering touches. Each one of her offers had made my skin crawl. I hadn't clipped my words, telling her that I'd never touch her or let her suck my cock again. I'd made that decision well before Alina showed up, but my connection with her only cemented my disgust at the thought of anyone else wrapping their lips around my cock.

Maybe that wasn't in the cards for Alina and me anymore, but I could be there for her as a...friend. Right? There was nothing wrong with lending my support to a friend in need. Lincoln and Dracula couldn't fault me for that.

Keep telling yourself that, dumbass.

Letting out a dark laugh, I realized I'd take any damn excuse to justify going to her room. I just needed to have a real conversation with her and see for myself whether she was hurting as much as I was with the chasm gaping between us. If she wasn't, then I'd back off, but if she was...I didn't think there was anything that would be able to hold me back from her.

After cleaning up the mess on my desk, I took a quick shower before tugging on black jeans and a plain tee. Spraying cologne on my wrist, I moved to notch my two slim chains around my neck before using some product in the longer bit of my hair on top that always threatened to fall into my eyes. Giving myself a quick nod of approval, I turned from my room, heading up the flight of stairs toward her door, full of confidence and the belief that everything would work out.

But the second my feet stilled in front of her door, I froze with my closed fist an inch shy of knocking. What if she told me to kick rocks?

Shit, what was I doing here? I'd just told her that I couldn't do this yesterday morning, yet here I was pining after her not even two full days later. Disappointment blossomed in my chest, causing me to lower my hand to my side.

I couldn't keep fucking around with her feelings whenever I ached for her. I condemned Lincoln for how he treated her, yet here I was playing a fucking game neither of us could ever win. I was pathetically lost.

Turning, I took a step before stilling as the door creaked open behind me.

"Andrei?"

My stomach flipped at the sound of her voice. She'd caught me, so what was I going to do now?

Clearing my throat, I glanced at her over my shoulder and barely stifled a groan at the sight of her long legs on full display in an oversized t-shirt that draped to her mid-thigh. Was she bare beneath it? Her wet hair looked fucking adorable, and I realized I loved seeing her in such a natural state. She was breathtaking in every way.

Focus, damnit.

"Hey, sorry. I shouldn't have come here. Have a good night," I offered, mentally cursing myself out for being such an idiot and giving into my impulses.

"Oh," she breathed out, confusion wrinkling her brow. "Okay."

She wasn't going to call me on my shit for once. I wasn't sure whether to be thankful for that or disappointed. I missed our banter more than fucking anything.

Nodding a goodbye, my lips thinned as I forced my feet to carry me toward the stairs. Each step I took away from her felt like a dagger twisting in my gut. It was the same thing I'd felt when she'd walked away from me yesterday all over again. Why did I keep doing this to us?

"Andrei," she called out, "wait!"

Curiosity stilled my feet, and I turned as I heard her feet pounding against the floor behind me. I'd barely faced her in time to realize that she was launching herself at me. Her arms wrapped around my neck tightly as her legs anchored her firmly around my waist. It happened so quickly that it was like our bodies acted on instinct. My arms pulled her to me even tighter, one of my hands going to the back of her head as she buried her face in my neck.

Swallowing the desire in my throat, I stopped my hand from trailing down to check to see if she wore anything beneath the t-shirt. Not wanting to take the risk of anyone seeing her if she wasn't, I walked us back into her room, kicking the door shut behind me.

Fuck, I was here now. What was I going to do about it?

"I missed you," she murmured, breath fanning across my neck in a way that made a shiver course through me.

Well, that answers my questions. Fuck it.

Moving both my hands to her head, I drug my fingers through her hair and pulled her head back until she was looking at me with those big, blue eyes of hers. My voice was rough with need as I growled, "Baby girl, if you want me to stop, you better say it now."

She blinked once in answer as a smirk curved her lips up.

Burying my hands in her hair, I erased the distance between us, losing myself in her soft lips that opened for me immediately and invited me in further. Our tongues tangled as I moved us until her back met the wall. Using my hips to hold her in place, I pushed my cock against her core, growling as she let out a soft moan that I swallowed.

Her nails scraped against my back as she attempted to pull my shirt off. I was pressed so tightly against her that she couldn't get her hands between us to give her the leverage she needed to strip me bare. Her frustrated huff might have been the cutest fucking thing I'd ever heard.

"Take it the fuck off," she snarled against my lips.

That was my feisty, demanding girl.

That was *my girl*—period.

My heart slammed wildly in my chest as my

body realized what it was going to do before my mind could catch and let me think twice about it. Ripping my face away from her, I stared at her as we breathed heavily. I groaned at the flush to her cheeks, the desire I saw burning in her eyes matching my own.

"Exchange blood with me, Alina," I demanded, conviction burning through my heart. I didn't give her a chance to consider my words before I continued, "I know it's damn near impossible to find one mate in this life—let alone three—but I know you're *mine*, baby girl."

If she was my mate, there was no way my father or Dracula could expect me to stay away from her. Mate bonds transcended all rules and laws. Surely they couldn't touch me, or either of us, then.

Her body stilled as she sucked in a sharp breath. I could feel her heart hammering against my chest as her eyes searched my face.

"I'm serious," I reassured her, moving my hand to cup her cheek and brushing my thumb across her plush bottom lip. It was practically begging to be bit. "Let's find out once and for all and be done with this back and forth, what-if bullshit."

Suddenly, her hands were flat against my chest as she seemed to struggle with whether to push me away or pull me closer as she asked, "But what if we're not? What then?"

I wasn't even going to entertain the thought. Because how could something that felt so goddamn right, be wrong?

What I realized as I forced myself to back away from her the past day, watching her from a distance and knowing I could never get rid of Lincoln, was that I'd take her in whatever way I could. If it meant sharing her, I didn't give a fuck anymore. I'd show him how to treat her, and he could take some fucking notes.

Hesitation swirled in her eyes before her nostrils flared as she breathed deeply. On her exhale, she let her fangs grow out before dragging one against her bottom lip, "Okay. Let's do this."

Crimson pooled before dripping down her chin, pulling my own fangs out with my desire to drink from her. Lowering my face slowly to hers once more, I ran my tongue up to lap at the spilled blood before sucking her lip into my mouth. A moan came from her as I swallowed the liquid and let go of her lip long enough to split mine open in return.

Closing my eyes, I moved my hand to grip her jaw as I deepened our kiss, pushing my blood into her mouth with my tongue. Something about it felt so fucking primal, making me growl at the sensation of marking her with my blood.

I knew the exchange of blood between vampires was reserved for mates. It was of the highest disrespect to let someone else drink it, but I knew this was it for me, and I wasn't afraid to tempt Fate and tell her to give me exactly what I wanted.

A burning sensation flooded my neck, and I hissed in pain as my eyes squeezed shut tightly. Her breathing came out ragged as I pulled back from her, forcing my eyes open to see her and make sure she was okay. As the pain faded, I felt both of our bodies relax against each other once more.

A hesitant smile tugged her lips up, and my heart soared at the sight of her excitement. I needed to see the mark for myself, though, so I dropped her feet to the floor before grabbing her hips to turn her around. Her hand lifted to pull the hair from her neck, revealing two black blood drops sitting atop one another.

A tingling sensation swirled through my head, taking me off guard right as I leaned in to press my lips against the mark reverently. I was a little hazy, feeling like there was a new component of my brain unlocking and waiting for me to use.

You were right.

I jerked back as her voice filled my head, clear and loud as if she had spoken out loud. She turned back around, pushing onto her tiptoes to wrap her arms around my neck and pull me back down to her. I melted into her lips, finally letting go of all the fears that had held me back from being with her.

You're mine, baby girl.

I'm yours.

CHAPTER ELEVEN
ALINA

I couldn't help but laugh as tears of relief streamed down my face, mixing between our lips as we lost ourselves in each other.

I'd been quick to solidify my walls with Lincoln in my mind as soon as I saw Andrei in front of my door. While Lincoln seemed to understand as best he could the position I was in, it didn't mean I wanted to rub it in his face that I was exploring it with Andrei now.

If there were any cracks in my mental barrier, I'm pretty sure I would have heard something shattering or breaking above us, so I let the knot of fear forming in my chest loosen for now.

I'd tell him tomorrow, but for now, I wanted to focus on Andrei.

He was my mate. I almost couldn't believe it despite the mark I knew was on my neck and the fact that we had spoken into each other's mind. For once...Fate had given me what I begged for as I swallowed his blood.

Maybe she wasn't such a massive cunt all the time.

At first, I'd been fucking terrified when he suggested we exchange blood. It felt like I'd just gotten him back for a minute and that the rug was going to be pulled out from beneath us again. I'd experienced too much loss in a short time, and I didn't want to grieve the loss of someone who'd brought a spark to my life during such a dark time. He'd been the first one to allow me a space to feel safe since the attack on my family.

But it was for that exact reason I decided to trust in the possibility. If he wasn't my mate, I'd kill the side of me that yearned for him. It would have been difficult, but it would have been the answer I needed to close that door and focus on Lincoln for good. It was the unknown of what lingered between us that fostered the hope within my heart for us, so I forced myself out of the safety net of uncertainty and took a leap of faith.

"I don't know why I'm crying," I admitted as I pulled back to stare up into the light green eyes that had enraptured me since I'd run into him for the first time. "I'm such a baby."

That was a lie. I knew why I was crying. The relief my soul felt with the confirmation that he was meant to be mine was immeasurable.

The self-hatred I'd felt for pining after him while having Lincoln had been insufferable. I'd already struggled with feeling like I didn't deserve to find such happiness, so to feel like I was being greedy with that happiness...by not being satisfied and wanting even more...

It was horrible.

But finally, I could lay my head down tonight and let all that go. I had been right to not give up on Andrei, and damn was I happy that he hadn't given up on me.

His lips found my ear as he bent down to scoop me back into his arms, easily lifting me and wrapping my legs around him before settling his hands on my bare ass. "I'll let you in on a secret," he murmured.

"Okay," I breathed out, curious where this was going.

"Are you sure you're ready?" he teased, splaying his fingers against my ass and rubbing circles with his thumbs. "It's a big one."

Thumping him on the back of the head lightly, I chuckled before saying, "Just tell me already, asshole."

He turned his head, pressing a tender kiss to my cheek before whispering, "Bad bitches cry too. It doesn't make you weak."

A sound came out of me that was the most horrendous mix between a snort and a sob I'd ever heard, his words hitting deep despite the subtle humor he infused within them.

Slapping a hand over my mouth as he pulled back to grin at me, I whispered from behind them with wide eyes, "Oh my god, that was so embarrassing. Erase that noise from your memory, right now."

"No. Fucking. Way."

The way he enunciated each word had me dropping my hands to lightly pound against his chest as I laughed freely, enjoying the excitement and energy flowing through the space around us.

Backing me against the wall once more, he quickly made a grab for my wrists, easily engulfing them both before lifting them above my head in a quick movement. The laughter faded between us as hunger for him came roaring back to my core.

Fates, thank you. She's so fucking perfect for me.

My breath caught at the whisper I heard from Andrei in my mind. It wasn't loud like he was projecting to me on purpose, more like I was hearing his passing thoughts, making it feel so damn pure.

Looking at him from beneath my lashes as my breathing became short, I batted them twice as I muttered, "Is the offer to get on your knees for me anytime, anywhere still valid?"

A grin so wolfish took over his face that my pussy clenched in response. "For you, new girl? Of course."

In less than a second, he had me flat on my back with his face between my knees, like he'd been waiting all his life for this moment and nothing would keep him from getting what he wanted.

While his enthusiasm was a damn big turn on, the second my eyes hit the roof, my palm flew down between my legs to stop him just as his hands found the edges of my thong.

"Can we go to your room?" I quickly asked as I pushed to sit up.

When I'd opened myself to Lincoln, he'd had my undivided attention, and I wanted to be able to give the same to Andrei. I was finding it incredibly hard to do so, knowing I lived right beneath Lincoln.

Thankfully, Andrei didn't even question me. He simply picked me up while tucking the hem of my shirt beneath my ass to cover me up before speeding us down to his room on the second floor. Thankfully, it was positioned on the opposite side of the building from Lincoln's quarters.

A squeal tore from my throat as he tossed me onto his bed. I had a few short seconds to orientate myself enough to look around, appreciating the tidy space. It smelled just like him, and as he lit a few candles around the room, I realized the scent wafted from them. They smelled like patchouli and sandalwood, both musky and subtle.

Pushing onto my elbows, I joked, "What are you doing? You don't have to impress me anymore. You already convinced me to drink your blood and all."

Turning on his heel, he tossed me a wink before flashing onto the bed and spreading my thighs to lay between them. His eyes danced with mischief and adoration as he responded, "Just because I've got you doesn't mean I don't need to put in the work anymore, baby girl."

And with that he ripped the sides of my thong before tearing them away from my body, wasting absolutely no time with placing his hands on my hips to tilt them up slightly. His tongue delved into my heat immediately, and he groaned as he tasted me for the first time.

The way he sounded like he was getting pleasure out of eating my pussy had my elbows giving out as I flattened against the bed. My eyes rolled back in my head as he dragged his tongue up to my clit, flicking over it with a featherlight touch and driving me crazy.

My hands found his hair, twining through the soft strands as I tried to push his tongue onto me more. His answering chuckle had my lips curling up in a wide smile. I knew what I wanted, what could I say?

And as I pushed against him, he gave me exactly what I wanted, flattening his tongue and stroking it over me in short, quick movements that left me in a frenzy. Crying out, I quickly bit down on my lip as two of his fingers plunged into me, stroking me from the inside and driving me to new heights of pleasure.

A feral growl came from him at my noise, and he doubled down, increasing the pace of his tongue and fingers in tandem as I felt myself continue to grow wetter.

My hips bucked, making him growl again but almost in a tone of warning, it seemed. As if I was going to get in trouble for removing his mouth from me for even a minute.

I was hot as fuck for it.

Impatience roared through me as the desire to feel him inside of me took over. "Fuck me, now," I pleaded breathlessly.

"No," he growled against me, voice gruff and heated, "not until you come on my fingers, baby girl. Give me what I want, and I'll give you what you want."

My tongue darted out to wet my lips. There was something so incredibly arousing about a man who found his pleasure in making his woman feel good, ensuring her needs were satisfied well before he thought of satiating his own.

He began to switch between long sucks against my clit before biting down lightly, making the world spin as my orgasm crashed through me out of nowhere, hard and fast.

"That's it, baby girl," he praised in a rough voice. "Get nice and wet for my cock."

My shiver ran through my body, thoroughly

lighting me up from the inside out. Hooking his arms under my legs, my body was pulled toward the edge of the bed as he demanded, "Touch yourself for me."

I didn't hesitate, knowing what I liked and being unashamed to show him. I watched as he slowly kicked his shoes off, eyes glued to my fingers swirling around my clit lightly. Slipping them down my pussy, I curled them inside of me and flicked the tips up toward my g-spot, moaning as I did.

My eyes drank in the hard planes of muscle that rippled across his body as he pulled his shirt over his head and tossed it to the floor. Bringing my other hand to play with my clit as I continued to pulse my fingers inside my pussy, he groaned low in his throat, the deep sound reverberating through the room.

"You're a fucking goddess, baby," he praised as he slipped out of his pants, quickly fisting his impressive length in his hand as he crossed the space to me.

Precum beaded his tip, and I ached to flick my tongue over it. He seemed to have other ideas, hooking his arms beneath me once more as he demanded, "Put your arms around my neck."

Doing as he asked, he quickly pulled me up,

holding me high enough on his body to line his cock up with my entrance. The way he could just toss me around like I weighed nothing, positioning me exactly where he wanted me, was so fucking hot.

Pressing his forehead against mine, his breath fanned across my lips. "I'm going to fuck you hard and fast, baby girl. That okay with you?"

I couldn't help but snark back, maintaining eye contact as I said, "No, I really was hoping you'd treat me like a virgin and take it nice and slow—" My words were cut off as he dropped me onto his cock, pushing his hips up at the same time to slide all the way into me.

My breath caught in my throat as he hit so deep inside of me that I wouldn't be surprised if I could see the imprint of his cock in my stomach.

The corner of his mouth lifted. "Too bad."

Flashing toward the wall, he let my upper body fall back against it for a second before he began to slam into me, making me cry out. My hands fell from his neck to grip his shoulders, holding on for dear life as he pounded into me over and over, muscles bunching and flexing beneath my fingers as he did.

I couldn't help but dig the tips of my nails into him as I moaned, "Fuck, Andrei."

I was lost in the pleasure, so I didn't think twice when he growled out, "Scratch me, baby girl. Mark me as yours."

Immediately, I raked the tips of my nails over his shoulders, pressing in until red lines lay in my wake as I worked them toward his chest. My pussy clenched at the sight, realizing I loved the idea of marking him as mine. It brought out an animalistic side of me I didn't realize I possessed.

"Harder," he groaned out as his head fell back, increasing his pace to a level that had my eyes crossing slightly.

Trailing them over his collar bone, I dug the tips in until bright crimson greeted me. Raking them down his chest, I moaned at the sight. A twisted part of me hated knowing that these would heal in a minute, leaving his skin smooth once more.

My pussy tightened as my core clenched, and I found myself pulling myself away from the wall and hanging on to him for dear life. Andrei's hands splayed across my hips and ass, pulling me up and down his cock in a punishing rhythm. My hand grabbed the back of his neck, and I smiled wickedly as I remembered he *did* have a permanent mark now.

He was fucking *mine.*

With that toe-curling thought, another orgasm swept through me, making my fingers dig into his flesh once more, dragging them down in the way I knew he wanted as my brain floated off into the clouds.

He grunted, "Baby girl, I'm going to come in your pussy unless you stop me."

"Do it," I responded breathlessly, wanting him to mark me in his own way. "Finish inside of me."

I had received my annual shot for birth control a month ago, so I had plenty of time to not worry about the repercussions of letting him fill me later.

"Fuck," he growled out. "Tell me again."

Holding onto his neck, I bit down on his ear before whispering, "Come inside my pussy, Andrei."

His hips bucked before he stilled and spilled his release inside of me. I wasn't sure how long we stayed like that, with me wrapped in his embrace, but I finally came about when I felt the spray of water running over my skin. Letting go of my tight grip on him, I slid down his front until my hands splayed against his stomach as I stared up at him.

Grabbing my chin lightly, he pressed a soft kiss against my lips before offering me a gentle smile and turning to grab something. He shocked me by pulling a loofah out of the corner, insisting that I let him wash me.

Letting him wash me felt somehow even more intimate than fucking. It was such a sweet and tender thing to do, and I found myself relaxing at his touch instantly, refusing to overthink it.

Before long, we finished our shower and climbed into bed. I couldn't help but lift the collar of the shirt he'd loaned me, insistent that I wear it instead of my own. Giving it a sniff, my toes curled as his scent wrapped around me.

"Are you sniffing that?" he asked, clearly confused by the action any sane girl would do in my position.

"Yeah, and?" I rebutted before dropping the shirt and smiling. "It smells nice."

Not saying anything, he tucked me against his side, and I burrowed into the nook of his neck, sighing in contentment at this turn of events. The tiniest part of me felt guilty still for being with him, knowing Lincoln would be upset, but the same could be said the other way. There was a reason that I felt an equal pull to them both—Fate had confirmed it.

"Do you want to...uh, sleep here tonight?" he

asked, the hesitation in his tone making me lift my head to look at him with a quirked brow.

A pink stain tinted his cheeks, and when I placed my hand above his heart, I felt it beating wildly beneath my palm.

He was nervous.

Andrei truly was a little cinnamon roll beneath the bad boy persona he portrayed around everyone else. It was like armor he wore to carry out his mission. He had the weight of his parent's expectations upon him, and I knew how heavy that burden could feel...How much it controlled who you were as a person.

While I missed my family immensely and still felt a fire within my soul to get my revenge, I couldn't help but wonder if I ever would have found the woman I was becoming if my life hadn't been completely derailed by the attack...Would I have lived forever in the mold that was provided for me to fill?

Did it make me a horrible person to admit that I preferred this version of myself after what it took to get here?

Self-loathing bubbled up within me at the happiness I felt now. My family had been slaughtered by vampires, and here I was, happily bonded to two that drove my mind and heart crazy. But they weren't just bloodsuckers to me anymore. They were individuals with their own scars, heartaches, and dreams.

Fingers lightly gripping my chin pulled me from my thoughts and forced me to look into Andrei's eyes. Gently, he demanded, "Stop that."

You heard all that?

I felt and heard it.

I found that I didn't mind him hearing my thoughts and feeling my emotions, which should have scared the shit out of me.

He continued out loud, "I may not know everything that's happened in your life, but what I do know is that you have a heart that wants to do good. I mean, look at Lincoln and I for instance. I don't think either of us have smiled in the couple years we've known each other. Then you show up and call us on our shit, and we're suddenly at your feet like tamed hellhounds, smiling with our tongues hanging out of our mouths as we beg for a pat on the head."

A snort came from me at the mental image, and I smacked his chest lightly, shaking my head. "Oh, stop, that's not true."

He tugged me back down onto him, grabbing my

face between his palms as his lips thinned. Tucking a strand of hair behind my ear, he said, his tone even and serious, "You deserve happiness, baby girl. In whatever way that looks for you.

My thoughts flickered to Lincoln and how he'd react when he found out about my bond to Andrei.

"He'll be pissed," Andrei muttered darkly. "But he'll eventually get over it."

"How do you know?"

Fingertips trailed up my arm as he answered, "Because it's exactly what I went through, even before knowing you were my mate. I realized that I'd rather have part of you than none of you."

His words tugged on my heartstrings, making my stomach erupt with butterflies.

"I think I'll stay here tonight," I finally answered while snuggling into him and pulling my mental barriers as I allowed myself one last thought on the matter.

Even if they learned to accept that they would each be a part of my life, I couldn't imagine a world in which they wanted to share me around each other.

Would I have to live two separate lives with them, splitting my time?

If so, would only a part of me always be enough for them?

As I closed my eyes, I smiled at the synchronicity of our hearts beating in time.

Please let it be enough for them.

CHAPTER TWELVE
ALINA

I couldn't recall the last time I'd ever slept as soundlessly as I had last night with Andrei. When his alarm had gone off this morning, I was shocked to see light streaming through his windows. I hadn't woken up once in the middle of the night, which was saying a lot as I had the smallest bladder ever. With a sweet goodbye kiss, I'd slipped back into my room, crossing my fingers that no one was up and milling about already.

After going about my morning routine and drinking my breakfast, I readied myself to face whatever today brought.

One day at a time.

I knew I needed to let Lincoln know about the

development with Andrei, and despite being nervous about his reaction, I kept reminding myself that I couldn't control that. He was in charge of how he responded, and I'd handle it accordingly. I wasn't going to hide Andrei like a dirty secret, and to be honest, I wanted to get back to a place where my focus wasn't so wholly on these bonds.

Killing Dracula needed to become central to my life again. I wouldn't give up my blood oath to my family just because I'd found mate bonds with two vampires. While I was *slowly* learning that I couldn't hate their entire species for the actions of the bad apples, my hatred for their leader still ran deeply through my soul.

While I'd been focused on handling these situations with Andrei and Lincoln, Dracula had been plotting away and advancing himself on the board. I'd yet to make a fucking play, and I needed to rectify that immediately.

Yanking my door open, I lifted my chin and descended to the main level where chatter flowed freely. The second I passed, voices lowered to whispers. I couldn't help myself as I pushed my stomach to distend as far as it would and shouted in a cheerful tone, "Did you guys know that I'm pregnant with Dracula's baby? The doctors said it's growing into the shape of a bat already."

Honestly, I wasn't sure what was funnier, the thin lips and faces that said they didn't believe my shit despite believing every other thing they ever heard, or the open mouths that soaked in my words. As ridiculous as it was, maybe that would give them something to foam at the mouth over for a while.

"Ridiculous," I muttered, shaking my head as Andrei strolled up to me with a shit-eating grin.

"I can't wait for that to get back to him," he mused. "I think his head might actually combust."

With a groan, I linked my hand into the crook of his elbow as we headed toward the door. "I don't know what I'm going to do about him. There's no way in hell that I'll ever consider exchanging blood with him to know if his claim about us being mates is true. Did you know that mates couldn't kill each other?" I asked curiously.

Pulling the door open, he waited for me to go through as he answered. "Truthfully, it sounds familiar, but mates are so rare that the ins and outs of it really aren't talked about often."

"What a shame that is, right?"

My mood instantly soured hearing his voice. Didn't he have a job to do as the leader of Sanguis or something? He'd transitioned into a full-time pain in my ass so seamlessly, I couldn't help but question if he actually had any responsibilities.

"What are you doing here, Dracula?" I asked callously, pulling to an abrupt halt as I faced him.

I felt Andrei's presence at my back, and it soothed the frazzled energy that always came with being around this maniac. I knew without a doubt that he'd have my back now. We really needed to discuss how our mate bond would impact his father's expectations of him, though.

Pushing off the barren tree he was leaning against, he spread his hands wide as he approached. "I really wish you'd call me Drake. Dracula is so formal, darling, and we're mates after all."

With a roll of my eyes, I crossed my arms and snapped, "And I wish that you'd leave me the fuck alone, but I guess that neither of us are going to get what we want, are we?"

His eyes narrowed dangerously as he closed the distance between us. I heard Andrei's boots crunch against the ground as he drew even closer to my back, making Dracula's fangs snap out as he hissed, "Did you not hear the news that she's my mate, boy?"

My lips pursed as I fought the urge to remind him

that our *fated bond* was *not* confirmed—at least not in my mind, but I didn't want to fuel an argument between us. In fact, I'd rather he just leave as soon as possible. Whatever he was here for, I just wanted him to fucking spit it out so I could go on with my day.

"I did," Andrei responded easily, showing absolutely no fear as he placed his hand on my shoulder and squeezed.

Dracula's eyes snapped to the touch, his face burning with anger as he ground out, "So back off!"

"No."

Andrei's simple response had my core heating with desire. It was attractive as hell to watch him stand his ground in front of Dracula now, in comparison to how he acted in front of him the first time I'd seen them together. Talk about a one-eighty.

Deciding to take over the conversation, I asked, "Why are you here? What do you want?"

His nostrils flared as he dragged his eyes away from Andrei's hand and back to my face. "Is it so hard to believe that I might just be here to check on your well-being?"

My answer was instantaneous. My gut burned as I seethed, "Yes. Yes it is."

With a deep sigh, he rubbed his hand through the scruff of his beard. "If you hate me showing up here so much, I'll make a deal with you."

I tried to keep my face void of all emotion, not wanting to give away a single thing. I was curious, despite wanting to instantly tell him to fuck off. As much as I hated to admit it, I potentially needed to get closer to him to learn more about this situation between us and gather intel about his life.

Perhaps it was finally time to play the game.

"What do you propose?" I asked, letting curiosity tint my tone instead of the malice he was used to with me.

The shock that I hadn't instantly told him to get lost was written all over his face. His mouth popped open before closing and opening again. After another moment, he finally cleared his throat and answered, "I'll stop showing up here if you spend your weekends at my castle with me. I want the opportunity to show you that your thoughts about me and my life are inaccurate, darling. Give me a chance."

Well, damn. This was exactly what I wanted, but was it worth the risk? I wouldn't have Lincoln or Andrei there to back me up if things went south.

But also, what were two days in the grand scheme of things? I could survive that…right?

He'd had plenty of opportunities to kill me before now. What was the point in putting on this show and letting the world know I was his mate if he was just going to kill me the second I got to his castle?

"Fine," I snapped, forcing myself to sound bitter, hoping like hell I'd masked the sinister joy I felt at being presented the opportunity to infiltrate his home. I couldn't clue him into my nefarious actions by suddenly jumping for joy at his offer. Alexandra's note popped into my mind, and I quickly tacked on, "But I have to meet my friend in the library for a study session on Sunday, so I can't stay all weekend."

If he wanted to play house with me, I'd go along with it to move my plan along, but I would do the bare fucking minimum. I hadn't agreed to be a cordial or kind house guest during my stay with him. All I had to do was play along, and I'd get what I needed this weekend, so I never had to go back again.

He faltered for a minute, likely as shocked by my agreement as Andrei was behind me, his rumbling discontentment bubbling through my mind. As Dracula's gaze ran over my face, I threaded my fingers together in front of me, squeezing them tightly to stop myself from fidgeting under his scrutiny.

"I'll be back after your strategy class to take you through the portal tonight, bringing you back on Sunday morning," he finally said, nodding once in agreement. "You won't need to bring anything with you. I'll have everything you need, darling."

I was about to mention that I had mentor training with Lincoln after that, but honestly, there was no way he didn't know that with how invasive he had already become in my life. He was purposefully cutting me off from spending one on one time with Lincoln.

"Okay," I offered weakly, unsure of what else to say to him when I was actively trying to refrain from insulting him.

He must have misread my soft tone for a friendly one, and my lips parted in shock as he smiled before leaning in quickly to press a kiss to my forehead. I was so shocked by the move that I stood there blinking at his back as he disappeared down the path to the portal at the pavilion.

Andrei was in front of me in an instant, shaking me by the arms. "What are you thinking, Alina? You cannot go there. It's a dangerous fucking place to be, and I'm sure everyone already knows exactly what you are to him as well as your birth right as a Van Helsing. There will be a target on your back that not even Dracula can guarantee you safety from."

I'd ensured my walls were firmly in place with Lincoln and him from the moment I woke up this morning. I wasn't quite ready for either of them to hear the streamline of my inner consciousness yet, not when so much of it revolved around planning to kill the leader of Sanguis. There was no doubt they'd try to get in my way and stop me, and I couldn't afford to have any more blockades in my mission.

I let a little bit of ice chill my words as I snapped, "Well, then it's a good thing I'm not some incapable damsel, now isn't it?"

The door to the building clicked open, Lincoln's voice filling the space as he stepped through it. "What's going on here?"

Fuck me. Of course he'd pop up right now.

I was hoping to hold off on telling him about the little deal I'd just made until the end of the day.

Andrei's eyes burned with fire as his jaw

clenched, looking back and forth between Lincoln and me. I realized what he was about to do a split second before he opened his mouth and blabbered.

"She just made a deal to spend the weekend at Dracula's castle if he'd stop showing up here during the week."

Goddamn traitor. Who the fuck did he think he was?

Silence filled the air, but I refused to turn around and look at Lincoln. I wouldn't be surprised to find steam coming out of his ears with the heat of the anger I could practically *feel* radiating from him.

"Alina," he growled. "Face me."

If these two assholes wanted to band together to try to control me, they had another fucking thing coming. Just because we were mates didn't mean they could suddenly tell me what I could and couldn't do with my own life.

"Don't talk to me like a dog," I snapped back at him, with my narrowed eyes trained on Andrei still. Hopefully my gaze conveyed that I wanted to kill him right now for spilling my business.

Fuck this.

Deciding to let them become butt buddies if that's what was suddenly about to happen, I left them in the dust as I sped toward the classroom. I knew I couldn't escape them since we were all going to the combat room, but I knew the other students would at least start trickling in soon, hopefully offering a buffer between me and the men.

They were right on my heels, giving me no reprieve as I drew to a halt on the mats.

"Alina, what the hell were you thinking?" Andrei asked as Lincoln spoke on top of him, "You are not going there with him!"

Whirling around, I held my hands up as I felt my face heating with anger. "Let me make something perfectly clear—I will never let a man control me, so be very careful with how you speak to me next."

"We're your mates, Alina!" Andrei yelled, throwing his hands in the air wildly, and my stomach swooped painfully with the force of him dropping that bomb in front of Lincoln before I could. "It is our job to protect you."

All the fight bled out of me as I watched Lincoln completely deflate.

"Is it true?" he asked in a tone so detached it fucking broke me. "He's your mate as well?"

Before I had a chance to speak, he flashed to Andrei's back and stared at the back of his neck, where we both knew the black drop signifying the mate bond would be.

My eyes bounced back and forth between them. Lincoln's face contorted from anger, to grief, and to disbelief, and back to anger as understanding dawned on Andrei's face, realizing what he'd done.

"I'm sorry, Lincoln," I whispered dejectedly, letting my eyes fall to the mat, knowing the damage was done. I couldn't shove the words back into Andrei's mouth, no matter how badly I wanted to. "I was going to tell you today."

This wasn't how it was supposed to be.

Of course, at that very awkward moment, the other students began to trickle in, leaving us in an awkward three-way standoff. Lincoln was the first to break away, taking his anger out on the class. "Warm up, now! You're the laziest damn class I've ever had. At this point, none of you will be ready to graduate no matter how many damn years you spend here."

Andrei stepped toward me. "Alina, I'm s—"

My eyes jerked to him as I cut him off, "I know. I know you're sorry and you didn't mean to, but I need space to process this, okay?"

Walking away from him, I let myself be swept

into the mindless motions of my stretching routine before starting my sparring session.

The rest of the day felt like it simultaneously flew by and dragged on, somehow. I felt so lost about what to do, hating the way Lincoln brushed me off when I tried to talk to him at the end of class.

In theory, I knew he wasn't going to take the news of yet another mate well, but I'd planned on reassuring him of my feelings for him when I broke the news. The way it actually happened? It was the most brutal bandage-being-ripped-away that I'd ever witnessed.

Deep down I think that when he mentioned not being afraid to fight for me, he didn't really think it would be a fight. He'd never considered the fact that Andrei could be my mate—after all, it was crazy enough to find one, let alone multiple. The news made it real for him, that there truly was someone on the same level as him, competing for my affection and attention.

As Professor Balan dismissed us from strategy, wishing us a good weekend, I grabbed my notebook and pen with the intention of bringing it with me to Dracula's castle. Just because this shit with Lincoln and Andrei had imploded in my face didn't mean that I was going to back out of going to the castle tonight. Hopefully when I came back, the situation wouldn't feel as tense, and I could have a rational talk with them both. For now, I was throwing all my frustrations to the side to dial in on my mission.

I was the last to exit the class, dragging my feet to prolong the inevitable of spending so much time alone with the man who'd killed my family. Rounding the corner and heading downstairs, I pushed the doors open to head outside. I found Lincoln and Andrei standing there, seemingly waiting for me as the rest of the students headed toward the dorms in the distance.

Glancing between them, I waited for one of them to talk, and thankfully wasn't left hanging for long. Lincoln was in my face in a flash, grabbing my face between his hands and pressing a long, lingering kiss to my forehead. "Open the mental connection between us if you need me this weekend, okay?"

I blinked repeatedly, shocked that the request was all he had to say. He was just going to let everything else go for now?

"I...I will," I murmured, finding comfort in that option. I'd honestly forgotten about that ability when I'd thought of being alone in the castle with Dracula.

"From what I've read, the further the distance between mates, the harder it is to communicate, so I'm not sure how well it will work. But it's something," he breathed out as he wrapped me in a hug. "I don't know why the hell you're doing this, but I know I haven't earned the privilege of knowing everything about your life yet. Just promise me to always keep your guard up."

Relief poured through me with the knowledge that he wasn't going to hold a grudge and give me the silent treatment any longer. I also appreciated that he admitted knowing that he needed to earn my trust to know more about why I was doing this. It went a long way to hear him say that, especially when he'd opened up to me recently about his past. I didn't want our relationship and communication to feel unfair, and I *did* want to open to them...eventually.

Pulling back, I pushed onto my tiptoes to press a quick kiss to his lips, needing to show him that I wasn't giving up on him just because Andrei was also my mate now. What I intended on being a brief peck turned into him grabbing my waist and tipping me back for a long, deep kiss.

I was breathless by the time he stood us back up and let go of me.

Andrei stood quietly, waiting with his arms across his chest and shaking his head at Lincoln, who grinned like an idiot in response.

Rolling my eyes at their shit, I walked toward Andrei and reached up for him, holding my notebook behind his neck. "Hey," I whispered as his arms wrapped around me. "I forgive you, okay? Don't beat yourself up for it."

We all made mistakes, but I knew he hadn't blurted about our mate bond maliciously, and that's what mattered.

Resting his forehead against mine, he smiled gently. "Thank you, baby girl."

Dipping his lips to press them against mine, he coaxed my mouth open to deepen the kiss the same way Lincoln had, but we were quickly interrupted by the loud clearing of a throat. Reluctantly, I pulled away from Andrei, turning to regard the actual bane of my existence, standing with his arms crossed over his chest in a suit he had no right looking so damn good in.

Bad, Alina. Stop thinking the enemy looks like anything other than evil reincarnate.

"I'm going to pretend I didn't see any of that," Dracula chirped in a cheerful tone, though his blood red eyes suggested otherwise. Extending his hand toward me, he asked, "Shall we go, darling?"

Swallowing hard, I forced my repulsion down as I stepped forward and placed my free hand in his, allowing him to guide me toward the gate to the pavilion. Glancing back, I watched Lincoln and Andrei's faces vanish as I crossed over.

Fates, please don't let this be a mistake.

CHAPTER THIRTEEN
ALINA

Stumbling through the portal, I instantly ripped my hand out of his rough one as soon as I knew I wouldn't be swept away to some unknown dimension. Looking at my hand in disgust as my lip curled up, I rubbed it against my pants before shaking it, as if I could so easily wipe away the feeling of disgust that filled me at allowing myself to be touched by him.

It had been a necessary evil to hold his hand in my mind.

Traversing portals alone for the sake of my independence wasn't a hill I was willing to die on just yet. Deep down, I knew that they were all set to go to a certain place, but the knowledge had never eased my fears. Skye had always secretly held my hand when we had to use them to go to Ordinarius since she knew I didn't want to look weak to everyone else.

The only time I hadn't been a little baby about it was when Estrid invited me to DIA. Looking back on it now, I realized the fear hadn't been there because I didn't care where the portal took me then...as long as it took me away from all the death I was running from.

"What is wrong with your hand?" Dracula asked, turning to look at me with his lips pressed together tightly as they twitched at the corner, like he was barely containing a laugh. Mirth danced in his dark eyes, and a dimple deepened the corner of his mouth, which was super fucking annoying.

Why give the villain in my story such an adorable mark?

Dropping my hand to my side, I couldn't help but scrunch my nose up at myself for doing something that made him want to laugh, even if it wasn't intentional. The last thing I wanted to do was do anything to pull out his damn dimple. I was not here to make him chuckle.

He should fear me, not laugh at me.

"Nothing," I snapped, forcing my gaze away from him to take in my surroundings.

"Where are we?" I asked, confused by the grandeur of the room we stood in. Large, vaulted ceilings spanned above our heads, coming to high points that were accentuated by the light spilling through the space. As I turned around, I gasped at the beautiful red and white stained glass that framed a single, black-iron door.

"My home," he answered, voice echoing through the expansive area.

Looking over my shoulder at him, I found him smiling at me. Literally, what could I possibly be doing right now to invoke that?

Refusing to let him distract me, I focused back on the mystery on my plate. I'd read a lot since getting to DIA, about how the school operated and each of the different sectors. This absolutely wasn't where the portal should have let us out. The portals in the school allowed large groups to come and go at the discretion of Estrid or a leader of the territory you were traveling to. They weren't just open for anyone to use, and I presumed they were somehow spelled to know the user, similar to how the barrier around the slayer territory read species.

Due to the nature of why they were used, the

entry or exit point should have been in a city or common area for citizens to get to. Without a doubt, there was no way Dracula was letting people come and go through his castle.

Arching an eyebrow, I couldn't help the scowl I gave his smile in return as I questioned him. "How did we end up here? This isn't where the portal should have let us out at."

His arms swept behind his back as he took slow, purposeful steps toward me, cocking his head lightly to the side. "I'll answer your question if you answer mine."

Why did I always seem to have to jump through hoops to get information from vampires? You'd think they were descendants of fae with the way they seemed to avoid answering things.

Shaking my head, I sighed, lifting my hand lightly before smacking it on my thigh in exasperation. "Fine!" I exclaimed before offering him a resigned sigh. "What's your question?"

As he came to a stop in front of me, I considered holding my breath as his warm, inviting scent wrapped around me, hating how I wanted to lean into the source each time. Reaching out, his hand brushed over mine that was holding onto my notebook still, making me instantly snatch it to my chest.

"Why did you bring the notebook when I told you that you didn't need to bring anything?" he asked as he dropped his hand behind his back and stared down at me expectantly.

I blurted out the first thing that came to mind. "I like to draw. It's my escape."

His brows rose in surprise. "Really? I'd love to see your work. I love to collect art from all over Praeditus."

Shit, was he trying to bond over a hobby that I most definitely did not have? I mean, I could draw a mean stick figure with some fangs and blood, and like a line for a dick with two dots for balls and circle boobs to represent my life, but I didn't think anyone would really consider it artwork. If they did, I'd title it, *Vampires who fuck,* since that seemed to sum up my life recently.

I tried my best to act coy, tightening my grip on the notebook that only contained notes from class as I cleared my throat lightly. "It's private."

I saw the suspicion creep into his gaze, making me quickly tack on in a softer voice, "But maybe... maybe one day I'll let you see."

"Okay," he answered with a nod before lifting a

hand to rub at his beard and cracking a smile. "As long as you aren't keeping it to take notes on my castle and everything you learn here, I guess that's okay."

Wait...was he joking with me despite me doing a horrendous job of hiding that that *was* in fact what I was doing?

Spluttering, I let my eyes widen like I was offended. "I would never."

His eyes narrowed on me before he let out a rumbling chuckle and turned around. "Yeah, of course you wouldn't, darling. But to answer your question, it's magic."

It's magic. That's the fucking explanation I was getting.

"I'll show you to your room," he called over his shoulder as he ascended the gorgeous sprawling staircase. It was split into two sides, arching to meet in the middle, and I followed behind him as he took the left side.

Letting out a huff at his lack of true explanation, I realized I was going to have to step my game up to try to lower his guard enough to get real answers. It was clear not one ounce of him thought I was here with the intention of giving him a chance like he wanted. Yet...he was still being respectful and even joking with me.

Why did he continue to try so hard?

Despite my suspicion for the man leading me through his home, I couldn't help but look around in appreciation of the gorgeous architecture. The space looked like a gothic cathedral that had at some point been converted into a living space. Candles were lit everywhere my eyes landed, lending an ethereal sort of beauty to the rooms we passed through. Black, marble floors laid throughout the halls, contrasting the natural stone the building was constructed of with an interesting mixture of old and new.

"This way," he called from ahead of me, drawing my focus to him.

There was another issue with him being the villain in my story that Fate needed to explain to me. Why did they have to make him so fucking handsome? When I pictured what Dracula looked like before meeting him, I imagined an old, pale wrinkled man who never saw the light of day; maybe even a man who was balding after being alive for so long.

Yet the version of Dracula that was real had deeply tanned skin, a neatly trimmed beard, and perfectly full, arched brows that added to his whole broody vibe. His black eyes were captivating, and his hair appeared to be thick and full, despite the product holding it in place. I found myself wondering what his hair would look like when it wasn't slicked back. Would it be soft and fluffy, hanging around his face?

"Darling?" he questioned, snapping me out of whatever trance had just overtaken me and rooted my feet to the spot as I inspected him.

Get it together, Alina. It's just the dumb fucking bond he keeps saying you have. It's getting to your head.

Without a doubt, I was looking for every reason possible to find him culpable of the crimes I accused him of, and while he annoyed the shit out of me with his overbearing presence and flexed his power in ways I didn't necessarily agree with, I'd yet to see the side of him that I'd built him up to be in my mind.

I desperately wanted to morph him into the vengeful, cold vampire that could order the massacre of my family. With his focus seemingly so intent on my well-being and wanting to get to know me, each passing day only added to my confusion.

Estrid's words played through my head, telling me how he was a generous, anonymous donor to the academy. Why didn't he want credit for helping students find a higher education and jobs that could elevate their lives?

And then there was the admission that he was holding an investigation and publicly searching for the vampires that killed my family.

Perhaps it wasn't the most tactful move, but I couldn't contain all the questions bubbling through me anymore, so I blurted out, "Why are you searching for those who killed my family? If it wasn't you, like you claim, why take a public stance that vampires will be held responsible for hurting slayers? Why go through all of this? That can't be a good look for you considering you govern vampires. Why stand up for the injustice done to my family?"

I was breathless by the time I spat it all out, my confusion and frustration twinging together to make my chest knot tightly.

If he wanted to keep playing the doting mate who was thrilled to find me, I expected him to have a prepared speech to feed to me, whispering all the things I wanted to hear to make me believe him. His answer was damn near the opposite of that.

"Your family is my family now, Alina. I told you I would help you get vengeance, and I meant it."

It was that simple to him if he was being truthful. There was no drawn-out anger about his name being dragged through the mud, nor did he seem to want justice for his name to be cleared. No bullshit about wanting to unite our people under the guise of peace.

"You're too wrapped up in your own pity party to see that maybe, just maybe, you played directly into some-one's hand, believing the shit they spoon fed you."

I couldn't stand to look at him as doubt began to surface within me, hating that he was either a wonderful actor playing me like a puppet master or that I actually had no idea who my true enemy was. It hit me then, that I was holding on so tightly to the first option being the truth because the second one... It was a bitter pill to swallow, admitting I was wrong, had been played, and didn't even know where to begin to fulfill my blood oath if that was the case.

As I stood here staring at him with all my cards on the table, I admitted, for the very first time, "I don't trust you. If it *wasn't* you, why the hell did they both send *your regards* for the massacre of my family as well as my forced turning?" I asked, voice tight-ening with emotion before cracking slightly. "I don't know why they'd leave me alive to be a pawn in whatever sick fucking game they're playing."

As soon as the emotion trickled into my voice,

he was on me, hands cupping my face gently as his voice echoed with a ferocity I'd never heard from him before. "I don't have the answers to your questions, Alina, but I swear to you, I will get them, even if I have to burn this entire place down to do so."

My mouth parted, and I inhaled sharply at the conviction in his tone.

His thumbs brushed my cheeks as he growled, "And don't call yourself a pawn ever again. You're a survivor, and the fucking Queen on my board."

I was a survivor, but the title didn't make me proud. It left me feeling guilty for being the one who was chosen to live. It shouldn't have been me. I was half the slayer of anyone else in my House. No one else would have found themselves feeling empathetic to vampires in the wake of their family's death. Nor would they have found themselves so far away from getting revenge.

I was doing my fucking best to cope and choose the right path, but how was I supposed to do that when my soul felt split on the correct way to lead myself each time I drew a breath?

I had no words for him, and he must have seen that because he dropped the subject. He simply grabbed my hand, gently guiding me wherever we were supposed to go...and, lost in my thoughts, I let him.

Was I ready to admit to myself that I might be wrong and open my eyes to other possibilities?

Was I ready to consider that maybe life wouldn't be so cruel as to forge a potential mate bond to the same person who ordered the slaughter of my family?

Letting go of my hand as we approached a large set of black doors, he pushed them open, gesturing with his hand to go through. "You'll find everything you need here. Come back down when you feel ready, and we'll talk more—or whatever you want."

I found myself letting out a massive exhale of relief at a moment to be alone as my thoughts lay scattered to the wind, swirling around just out of reach.

As soon as I walked past him and over the threshold, the doors creaked behind me. I whirled around, stopping him before they could close completely. "Hey!"

He paused, concern pinching his brow as he asked, "Yes?"

Fuck, why couldn't I have just let him close the doors and walk away?

Awkward silence stretched between us as I

cracked my knuckles at my side nervously before finally settling on saying what I initially was going to anyway. It was time to put my ego to the side and figure shit out.

"Thanks, Drake."

CHAPTER FOURTEEN
DRAKE

Every night since meeting Alina, I'd gone to sleep with fury burning through me for so, so many reasons. The most important being that she'd been harmed and her entire family had been killed. Without a doubt, her becoming a vampire worked in my favor because I wanted us to have eternity together but turning should have been a choice for her to make.

The second reason fury pounded in my skull during every waking moment was that the massacre meant there was a rebellion brewing in my city. Whether it came from the inside, led by someone on my board, or by someone on the outside remained to be seen, but I had an extreme suspicion.

While the slayers' territory was within the

boundaries of Sanguis, there was a sizable enough distance between us to staunch the number of fights erupting between our two people. Even with the distance, never had something with such high repercussions happened without me knowing about it within an hour. Hell, because I was a ruler who didn't want to lock himself away, not dealing with day-to-day tasks, I typically heard about the most mundane activities each day.

Keeping the attack secret from me for fucking *days* meant that it had to be someone on the inside. I couldn't imagine how someone from the outside would have been able to amass the power and connections that it would take to stop that information from reaching me.

Each person I surrounded myself with was carefully selected for their role, and I never rushed to fill an empty slot just to have a body occupying it. No, I waited and watched, learning everything about the person I was selecting before extending the invite to join me.

The thought of one of them spitting in my face like this...it had my body shaking with fury at the disrespect. I'd given them status, wealth...*power*. I put them where they were, and this is how one or multiple members were going to show me their thanks?

Lifting the glass of scotch to my lips, I downed the golden liquid before slamming the glass down onto the kitchen island, shattering it as my rage consumed me.

"Drake! We're going to run out of glasses if you keep this up."

Slowly turning my head, I glared at Lo as she grabbed the most expensive brand of rum I had and swigged it directly from the bottle before jumping onto the counter top. Her dark curls bounced with her movement before she settled in with a smirk on her adorable face. Somehow, those large brown eyes always got me to crumble and let her do whatever she wished to in my castle.

Rolling my eyes in jest, I murmured, "Doesn't look like that's going to be a problem for you, you heathen."

Sticking her tongue out at me like a child in response, my heart warmed at our easy banter.

She was a little rough around the edges, never once conforming to what was proper or expected of her, but that's what made her my most valued friend and confidant. What you saw was what you got with her, and if her mouth didn't say it, her face sure as hell would. She was an open book, for better or for worse.

There wasn't a number large enough to account for all the times she'd refused to blow smoke up my ass. She always gave it to me straight, sometimes to the point of *really* pissing me off until I would need to step away to calm down before continuing our conversation, but she was always right. Well, she was *usually* right.

Swallowing, she winced and beat her hand against her chest before a little burp escaped her. Lowering the bottle to her side, her eyes darted to the shattered glass scattered across the marble island and floor. "You better clean that up before your *bride* comes down here. You don't want her to think you have an anger problem."

"Oh, shove it," I snarked back. The terrible book and movie adaptations about *me* that have floated around our sector ever since they'd been discovered in the human plane were the reason Lo had insisted on calling Alina my *bride*. Much to my utter fucking annoyance.

Grabbing the handheld broom and pan from under the sink, I gathered the pieces before dumping them in the trash. Discontent swirled through my gut as I shoved everything back under the sink. Who the hell had I misplaced my trust in?

Eyeing the bottle of scotch, I murmured, "Fuck it," before following her lead and taking a swig directly from it.

Lo was the only person I let my guard down with completely, not caring about appearing like a proper leader to her. I hoped to add Alina to that small list of people after tonight.

I couldn't explain the relief I'd felt in her acceptance of my trade for her to come here on the weekends. While I'm sure I would find it difficult to not visit her during the week, I'd take what I could get, and having her in my space, where I could truly show her who I was, felt like the biggest victory.

"Yes, Dracula," Lo whooped, pumping her hand in the air. "Let your hair down and relax."

Why did I keep her around, again?

"Are you leaving anytime soon?" I asked in jest as I pushed to sit on top of the counter next to her, flicking her arm lightly.

She'd been with me so long that I might as well call her my sister at this point, and she was about the only person in the world who could have convinced me to let her live here with me.

"Oh, no, honey," she chuckled before taking

another swig and looking toward the archway of the kitchen like she expected Alina to appear any moment. "I'm not going anywhere until I see if I won the bet or not. I'm invested."

"Mhm," I retorted while fending off the hand that she was slowly moving toward me to try to flick me back. "Sure you are, Lo."

While we did have a bet on whether Alina would wear the dress I'd bought for her, with me betting that she wouldn't and Lo thinking she would because of how beautiful it was, I knew that wasn't why she was really hanging around, but I didn't mind either way. She was family, and I wanted them to meet.

More than anything, I knew Lo wanted to see for herself if Alina was everything I'd said she was after I'd told her I'd found my mate.

I could have kept my knowledge of finding her a secret, but Alina's safety was of the utmost importance to me. Announcing our bond would hopefully make whoever was behind this think twice about inciting my wrath if they hurt her. There was nowhere they could run that would prevent me from hunting them down and tearing them apart mercilessly once I found out who was responsible for my mate's pain. It would be a slow, painful process that lasted weeks. I knew *exactly* how far I could push the limits of a vampire's regeneration and healing capabilities before they succumbed to their wounds.

Hearing footsteps echoing in the distance, I called out, "In here, darling!"

My eyes flickered to the arched doorway, hating the nerves that suddenly made my stomach drop. I wanted Alina and Lo to get along so badly, but they were both in possession of big, bold personalities. Their introduction would either be like two forces of nature colliding, or they'd be thick as thieves, one adding gasoline to the fire the other started.

Both options honestly terrified me a little.

"Here we go," Lo mumbled as she leaned her back against the cabinets and swung her dangling feet.

Alina's head poked around the corner. All I could see was the collar of a shirt, but it was enough to make me grin at my victory. I knew she wouldn't wear the dress, but I'd made damn sure I'd enjoy the only other options I left for her.

I'd put her in my room, so it was either the dress or my clothes. Both were perfectly fine options in my opinion.

"Is there a bottle for me?" she asked, taking the scene before her in stride as she padded into the rocm fully, with absolutely no shame over the fact that all she wore was a long sleeved, black dress shirt that draped to her mid-thigh.

I watched Lo from the corner of my eye, her warm, beige skin glowed under the soft light in the kitchen, illuminating the smile that tugged her lips up. Reaching into her pocket, she chuckled as she slapped the money onto the counter between us, admitting her defeat silently.

"What's mine is yours," I answered, jumping off the counter and sweeping my hand out to the liquor cabinet off to the side. Surprising me, instead of heading toward the liquor, Alina walked right past me and stopped in front of Lo.

Extending her hand out and lifting her chin, my beauty offered, "Hi, I'm Alina."

Lo's silence paired with the weight of her gaze would have made anyone else shuffle around awkwardly, but not my mate. She continued to hold her hand out, unblinking as she held Lo's gaze, letting her know she wasn't going away without being acknowledged.

Right as I was about to yell at Lo to play nice, she hopped off the counter and bypassed Alina's hand entirely, engulfing her in a hug and sloshing some of the rum over Alina's back with her quick movement.

Alina remained stiff as a metal pole as Lo cheerfully answered, "I'm Lo, also known as the main pain in Drake's ass, as well as the only Bishop on the board, I suppose."

My breath caught in my throat as I waited for Alina to return the gesture, and I could help my audible sigh of relief as she finally encircled her arms around Lo. But more than that, I thought my heart might actually explode when I saw a smile appearing on Alina's face. It was a small one, but it was there, and I was suddenly so damn thankful for Lo sticking around to meet her.

All I'd wanted since meeting Alina was to make her smile. Everything she'd been through—the pain, the rage—it was too much for her to carry alone. I wanted to take some of that burden off her shoulders, giving her the freedom to feel like she could truly smile again.

"Nice to meet you, Lo," Alina murmured as they pulled apart, her amused gaze tracking the smaller vampire as she practically danced over to the liquor cabinet.

Without turning around, she called out, "What's your choice? He has some good shit in here, so don't feel like you need to be stingy."

Yup, they were going to be thick as thieves in no time.

And just when I felt like my night was made from seeing Alina smile, a tinkling laugh came from her, floating through the air like the most beautiful song I'd ever heard.

"If that's the case, give me the finest whiskey," she chuckled, padding over to join Lo as she rummaged through the rows of bottles before pulling the bottle of Macallan 1926 from the very bottom, where it was supposed to be kept safe.

"Aha!" she exclaimed before turning around with it and presenting it to Alina.

Letting out a sigh, I called out, "While it is the most expensive one I own, it's more of a collector's item. That's the only hand-painted bottle that remains. So if you do decide to take it, the only thing I ask is that you not damage the bottle."

If Alina decided to be stubborn and drink it despite that, I wouldn't be upset. She was worth so much more than that bottle—I just happened to love the artwork on the bottle. When I told her I was a collector of all kinds of art, I had left out that quite a bit of my collection was from Ordinarius. I wasn't sure how she'd feel about all my non-sanctioned trips to the human world since it was technically illegal to go there without garnering a political invite from the leader of their government. She had been raised a slayer, after all.

Turning to look at me over her shoulder, she asked, "How much was it?"

Shrugging, I answered nonchalantly, "Two point three million human dollars."

Her eyes bugged out of her head as she turned back to Lo, holding her hands far away from the bottle as she hissed, "Put it back, oh my god!"

"Fine, fine," Lo mumbled before putting it back and pulling out the Macallan 25 bottle instead. "Here!"

It was adorable as hell how Alina looked back to me with eyes as wide as saucers as if she was waiting for me to confirm it wasn't another expensive bottle.

Shaking my head, I reassured her, "It's fine, darling. Take it."

Now compared to when I picked her up at the academy earlier in the day felt like a massive jump forward. It was as if she was letting down her walls slowly but surely, and my hands trembled around the bottle grasped in my hands, scared of fucking up our unspoken truce.

I got the feeling if I moved too quickly, even

more walls would spring up than had been there originally. If that were to happen, I was afraid they'd never come down again.

"Alright, alright, I'll leave you two alone," Lo announced before sashaying to the fridge to grab the O-type blood I kept in there for her.

It was one of the only rules I had of living here, we never allowed human donors in. It was much too large a risk. Without Alina here, if I died, Lo was set to take over the board. It would be far too easy to take out the two most powerful people in Sanguis with a poisoned human donor.

Call me paranoid, but I hadn't lived all these years by being an idiot.

After the two women exchanged their good-byes, Alina turned toward me and cocked her head. "Now what?" she asked, blinking at me owlishly as she gripped the bottle of whiskey in her hands.

If she didn't want to talk about anything personal or serious, I wasn't going to be the one to bring it up. I brought her here to get to know me, to try to make her feel more comfortable in my presence.

"Want to watch a movie?" I offered.

"A movie?" she parroted back, as if it was the

most absurd thing I could have offered. "Who are you, and what have you done with Dracula?"

My chest rumbled with my chuckle as I walked toward her. I tucked a strand of her silver hair behind her ear. "He's tucked away for the night, and he won't come back out until I have to be in public again. This is the real me—I just have to be careful of who I let my guard down around."

Her pupils dilated at my words as she whispered, "You shouldn't trust me."

Her honesty was endearing, but it didn't change the fact that she was worth the risk. I already knew she couldn't kill me, but there were plenty of other ways she could hurt me if she tried. Several of those would eventually lead to my death if executed properly. There was no way in hell I would ever tell her that, though.

"Maybe not," I murmured, "but here we are."

She seemed to snap from a trance, stepping back and lifting the Macallan to her lips. My eyes traced the way she wrapped them around the glass opening of the bottle before taking a long gulp.

My cock hardened painfully in my pants as I watched her drink that whiskey like a pro, all while wearing my shirt.

"Lead the way," she announced, sweeping her hand out to spur me on.

Even if we didn't speak another word for the rest of this night, this would absolutely go down as the best day I'd ever had in my long existence because it marked the day I saw even the smallest sliver of a chance to earn her trust.

CHAPTER FIFTEEN
ALINA

Settling into the furthest corner of the large, red sectional in the room, I watched as Drake piddled around with the projector.

I didn't know what to make of this version of him. He seemed...normal. It was a jarring change from the put-together and frankly intimidating image he'd worn every other time I'd seen him. It was such a severe change that it wouldn't have surprised me if he told me he was the nicer twin that was kept locked in this castle while his evil twin prowled the world outside.

Lifting the collar of the shirt I wore inconspicuously, I inhaled a scent that was all Drake. The one I knew, not some nice twin who dwelled in a castle and plied people with his expensive liquor collection. Dropping it back down, my eyes continued to track his every move as I nervously played with the cuffs of the long sleeves.

I didn't know how to act around this version of him. Hell, I didn't know how to act around the other version of him either anymore. I was so worried about being duped by him that I was still struggling to believe anything he said despite how much truth I sensed in them. The conviction in his words had never once wavered from my first time meeting him all the way to now.

I pictured a lot of different ways that this weekend might go, but this sure as hell wasn't one of them. I'd imagined a cold, disenchanting home that had waitstaff and maids who all cowered in fear of Dracula. Instead, the castle was warm and inviting, completely void of the evidence of a staff that waited on his every whim and desire.

As was typical of the version I did know, though, he'd left a gift for me in his room. As soon as I'd been left alone, my eyes had fallen to a gorgeous red dress with a slit up the thigh that would surely turn eyes. There was a note laying on top of it in a sprawling script, saying he'd bought it specifically for me and hoped I loved it.

The fact that I didn't immediately huff at his gift

was a sure sign that I was softening toward him. While I certainly thought it was beautiful, the dress felt like too much, too soon. Even after searching the room and expansive closets and not finding any actual clothing for me to wear, I didn't feel comfortable caving and putting the dress on. I could have stayed in my skirt and blouse, but I didn't want to put them back on after cleaning up in the shower, so a big dress shirt it was.

Tucking my feet beneath me, I squirmed for a moment in the awkward silence before caving and asking, "Why that dress?"

He didn't stop working on connecting the projector as he said, "I thought you would love it, and Lo convinced me to give it to you as a present, though I wanted to wait to give it to you. You weren't very receptive to my last gifts, after all." The machine kicked on then, and I winced at the bright light shining in my direction. "I told her you wouldn't wear it tonight, and she bet me that you would."

The mention of the tiny, beautiful vampire left my heart feeling warm and a little gooey. Like Alexandra, there was something about her that put me at ease instantly. She just had that effect on me, and I obviously wasn't the only one. They had a sweet relationship, and it was clear they were close. The way I watched them sitting together so casually as well as the way she spoke around him made me think that they likely had a familial bond.

I hated to admit that my gut had clenched when I first popped my head into the room and saw her sitting so close to him on the counter. It was the first time I'd ever seen him so relaxed, and he'd seemed like a completely different version of himself in general. It didn't help that Lo was drop dead gorgeous with dark curls that contrasted her light brown skin. She had been practically glowing beneath the warm lights of the kitchen, and it only took me a few seconds of interacting with her to realize that she had a great personality.

If I cared about who he occupied his time with, she held all the qualities to make me jealous...which I totally wasn't. He wasn't mine, despite his adamance that he was. I hadn't claimed him, so he could spend his time with whomever he chose. And I couldn't give a shit about it.

I glanced away from the bright light, dropping my gaze toward my hands twisting in the sleeves of his shirt as he moved to sit on the other side of the couch. It was thoughtful of him to allow me the distance I wanted between us, but it didn't stop the twinge of want deep in my stomach. *Fuck that.*

Forcing myself to think about literally anything else, I allowed my curiosity of their bond to lead me forward. I asked, "How did you meet Lo?"

My brain was adamantly trying to convince me that this information would help me learn about his exploitable weaknesses, but the truth was that I wanted to learn more about this version of him, whether I was ready to admit that to myself or not.

Pulling my knees up to my chest, I rested my chin on the tops of them as a wicked grin pulled at his face. A dark chuckle rumbled from him as he shook his head. "Oh, Lauren...We've been together ever since she tried to kill me as a fledgling who had been turned and left to her own devices. She didn't care where she got her blood from as long as she got it."

My own smile threatened to spread over my lips at his words. So, we'd both tried to kill Drake when we first met him. I knew there was a reason I liked her.

Letting out a sigh, he relaxed into the couch, tossing his arm over the back as his gaze swung to me. "Thank you for giving her a chance. I know it's probably hard to meet new vampires with your upbringing and to not judge them off the bat based on what you'd been raised to believe about them."

His voice was gentle and kind as he thanked me, once again making me wonder how I was supposed to hold the grudge of my blood oath against this version of him. But what was more shocking than that was that his words made me realize I hadn't assumed anything bad about her just because she was a vampire. For the first time, probably, it hadn't been the first thing to come to mind upon meeting a vampire. I'd simply wondered who she was and what she was like, like I would a fellow slayer or human that I didn't feel threatened by.

My lips thinned. "Yeah, well, I'm not sure about anything I was taught anymore. Things used to be so simple and straightforward, and now...It's one hell of a messy, overgrown maze up here," I admitted, pointing at my head.

Should I be admitting things like that to him? *Probably not.* He could easily use my confusion to advance in whatever his grand plan was, but I suddenly found myself very tired of carrying and forcing so much anger and hatred toward him. The rage was like a festering beast within me that I had to constantly feed to keep alive.

"I say this with the utmost respect," he muttered

before taking another sip from his scotch. He let out a huff before saying, "But fuck what you think you know."

It was such a crass and informal way of speaking, and the unexpected words made me laugh as I reached for my own bottle on the small table next to me. Lifting it toward him, I muttered, "I can cheers to that."

Fuck what I think I know. Amen. I had so many thoughts in my head that I felt like I couldn't possibly control them all. I just wanted to let go of them all, to feel like I could breathe again without the weight of them bearing down on me constantly.

We shared a moment of easy laughter that felt so damn comfortable it startled me when I realized it was happening.

Cuddling the bottle to my chest, I snuggled into the plush cushions of the couch and considered him. "You're not what I expected. Why do you seem to have two separate personas?"

Hell, if he was in the sharing mood, I was going to take advantage.

"Heavy is the head that wears the crown," he muttered, staring at me with an unnerving focus that made me fidget. "When you're at the top, you're hated. If you show weakness for even a moment, they're out for blood. This castle is the only place I can take off that mask. It's why only Lo and I live here—I can't handle being that version of me all the time. After too long, it starts to make me feel like that is who I truly am, and I hate it."

"That sounds really lonely."

I wasn't certain how old he was, but I knew there were whispers that he was the original, the very first vampire. And according to the history in the Van Helsing books, we knew that vampires had been around for at least a millennium.

"It is," he whispered in a broken tone, staring unblinking at me for a few seconds before the unthinkable happened. The black that obscured all of his eyes began to bleed away, revealing white until the center of his eyes finally appeared.

His eyes were strikingly bright blue, and my mouth dropped open with surprise as he stared at me, honest and open.

"How...how do you do that?" I asked, still reeling from the knowledge that he could somehow control the black that obscured his real eyes.

With a single shrug of his shoulders, he glanced away toward the screen in front of us. "For as long as I can recall, I've carried around a part of me that I keep locked up. With time, I've learned how to control the bits and pieces of it that lend me help. Fully black eyes keep anyone from being able to read me easily, which allows me to appear colder and more neutral than I really feel inside."

I snorted, glancing at him sidelong as I admitted, "I've always been able to sense emotions by looking into your eyes, despite them being fully black. I thought it was strange how emotive they were given the lack of iris."

He seemed to fight the smile that threatened to brighten the part of his face I could see. "That's because you're my mate. You can naturally sense my moods and underlying feelings if you really try. Even naturally, you'll begin to pick up on them without trying."

That made me sit up straight. "What? Seriously?"

That new tidbit had me replaying all the times I'd been around Lincoln, Andrei, and Drake.

Is it why I sensed that there was so much more to Andrei even when he had that shitty, cocky exterior locked firmly in place? I'd felt adamantly that there was something broken in him that he was hiding...a softer side that was protecting his heart.

And fucking Lincoln...Fates, it had been so toxic between us with the hatred at first, but there had been an underlying desire that consumed me no matter what. Had it been his own desire adding to mine, allowing those moments to take over everything I felt and obscuring the hatred that burned so brightly within me for vampires? Neither of us had seemed to be able to walk away despite the rage and disgust we felt for one another.

Perhaps the most polarizing moment I felt had been with Drake, though. When I'd been trying to kill him...I'd felt moments of attraction before it was replaced with such gut-wrenching grief that I'd been brought to tears. It had thrown me then, tears when I wasn't sad at all over the thought of killing the monster I'd believed him to be back then.

But if his words were true...then that meant...*No.* I was not ready to accept that he was truly my mate.

We were moving into topics of conversation that no part of me was ready to have or to process, so I burrowed back into the corner of the couch and asked, "Are you going to play the movie?"

My hand tightly squeezed the neck of my liquor bottle, prepared for him to push the topic with me. Instead, he reached over and clicked a button wordlessly to play the movie, and my hand relaxed with each passing second.

He didn't speak another word for the rest of the

movie, which was one I'd never seen before, but that wasn't surprising considering we hadn't possessed much of a collection from Ordinarius. The strictly regimented routine of the slayers didn't allow much time for such entertainment.

The movie Drake played for me was called *The Fellowship of The Ring*, and clearly showed what humans pictured our fantasy worlds to be with their limited knowledge of the supernaturals. Watching the way-out-in-left-field film allowed me the chance to relax as I let my brain numb out with the help of the alcohol. Silently, he'd moved onto playing the second movie in the series, and about halfway through, my eyes started sagging.

I'd quickly lost my fight against sleep but roused for a moment when I felt the bottle being pulled from my grasp before a soft blanket was laid around me. I snuggled into its warmth as it was tucked under my feet and my sides to cocoon me. The warmth quickly lulled me back to sleep, and perhaps I'd dreamed it, but at some point, I'd felt a heartbeat thrumming steadily beneath my ear.

CHAPTER SIXTEEN

ALINA

The smell of coffee roused me from my dreamless sleep, reminding me of how much I missed the hot, comforting liquid from my time as a slayer. I hadn't even thought about the warm, caffeinated brew with it out of sight, out of mind since at the academy, but suddenly, I had to satisfy the craving.

Wait, where the hell was I?

Glancing around, I recognized the theater room with a start. The fuzzy feeling of a sleepy brain quickly wore off, and I recalled falling asleep during the movie last night. I hadn't expected to sleep peacefully here all night, but this couch was like a damn cloud. Tossing the soft blanket off, I pushed to my feet and headed in the direction of the glorious scent.

My nostrils flared as I took a few quick breaths, scenting the air for a second smell I recognized. Was that...*bacon?*

Why would either of these scents be wafting through the castle when no humans lived here? What went on here continued to surprise the hell out of me. Drake's sentiments from last night played through my mind, and I chuckled with the realization that I could apply it to just about anything in my life right now.

Fuck what you think you know.

Using the scents when I was split on which way to head through the maze of the castle, I quickly found myself approaching the kitchen. A gentle hum floated through the air, and though I could be mistaken, I was fairly certain it sounded like Drake's deep, velvety tone.

Sure enough, when I padded into the room, I spotted him in front of the gas stove, flipping bacon with a pair of tongs and softly humming a song I didn't recognize. My question from yesterday about what his hair would look like without the product in it was answered, and I was correct. It was soft and messy like he'd let it air dry—it softened his look, and I found my traitorous body feeling an overwhelming attraction to this version of him.

Fuck, I was in way over my head with my stay here. Everything was completely opposite of what I'd expected to find here. Instead of dodging fists, weapons, or fangs, I was bobbing and weaving around emotions I wasn't even close to being ready to accept.

Bob and weave, girl. Bob and weave.

"Good morning," he greeted me, glancing up for a second before returning his focus to the food. "There's fresh coffee in the corner. I wasn't sure if you were at a place in your transition where you could stomach anything other than blood, but Lo demands coffee every morning or else she is a total grouch, so it'll always be here if you decide you want to try."

Was this...domesticated Dracula? It couldn't be.

Thinking back to his musings from last night, I knew he was right. If he showed this side of himself, people would circle him like vultures, thinking him weak. I found myself respecting him more for showing me this part of himself. I knew others wouldn't share the sentiment.

To me, it took a lot of balls to let your guard down enough to show someone else that you weren't all rigid, jagged corners that would pierce a person if they got too close to you. I'd spent so much of my life living that very facade to cope, and I found myself still falling into those tendencies as a knee jerk reaction a lot of times.

Even after seeing the gentler sides of Lincoln and Andrei that they hid from everyone else, I was surprised to find an even softer and tender side of Drake than anything I'd seen from my other guys.

Wait. Fuck. No! He was *not* one of my guys.

Breezing past him, I desperately pushed my mind back in the direction of hoping I'd be able to drink coffee again. I grabbed a white mug dotted with flecks of blue and green and filled it to the brim. "I loved coffee before..." I started but trailed off as I realized how nonchalantly I was about to say before I was turned.

It was becoming so second nature to think of myself in that way—as a before and after—but I wasn't sure if that was a good or a bad thing.

He cruised past my stalling. "Everyone moves at a different pace for what they can stomach, but with time, you should be able to enjoy some regular food and drinks again. You didn't hate the whiskey last night, so I'm thinking you might be able to stomach the coffee and maybe even some food now."

I had no idea that vampires could ever enjoy food again, and the newfound knowledge brought me a level of comfort. What I wouldn't give to feel a semblance of normalcy again.

Grabbing a few sugar packets, I tore them open and poured them in as he added, "There is still animal blood in the fridge for you, though."

After stirring the sugar in, I raised the cup to my lips before murmuring, "Thanks." After taking a sip, I stuck my tongue out in disgust as my nose curled. Even as a hardcore, badass vampire, I couldn't stomach almost-black coffee.

"Cream, Alina?" Lo called out, startling me with her unexpected appearance. My heart jumped in my chest as my grip tightened on the mug. I suppose the ability to sneak around came with the territory of being older and more powerful, better equipped with a level of agility and swiftness that I didn't yet possess.

Turning around, I offered her a soft smile as my racing heart slowed down a beat. "Please."

She was so subdued in comparison to the

woman I'd met last night, but perhaps she wasn't a morning person. My eyes flicked to the clock on the stove, finding that it was almost one in the afternoon. Well, this was our version of morning anyway.

As she rummaged around in the fridge, I took a moment to appreciate her beautiful curls that had been swept up into a ponytail. My hair was naturally straight, but annoyingly so, in that it took so much product to hold a curl. A beautiful, red cloth was wrapped around the top of her hair and tied in the back, matching her red top and black leather pants perfectly.

I had to give it to her, she had style.

"Here," she mumbled, struggling as she tried to carry six bottles as she turned toward me.

I rushed to grab two from her before they slipped from her grip as Drake sighed heavily. "You could have just asked her what flavor she wanted instead of pulling your entire stash out, Lo."

Sure, she *could* have just asked, but I still found it so endearing that she was trying to accommodate me.

Drake sounded nothing short of an exasperated father, and the absurd thought had me giggling as I walked back toward the coffee station and put the bottles of creamer on the counter. My laughter only increased as I saw Lo mocking him quietly, eyes comically wide as she tilted her head back and forth.

When she realized I was watching her, her eyes turned mischievous, and she sent a wink my way. Yup, I saw why it was so easy for him to be himself around her. Any of the lingering jealousy I'd felt faded away in an instant. The uncomfortable truth was that I had been jealous that she somehow managed to bring out a side of Drake that I actually liked. But the more I was around her, the more I realized she just seemed to exude that same calming energy toward everyone around her, allowing them to feel at ease enough to be their true selves. If I didn't know better, the magic of it would make me believe she was a witch.

The world needed more people like Lo, no matter their species. Perhaps if there were more people like her out there, we wouldn't all be so damn quick to anger and judge.

A sad thought struck me as I watched her. I would have never given her the chance to show me who she was before I was turned. I would have laughed in someone's face had they told me that I needed to give a vampire a chance, that any single bloodsucker possessed a gentle, light soul.

Guilt churned through my gut, the realization that I had been part of the problem eating away at me as I clenched my jaw and stared at the collection of creamers before me. The longer I was away from the slayer lifestyle, the more I realized that we truly needed to change how we did things. All of us. Not just slayers. Not just vampires. But everyone.

After selecting our creamers, I followed Lo to sit on the slim bar stools tucked beneath the island as Drake finished with the bacon and began to crack eggs. Testing my hazelnut coffee, my eyes went wide with joy as I moaned around the sweet liquid washing delightfully over my tastebuds.

A growl tore from Drake, his head whipping around so fast I was surprised the force of it didn't snap his neck as his eyes settled on what had pulled that satisfied moan out of me. His eyes had slipped to their black state as if the beast within him couldn't stand the thought of anything besides him making me moan.

My thighs shifted together at the unexpected heat that built between them.

"So," Lo drawled, breaking the tense moment. "What's on the docket for today's schedule, Daddy Drake?"

Spluttering at the nickname, I choked on the

coffee halfway down my throat, completely killing the desire I'd felt. A thump came from her lightly on my back. "Don't die on me, Alina. I actually like having you around. You can't leave me with him alone anymore. He gets so moody and grumpy, but not when you're here."

The nickname felt so on brand with the way he scolded her but to me, it would feel beyond sexual if I referred to him as that.

After clearing his throat, he turned back to his eggs, whisking them as he spoke in an even tone, "I'm having the event planners come in today. We need to finish planning Monday night's ball if we're going to officially introduce Alina to the board members there."

"Excuse me, what?" I asked, voice barely more than a screech as I rocked back in my seat. Surely I'd misheard him.

Lo mumbled around the mug at her lips, "I told you to ask her first, bud."

I glanced between them, desperate for someone to explain what the hell was happening. Lo instantly bowed out, hopping down from the stool before grabbing two pieces of bacon and waving them in the air in a goodbye. "Have fun with that, Drake! Alina, when you're ready to get dressed, go to the room on the left just before the suite you were in last night. I filled that closet and fixed up the room for you to use!"

I wasn't sure what to focus on first: the fact that there was a fucking ball planned with the intention of introducing me to a bunch of bloodthirsty vampires at, or the fact that there had been a whole ass room prepared for me and he'd shoved me into a room with only a dress or his clothes to choose from last night.

That cheeky fucker. He admitted to knowing I wouldn't wear the dress, forcing me to wear his clothes. It was so fucking similar to Andrei's insistence that I wore his shirt. It must be a weird alpha thing to have me wrapped up in their scent.

"Care to explain?" I sassed to his back as he let silence fill the air in the wake of Lo's departure.

He separated the eggs onto two plates before turning around and dropping a few pieces of bacon onto both. Leaning against the large island, he pushed one plate toward me before placing a fork next to it. "Try them," he insisted.

While biting into his bacon and munching on it, his bright blue eyes ran over me, brows pinching together like he was carefully mulling over his next words.

Perhaps he wasn't an idiot after all. Only time would tell.

Lifting the strip of bacon to my mouth, I bit into it, chewing a couple of times before a rancid flavor filled my mouth. Fighting a gag, I spit the bacon out, resisting the urge to hurl.

Giving a sad look at the plate, I mentally said goodbye as I pushed it across the island toward Drake. *One day we'll be reunited, old friend.*

It seemed liquids were a yes, and solid foods were a hard no.

He chuckled and took it away from me before going to the fridge. A moment later, he turned, tossing blood bags in front of me. "Maybe next time, killer."

Killer? Now that was a nickname I could get down with. It was about time he recognized what a threat I was.

"Controlling introductions is necessary here, Alina. A ball is the best way for us to introduce you to the board and show that we are a united front, even if you don't feel that way yet, darling."

"Why do we need to do that so soon?" I asked, voice high pitched nerves filled me at the thought of being forced into a room with all those vampires. "What does this gain me?"

"Protection, hopefully," he mumbled, arching a brow. "I have a sinking suspicion that one of them is the source of the rebellion stirring in my lands as well as the attack on your family."

I set my coffee mug down at that admission, the ceramic clattering against the hard, marble countertop. He thought one of his most trusted members could be responsible for the attack on my family?

Now this...this was information I could work with. "Who? Why?" I rushed to ask.

"I'm not sure who, which is another reason we need to have the ball. I want to observe their reactions to you to try to get a lead."

Fuck, he was really putting his money where his mouth was. If I chose to believe his insistence that he wasn't the one behind the attack and that he only wanted to help me, this would absolutely be the way to quickly get the information I was desperate for.

"Okay," I answered, confidence pulling my shoulders back. "Let's do it."

Maybe if I was actively trying to investigate my family's demise, I wouldn't feel so confused about my feelings toward him. Undoubtedly, if it was him, surely the ball would help me figure that out. I'd at least get the chance to talk to all the members on the board to try to see if any of them had loose enough lips to mention anything regarding the attack.

I was willing to accept other people as suspects in my family members' murders, but I wasn't yet willing to entirely cross Drake off my list.

"I'll leave you to make your choices for the ball with the event planners. I have a few things I need to take care of before I can come back and relax tonight, but feel free to roam the castle or use the heated pool in the back once you're finished. This is the only place I trust that you are safe."

Me, plan a ball? I didn't know where to even start with that. I'd probably just tell the planners to choose whatever they wanted. If I had my way, it'd probably look more like a gothic funeral than a ball. Well, maybe that was accurate for what the event symbolized now that I thought about it...

Nodding, I allowed myself a moment to ruminate, fingers tapping the countertop as I considered everything I'd learned since being here. The burning fire of vengeance within me flared to life, but this time, I didn't feel like it was in control of my actions and decisions, only lending to my strength to do what needed to be done.

"It's time to make our first move as the King and Queen on the board. Are you ready?"

Staring into his bright eyes, I let all my strength fill my tone as I nodded. "I'm ready."

My body felt like it was tingling with anticipation of what was to come. One way or another, I was going to get my answers.

I *would* fulfill my blood oath.

CHAPTER SEVENTEEN
ALINA

In the end, Lo ended up taking pity on me and planning the ball with the event planners as I watched, completely disinterested with the whole process. We'd fallen into a companionable silence for the rest of the day, both of us content with the easy surface level conversation as she took the time to show me the castle before we'd gone for a dip in the pool.

We spent most of the night out there. I'd been so enraptured by the cliffside that the estate was tucked into. The view was breathtaking. We were completely removed from civilization, with only the tiniest pinpricks of light in the distance showing where the main population of vampires lived.

"I'm sorry I couldn't come back earlier last

night," Drake muttered with a bit of bitterness in his voice as we returned to the pavilion at DIA. "I came to check on you when I got back, but you were asleep already."

I turned my head downward, fighting the blush that threatened to creep into my cheeks. The memory of the way he'd brushed the hair out of my face and pressed a kiss to my forehead before leaving the room had been on replay in my head all morning long.

"It's okay," I answered quickly, not wanting to give away that I'd been awake because then I'd have to face my own questions about why I didn't stop him or say something in the moment. "I was super tired after such a long week."

Rocking on my heels at the awkward goodbye bearing down on us, I tucked my hair behind my ear, an old nervous tell of mine. He reached for the hand resting at my side, glancing around like he was worried about anyone seeing him like this with me.

"Thank you for taking a chance on me," he breathed out, and I found myself wishing he didn't have to cover his eyes in darkness as he stared at me. "I know that I have a long way to go to prove to you that my words are the truth, but all I can ask is that you continue to try to have an open mind. I only want what's best for you, darling."

His lips pinched together, his eyes creasing at the corner as if he was in pain before he seemed forced himself to speak through clenched teeth. "Even if you find that what's best for you isn't with me, I'll still fulfill my promise to help you find justice for your family."

I was blown away by his admission. So much so that my eyes danced around his face, searching for the smallest tell that he was full of shit because I just couldn't believe it.

He'd practically been a caveman the first few days I'd known him, back when I'd absolutely loathed him with everything inside of me and refused to even acknowledge the possibility that he might be my mate. But now that I'd softened toward him and only occasionally thought about trying to hurt him, he was telling me that he wouldn't force the bond on me?

"I, uh," I started to respond but found myself quickly nibbling on my lip instead as I struggled to think of the right words to convey what I was feeling. There were so many layers to his admission, so I settled on, "Thank you," before pulling my hand from his.

I needed some space from him to sort all of this out in my head, so I was thankful to be back at the academy and able to spend time with Alexandra today.

He threaded his fingers together in front of him, and he inclined his head in response. "Of course, but darling, you should know that I won't give up on you until I know there's absolutely no hope left. I've waited thousands of years to find the one the Fates chose for me, and I won't let you slip through my fingers without giving it my all."

Now *that* sounded like the Drake I knew.

"May I walk you back to your dorm?" he asked in the polite, refined tone he took on outside of the castle.

"Actually, would you mind if we said goodbye here?" I asked, wincing slightly at how bad that sounded. I just really wanted a moment alone before I reached my sector at the academy, where I had no doubt Lincoln and Andrei would be lying in wait for me.

"Of course not," he bit out through a tight mouth, as if he was trying to physically stop himself from frowning. His jaw ticked as his nostrils flared with a deep intake of breath. Had I hurt his feelings with my request? "I'll be back Monday after your strategy class to collect you, as well as Andrei, for the ball."

A joke about how he seemed to conveniently forget that I had another class with Lincoln after strategy was on the tip of my tongue, but my brain short-circuited at the mention of Andrei.

"Andrei has to come?" I asked, my brows pinched together as my stomach churned with the thought of him having to be around his father any more than he had to be.

"Of course," Drake responded easily. "All board members, as well as their significant others and families, will be in attendance. That should have been mentioned during the event planning when discussing the arrangements for the number of guests we were expecting."

I winced before admitting, "I really didn't pay attention. Lo did everything with the planners for me after I begged her to."

His mask slipped for a moment as a true laugh began to bubble out of him, but he quickly swallowed it, a look of alarm crossing his face as he realized what he was doing.

Knowing I needed to get going, I mumbled a quick farewell, "Okay, I'll see you then."

Nodding his head once, I took that as my cue to

turn on my heel and walk toward the gate back to my sector. I felt the heat of his gaze on my back the entire time, and I occasionally peeked over my shoulder to see him stoically standing and watching over me like he needed to see me to the gate safely before leaving. When I finally reached it, I gave him a brief wave before walking through.

The brisk chill of our sector welcomed me, and my body seemed to exhale in relief at being back in the territory I realized I truly felt comfortable with in every aspect. How quickly things could change.

On my stroll to the dorm building, I found my head shaking repeatedly as I tried to think of what to tell Lincoln and Andrei about my time with Drake. I mean, hell, even the fact that I was referring to him as Drake instead of Dracula would be a huge giveaway about how things had shifted.

"What's a girl to do?" I asked the universe. "You wanted to give me three mates, so I think it's only fair that you should tell me exactly how I'm supposed to juggle them."

Of course I got no answer in return, that fickle bitch.

Turning my doorknob, I grappled with the sadness sitting in the pit of my stomach. Having expected to see Andrei and Lincoln waiting for me as soon as I crossed into the vampire sector, I was disappointed that I hadn't spotted them *anywhere* on the walk to my room. Despite trying to keep my focus on Drake and the information I could absorb at his castle, I had found myself missing my other guys immensely.

"Took you long enough," Andrei's voice called out as I pushed inside my room.

A shit-eating grin crawled over my face as I rushed in to find him sprawled on my bed, tossing a ball at the ceiling and catching it repeatedly. Putting on an extra burst of speed, I launched myself at him, making him laugh and question, "Miss me, baby girl?"

I hadn't realized just how damn much until I was melded to his chest and pressing my lips to his. After a few seconds, I pulled back and flicked his nose for that cocky attitude of his and answered nonchalantly, "Nah."

His mouth popped open dramatically, and he gasped. "You take that back right now."

I mimed zipping my lips shut and throwing away the key, and he responded by flipping me beneath him and tickling my sides until my laughter bounced off the walls filling the space around us with merriment.

"Mercy!" I screamed, thrashing beneath him, "Mercy!"

"Admit it!" he yelled back, doubling down by digging his fingers into my upper ribs where I was the most responsive to his torture.

"Fine! I missed you, fucker!" I finally relented.

Bliss settled over me as he pulled his fingers away from my sides and I finally relaxed. Taking a few deep breaths while still smiling at our goofy exchange, I smacked his hand lightly as he flopped over onto the bed next to me.

Grabbing my hand, he twined our fingers together before asking, "So, how did it go?"

Letting out a deep breath that made the few strands of hair that had fallen near my mouth flutter, I admitted, "Honestly? It was nothing like I thought it would be, but in a good way."

Turning onto his side, I felt his eyes boring into the side of my face as he asked, "Oh? Do share with the class, new girl."

"It was just me, him, and Lo. It was easy and nice. Relaxing, even, albeit very confusing."

He bolted upward, and I tensed in alarm, heart beating erratically in my chest as he frantically asked, "Lo as in Lauren? The Bishop?"

Pushing up to lean against my headboard, I

nodded and shrugged, not understanding the big deal. "Yeah, that's her."

He blinked around bulging eyes, disbelief saturating his words as he said, "You had a relaxing, nice, easy time with Dracula and Lauren. My mind cannot even begin to comprehend how that's within the realm of possibilities with the two most ruthless, cold vampires I've ever met. That's saying a fucking lot considering who my dad is."

I snorted as I tried picturing the small vampire who had literally waved bacon in the air as she said her goodbyes while escaping the awkward moment between me and Drake as anything other than jovial.

Ruthless and cold? I hadn't seen a lick of that side of her, but maybe what Drake had said to me about being at the top and having to show no mercy or weakness applied to her too. If my memory of chess was correct, the Bishop was the third most powerful piece after the King and Queen.

I opened my mouth to expand upon how kind and different they were from his preconceived notions of them but found myself feeling guilty at ripping their carefully constructed mask away without their consent. Snapping my mouth shut, I decided against it, feeling like it was a betrayal of the faith they'd placed in me by showing me that glimpse of themselves.

All I could do was hope that one day I could pull all these pieces of my life together and that they could all see each other in the same way that I did.

"I have some news that I don't think you're going to be very happy about." It was an abrupt subject change, but I knew I needed to give him a heads up about the ball.

For some reason, it felt important for me to be the one to tell him and not his father. If he had an adverse reaction to the news, I wanted him to feel like he was in a safe place to talk about it and figure out if we needed to change the plans.

"What?" he asked hesitantly, sweeping his fingers through his messy hair.

"Uh, so, there's going to be a ball Monday night for me to be officially presented to the board members and their families as Dracula's mate," I said, not taking a single breath between my words and wincing at the end as I waited for his response.

"No!" he roared, jumping to his feet and pacing in front of the bed, running his fingers into his hair more urgently and tugging on the roots. "I don't want you anywhere near him, Alina."

Well, shit. He'd said my name. He was truly freaking the fuck out over this.

Trying to be a calm pillar for him, I slowly stood and padded over to him, stopping him in place by grabbing the front of his shirt. "Hey, look at me," I commanded gently, repeating myself with a bit more bite to my tone when his eyes remained on the ground. "Look at me, Andrei."

His eyes slowly trailed up to settle on mine, but it was like he was looking straight through me with the lack of light in those green eyes. They were completely flat and void of emotion, as if he was completely lost in the thoughts going through his mind.

"I am capable of fending for myself," I reassured him before swallowing my ego and adding, "And I will have you, Dracula, and Lo there to back me up, okay? No one is going to fuck with me with that show of support behind me."

It wasn't even a question in my mind when I said Drake was on my side as the words fell from my lips. *Shit.*

Shaking his head, his mania seemed to bubble up as he tried to pull from my grip and dropped his gaze back to the floor. "No. No, you don't understand, Alina. I cannot show support for you yet until

I *know* it's safe to do so. Dracula clearly doesn't want to share you, and my dad *will* pick up on that."

"But we're mates, Andrei," I argued, regurgitating what little I know about what the hell that even meant. "That transcends all laws and rules. How could he possibly try to hold you back from me?"

A dark chuckle bubbled from his lips as he began to pace again, just beyond the circle of my reach. "I couldn't begin to explain my father's actions or why he thinks the way he does, but just trust me on this, Alina. We have to keep our distance while we're there."

All I wanted to do was calm him down, hating that I had caused him to feel this frenzied kind of fear. My gut churned at seeing him like this, so I was quick to agree. "Okay. We'll keep our distance. It will be okay. Do you hear me?"

He seemed to be soothed by my words, halting his pacing before taking a deep, shaky breath and nodding. I felt the tension in my shoulders loosen the tiniest bit as he drew in another breath.

Fates, his father had really done a number on him. I made a mental note to ask Drake about Andrei's father in private. From the glimpse of him that I'd seen this weekend, I couldn't imagine him tolerating someone that seemed so abusive within his trusted circle.

Closing the distance between us once more, I ran my hand up his torso to rest on his chest. "It'll be okay. I promise, Andrei," I whispered with the utmost faith in my words, knowing that I would jump through fire to ensure it truly did end up okay in the end.

Finally, it was like the haze lifted from his eyes as he looked into my eyes and nodded. I heaved a sigh, relief flooding my limbs as he wrapped his arms around me loosely. "Okay," he agreed breathily, but I could tell he still wasn't fully settled on this topic. His eyes began to shift around again, as if he was constantly on the lookout for the next threat.

I wasn't sure how I'd remain polite around his father, not with the extreme reactions I witnessed from Andrei at the mere mention of upsetting his father. Everything in me wanted to pop his father in the mouth and demand to know why he thought he could treat his son that way.

A knock sounded at my door, startling Andrei into a rigid stance as he tightened his arms around me. Glancing over my shoulder as the door opened, I saw Lincoln leaning in the doorway, looking us over with an unamused grimace.

"How cute," he muttered dryly.

Rolling my eyes at his antics, I patted Andrei's chest before pulling myself from his grasp to face my favorite professor.

"Has anyone ever told you that you're a grouchy old man before?" I asked sarcastically as I sauntered over to him, reaching up and wrapping my arms around his neck when I stopped just in front of him.

His voice dropped an octave as he answered, "Treat your elders with respect. You may refer to me as *Sir,* Ms. Van Helsing."

I think this was maybe the first time I'd heard my family name uttered by him without disgust or contempt lacing his tone, and the acceptance, conscious or not, warmed my heart for him.

"Okay," I agreed before pressing up onto my tiptoes and hovering my lips an inch from his as I looked up into his hazel eyes, "*Sir.*"

A rumble of appreciation rumbled from him before he sealed our lips together in a toe-curling kiss.

Damn, it felt good to be home with my guys.

CHAPTER EIGHTEEN
ALINA

It seemed like Lincoln was truly *trying* to not look like a petulant child seeing his favorite toy being used by someone else when I was in Andrei's arms, but he clearly had no issue with putting on a show when the positions were reversed.

Sucking my bottom lip into his mouth, he nipped at it as a growl rumbled through his chest. I was sure it was because of my use of the word Sir, and I knew I would never tire of teasing him with the title.

"Gentle," I murmured, forcing him to release my lip and pointing a warning gaze at him.

The only reason I wanted him to be gentle with

me was because Andrei was in the room, and I was not in the mood to explain that our rough behavior was not abuse, but something that I both consented to and enjoyed. I also didn't want him to think that he needed to change what he gave me to fit whatever Lincoln did. I enjoyed our time together just as much and for different reasons. Each man satisfied vastly different parts of me.

After disentangling my arms from around his neck, I fell flat on my feet but kept my gaze trained up on him. "Hey, are you busy right now?" Glancing at the clock next to my bed, I noted I needed to get going before looking back to Lincoln. I was a busy, busy girl these days, and I detested being late for anything. "I need to go meet Alexandra in the library, but I don't want to get in trouble for going into their sector, so I was thinking you could go with me?"

"Yeah," he answered with an easy, loose shrug. "Let's go."

Despite the nonchalant tone and body language, I saw his eyes light up and widen at the offer. I didn't actually give a shit about being caught going to the library because I knew that we didn't need a pass to go, but it gave me an excuse to give him some one-on-one time for a little bit.

Reaching back up to press a quick kiss to his lips, I murmured, "Thank you. Just give me one sec."

Andrei and I exchanged a quick goodbye, agreeing to talk about the ball before we were both whisked away by Drake. When I turned back to Lincoln, it was to see him grinning like an idiot. Rolling my eyes, I grabbed his arm and dragged him out of the dorm and toward the demon sector. As we walked, I took the chance to briefly catch him up on how my time was at Dracula's castle. I could tell he had a hard time believing that it was as laid back and easy as I made it sound, but in the end, he said he was happy I wasn't hurt and that I was back with him. Surprisingly, he let it go after that.

As soon as we passed into the demon sector, the dry heat engulfed us. I couldn't help but smile at the change in the environment, enjoying getting a taste of something different for once, but Lincoln seethed at my side. "I fucking hate this sector. I feel like I'm going to burst into flames."

"So dramatic," I tsked, sending him a cheeky wink as he narrowed his eyes at me.

It was laughable coming from the most dramatic woman he'd ever met, I'm sure.

We traversed the path to the library within minutes, enjoying companionable silence after a while. It felt like my head was on a swivel as we stepped into the library, eyes widening at the rows and rows of books. After offering a cursory greeting to Ms. Felicity, the librarian, Lincoln nudged me toward the winding staircase in the corner. A soft voice floated down from the level above, and I instantly recognized Alexandra's voice despite only having been around her briefly.

As we reached the top, I let out a smile as a man I didn't recognize reached out to grab her knee and said in a compassionate tone, "Darling, please try to relax."

Darling…I hated that it instantly made me think back to Drake and wonder what he was doing right now.

"Yeah, buttercup," I parroted, "relax."

Her entire face lit up as she turned around and saw me before launching herself at me, engulfing me in a hug. I didn't realize we were quite on that level yet, and I stood completely still until the shock began to wear off.

"I'm so happy you came, Alina!" she gushed with such honesty ringing in her tone that I felt the tension quickly leaching from my body.

Wrapping my arms around her a bit awkwardly

with how long this hug was going on, I patted her back lightly before screwing my face up at how dumb I probably looked for patting her like a pet.

This is why I didn't make friends easily. This type of stuff did not come naturally to me, and I found myself second-guessing everyone's intentions.

She pulled back, letting out a chuckle as she smirked. "Dude, I'm not a big hugger, but even I know that was a shit hug. We've gotta work on that."

It wasn't deniable, so I shrugged and laughed as I heard Lincoln chuff behind me. She peered around my shoulder with curiosity in her eyes.

Was this asshole laughing at her saying I'm a bad hugger? Fuck him. I was so goddamn affectionate. I gave him great hugs...with my vagina...on his cock.

Why did I invite him to tag along again?

Turning on my heel, I held my fingers to my lips as if I was going to blow him a kiss, making his head cock to the side in confusion. As I blew out, I closed my hand into a fist, but left my middle finger up, blowing it at him.

Yeah, how was that for affection? Jerk.

He played along perfectly, though, reaching into the air like he was grabbing it and pulling it to his chest. He held it over his heart for a moment, like he was cocooning the gift to his chest before he let his face fall flat, killing the joke and flicking me off right back.

A coy smile tugged at the edge of my lips as Alexandra taunted, "Oh yeah?" while grabbing my elbow and dragging me toward an empty table. "Is a teacher-student romance against the rules of the academy? I can totally keep a secret, dude."

Fates, was I ready to admit to someone out loud that I had not one mate, but two...with a possible third? Well, I could use a good girl talk, but maybe I'd leave out the whole mate aspect of it for now.

With a dramatic eye roll, I sighed heavily and all but melted onto the table, laying my chest and head onto it. "Girl, you wouldn't believe the fucking week I've had. Suddenly, I'm juggling three men, just like you, when I thought it was only going to be one, maybe two. How the fuck do you manage? I am exhausted."

"Three!?" she squealed so loudly I wanted to throttle her. Girl talk was supposed to be sacred and private.

Flicking my eyes to Lincoln, I noticed him

fiddling on his phone and hopefully *not* eavesdropping on our conversation.

Ducking her head in shame after I glowered at her, she whispered, "Welcome to the slut squad. Isn't it fantastic? We aren't the only women on campus with a harem! I met a witch named Deva who has *five* at the party Monday night, and we decided to own the slut jabs and named our squad that."

Lifting my head up from the table in shock, my mouth dropped open. "Five? Fuck that."

She chuckled and nodded in agreement before changing the topic quickly. "Speaking of the party, I know I said it in my note, but I'm so sorry I didn't find you if you showed up—wait, did you go to the party?"

Pushing to sit up straight in the chair, I sighed, remembering what a clusterfuck that night had been. With a nod of confirmation, I responded, "Yeah, I did. It was an interesting night for me, to say the least. Trust me, I understand that shit happens. We're all good, buttercup."

I wasn't sure where the nickname came from, but as soon as it came out I decided to keep it.

She raised a single brow. "Buttercup?"

Shrugging my shoulders, I tried to respond as a

small yawn overcame me, muffling my words slightly, "Yeah, it fits. Sorry, it's still early as hell for me. Our classes run a bit later than yours do, so our days start later to try to accommodate a bit more of the night into our routine—like the regular vamps are used to back in Sanguis."

"Shit," she said, jolting up at my words. I felt my brows wrinkle in confusion. "I was in class the other day, and we've been learning about your sector, actually. I didn't realize…" she trailed off, flicking her eyes toward Lincoln.

Where was she going with this? Color me intrigued.

Dropping her voice to a whisper, she continued, "I didn't realize Dracula was at the fucking top of the government there. How the hell are you going to get your revenge, Alina? He's surrounded by so many powerful people on his board."

I was so not getting into that cluster fuck right now, so I held up a hand as she opened her mouth to continue rambling about it. "Like I said, a lot can happen in a week. I know exactly what I have on my plate and what I'm up against. Don't worry about me, buttercup."

It was seriously adorable that she thought about what I shared with her in detention and was concerned about how I was going to achieve it, though. One day when we had time where we were truly alone, I'd fill her in on it all, but I wasn't willing to risk Lincoln overhearing all the details before I even knew how I wanted to handle it.

She took a deep breath before a somber look crossed her face. She muttered, "I just don't want to see you get hurt, okay? I have a lot on my plate right now as well, but if you need me and my monsters, let me know."

She...she was offering to help me fight against him? After learning that he was at the top of the food chain in my world? Fuck, she was so pure it made my heart squeeze. With jealousy? Affection? I wasn't sure, but it was an instinct that I didn't fight, feeling warm and gooey just from being around her for a moment.

My hand shot out reflexively, gripping her hand before I realized what I was doing. Snatching my hand back, I cleared my throat and responded, "Thank you, Alexandra. I promise I've got it handled. You said you have a lot on your plate, though. Anything I can do?"

It was clear she was trying to truly be my friend, and a good one at that, and I didn't want her to think it was all one-sided.

"Actually," she hedged nervously. "Do you remember when we met in the naughty bin, and you said it felt like I coerced you into telling me about what you were going through, and how it dredged up all that anger you felt?"

Cocking my head to the side, I pursed my lips at the uncomfortable memory before nodding. "Yeah, of course. It felt like I wasn't in control of my emotions. Why?"

"Do you feel that way around me now?" she quickly shot back, and I narrowed my eyes as I considered her.

Was she trying to do something to me right now?

I flicked my eyes over her as I tried to sense anything overwhelming or out of my control bubbling up through me as I had during our detention together. After a tense moment, I shook my head "no" and relaxed again.

"Okay, so hear me out...We have no fucking clue what I am, only an idea, and I'm still learning what I can do with my powers," she offered before dragging her hands into her lap. "But we came to the conclusion that we think I subconsciously pull on the negative emotions in people, an example being the anger I pulled out of you in detention. Turns out,

I've been doing it my whole life with humans who don't have mental shields to protect themselves."

Holy shit. That was absolutely wild, but I did actually have a reason to explain why her powers wouldn't be working on me now.

My lips parted slightly as I chuckled. "Believe it or not, since I've seen you last, I've had to seriously work on my mental barricade in order to keep some vampires out of it. So it's entirely possible that's why it's not working on me anymore if that's what happened the first time."

She sat there for a few seconds, clearly lost in her thoughts before she came out of it. "Damn, do you remember how you broke out of it?"

Contemplating her question, I reached up with my hands and stretched against the back of the chair. "Fuck, that feels like a lifetime ago, despite only being about a week now. I want to say that it was the fear of telling someone my plans that pierced that veil of anger that clouded me. Seeing your fear of me did wonders too if I'm being honest. I felt like I was turning into the monster I hated."

And now I'd somehow accepted that I was a bloodsucker.

Her eyes shuttered, pain filling their depths at my words. Her shoulders tensed, and she sucked her bottom lip into her mouth before biting down. Her brows pinched together, and it was clear that my admission had hurt her deeply. "I'm so sorry I did that to you. I truly didn't mean to, and it's such an invasion of your privacy. I don't think you're a monster, Alina, but I'm hoping you don't think I am either."

Oh, absolutely not. I was not going to let her go down that path. Monstrous was the exact opposite of what I felt about her.

"Buttercup," I started, with a take no shit tone to emphasize how serious I was, "the first time I saw you in the naughty bin, I thought there was no way in hell you belonged there. You radiate this pure kind of energy, despite saying you pull negative emotions out of people."

And honestly, one of the things that I remember best is that I'd wanted to crush her as her kindness radiated toward me.

I hesitated for a moment before asking, "Did you ever think that it was maybe just a reaction to the immense amount of good I feel in you? It goes without saying that darkness will always want to snuff out light."

Her jaw dropped open, like she'd never considered the possibility before. It was as if I'd created an entirely new avenue for her to look down.

My attention was pulled as I heard the soft chime of Lincoln's phone ringing for one beat before he answered. Turning to look at him, I saw shock flitter across his face before it was replaced with rage, his brows slamming together.

My gut churned with uncertainty at the unusual reaction from him.

"We have to go, now!" Lincoln yelled, scaring the shit out of all of us as we jolted in our seats, gasping from the sudden outburst.

He could be bossy, but it was always in a way I loved to hate. This was not that, though. His voice, filled with genuine concern, had me jumping to my feet at the same time Alexandra and her men joined us.

I really needed to introduce myself to them and be polite, but it looked like that would have to wait for now.

He held a hand up as his lips thinned. I wanted to tell him to just spit it out already, but he spoke a second later. "What you see next, you cannot repeat to anyone. The only reason I'm bringing you is because Estrid requested it, understood? This is confidential and cannot get out to the students, or there will be hysteria."

Alexandra nodded and leaned into her men at her back. "We understand."

I wanted to ask more questions, but this seemed like the type of moment where I needed to shut my mouth and listen to him for once. We followed behind Lincoln as he headed quietly and with steadfast determination toward the dorm houses in the demon sector. He never even turned to look over his shoulder to make sure I was following him.

What the hell was going on? I mean, seriously. I'd never seen him act like this. Whatever it was, it left a sinking feeling of dread in my stomach.

Slowing down as we approached a dorm house in the back of the clump of houses, Lincoln held a hand up, indicating for us to stop. I shared a worried glance with Alexandra who came to a halt at my side. Suddenly, it was like a veil was ripped away from the house, revealing the real scene before us.

I couldn't help but jump a little at the sudden change but didn't have a moment to take it in before Victoria was calling out for us to quickly come toward them. As soon as we crossed a certain point, a man at her right waved a hand, dropping the illusion quickly back into place.

"It's not good, Linc," Victoria whispered so softly that I wasn't sure Alexandra or her men could hear as she walked in the front with him, heading up the stairs and opening the door for us to step through.

The first thing I saw after Lincoln stepped to the side once we walked in was Estrid staring at the ground with grief and anger swirling in her eyes. She stood rigidly with her arms crossed over her chest and a frown pulling her lips down severely.

Following her gaze, I couldn't stop the small gasp of horror that escaped me at the sight of the dead body I saw sprawled on the floor. It was a petite student I didn't recognize, but that didn't stop a wave of regret for a life stolen so young from crashing into me. Her eyes were wide, staring lifelessly at the ceiling. Her pale body was covered in black veins, giving a horribly sick contrast to her.

I'd seen a lot of dead bodies before, slayer and vampire alike, but there was something haunting about knowing this murder carried out at the academy, a place that was supposed to be completely neutral. She should have been safe here, able to focus on her education and finding the path for her future rather than fearing for her life.

Naturally, I found myself gravitating toward Lincoln and tucking myself against his side as Estrid looked up to look at Alexandra. "Elwin, Alexandra, can either of you confirm if this is the same magic that we saw before?"

Wait, what? This had happened before?

Lincoln's arm draped over my shoulders, dragging me closer to his warmth before he squeezed me to him tightly.

Alexandra took a beat, staring at the body before nodding and confirming, "It was her."

Who the hell was doing this to students? My hackles rose at the thought of them being preyed upon. Instantly, I was overwhelmed by the urge to step forward and demand answers, to offer to help hunt them down, but Lincoln was quick to pull me back the second I tried.

His lips brushed my ear before he muttered, "This isn't the time or place, Alina. Leave it to them."

My jaw ticked, but I nodded, understanding his point despite not liking it. In fact, I fucking hated it. I'd been raised to act at injustice, and the thought of sitting back and letting others handle it was making my stomach churn.

After waiting around long enough for Alexandra to answer all of Estrid's questions, we found ourselves all back outside and I wasted no time in snapping into action.

"Go to your dorm, now," I ordered. "We will escort you there."

I didn't care if I sounded bossy. I wasn't willing to risk her life.

She nodded quietly, turning on her heel before she was quickly surrounded by her men, who kept their eyes peeled, heads swiveling around constantly. It was a very short walk, with all the small houses being bunched together.

Lincoln stepped forward as they walked up the steps toward their door, instructing them, "Stay in the dorm. All students are under mandatory curfew right now. A professor from the witch sector will be by to place a security barrier around your home, so don't be alarmed if you see a person waving their hands around or whatever the fuck they do. Just do not leave, okay?"

My heart ached at how hollow Alexandra's eyes looked as she nodded before giving me a small wave and turning around to go in. Her men gave us waves and thanks of their own before joining her.

As soon as they were safely tucked inside, I whirled on him. "What the *fuck*, Lincoln? What is going on?"

"Let's get back to our sector, and I'll tell you what little I know, okay?"

With a nod, we sped back toward the pavilion and quickly crossed into our territory, not stopping until we reached the dorm building. We didn't utter a single word as we sped up to his room on the top floor.

As soon as the door was shut, I whirled on him, tapping my foot impatiently for answers.

Holding his hands up defensively, he started, "You've been with me since I found out, so there wasn't much more than what you saw, but Estrid told me on the phone that there were two witch students attacked. I didn't want to mention it in front of Alexandra because Estrid thinks they are different threats between the two sectors."

My heart felt like it careened to a dead stop before dropping into my ass. "What the fuck!" I hissed, confused and angry at the thought of this place I was beginning to think of as my new home being attacked. It didn't matter that it hadn't yet spread to our sector. My friend was under threat, and that hit too close to my heart.

Running his fingers through his hair roughly as he paced in front of me, he admitted, "One of the witch students was found cut up and tied to a post outside of the dorm. There were no black veins running through that student. The methods of the attackers are too different to think they coincide, but I'm not sure that's actually good news. It means we have two different threats working against us at the academy."

We didn't know enough to strategize a proper defense without knowing who or what we were fighting against. *Fuck.*

I didn't realize I was shaking until I felt Lincoln running his hands up and down my arms soothingly, "I know, Spitfire. I know. We're going to handle it, though."

It really hit me how triggering it was to think of this place being attacked. The same fear that I felt as I rushed toward my family's home, feeling helpless and too late to do anything helpful, was dredged to the surface. My stomach turned as a familiar panic worked through my veins.

Gently guiding me toward the bed, he lifted the cover for me. I wordlessly climbed in, and as soon as he settled into the other side, I cuddled against his chest, needing his warmth and presence to ground me right now.

Running his fingers through my hair, he asked, "Will you please stay with me tonight? I don't think I could sleep if I didn't have my eyes on you right now."

All I could manage was a nod as I fisted his shirt in my hand tightly. I hated how much I needed him right now. He'd officially claimed a piece of my heart and there was no fighting the trust I felt in him any longer. He was my anchor.

CHAPTER NINETEEN
LINCOLN

A loud, frenzied banging sound woke me up, making me jolt in alarm as Alina roused at my side.

No one who lived in this sector would dare pound on my door like that.

Had somebody breached *our* security?

"Linc?" she asked sleepily as my fangs lengthened, my senses going on high alert.

Before I could answer her, the banging started up again, booming through my room. Truly, I wasn't sure how the door hadn't been split in two with the force on the other side of it, especially considering that I'd already cracked it after Alina kicked me into it the other day.

She bolted to her feet at the same time that I did,

both of us dropping into defensive stances to prepare for whatever was on the other side of that door.

Whatever it was, I wouldn't rest until it was eviscerated and my spitfire was safe.

"Lincoln, I'm giving you two fucking seconds to open this door before I throw respect and privacy out the window and break this fucking door in two!"

Alina let out an audible gasp as the source of the disruption was revealed.

Dracula.

My eyes narrowed at the door as some of the tension bled from my body. He was an entirely different kind of threat—one I wasn't sure how to react to anymore, and I hated that.

After our tiff in the combat room, we'd gone our separate ways with the promise to each other that Alina would only be one of ours in the end. Yet here we were, with split custody of her like divorced parents shuttling their child back and forth.

Alina rushed to the door, yanking it open. Quickly, he filled my room with his menacing presence, grabbing her arms roughly before crushing her to his chest.

"What are you doing here, Drake?" she rushed to ask as his hands moved up to her face, holding her gently as his crimson eyes ran over her body, as if reassuring himself she was real. And safe. And whole.

What kind of incompetent fool did this asshole take me for? Anger burned in my gut as her words permeated the haze of sleep still clinging to me.

Oh, so she had moved from Dracula to Drake after her time with him. How fucking enlightening. My jaw clenched, the muscle ticking with the force.

A low growl rumbled through my chest at the sight of the tender affection he showed her. I tolerated Andrei like I would an annoying pet that made Alina happy, but this asshole? Not going to fucking happen.

I knew the world he would inevitably drag her into if she chose to explore his claims of their mate bond. Nothing good waited there for her, and there was no way I could ever hope to protect her from it, which was what frightened me the most. I wasn't welcome in their world anymore, and until my mate was sucked up into the void of that dark, pit of hell, I hadn't given much of a shit.

But how was I supposed to simply accept letting her walk into that nest of vipers?

"Estrid alerted me to the attacks on students, and I came immediately," he answered, completely focused on her, like she was the center of his universe. Rage boiled within me, and I struggled to keep a sneer off my face. "I know we made a deal that I wouldn't show up here during the week, but I had to make sure you were safe, darling. When you weren't in your room, I lost it."

I couldn't stand here in silence any longer, letting my disgust for him flow out. "Yeah, she was in my room, you fucking bastard. Because I'm perfectly capable of protecting my mate."

Who the hell did he think he was, storming into the academy where I was responsible for her safety, acting like I'd ever let a hair on her head be harmed? But perhaps what infuriated me most was that she allowed him to hold her like that. Why wasn't she pushing him away? When she told me the time at his estate had been easy and hadn't dragged on, I thought that maybe she had kept to herself, and he hadn't disturbed her. The easy way she regarded him and accepted his touch made it more than clear that there had been a drastic change in how she viewed him.

"Watch yourself," Dracula responded in a tight, snipping tone. The hairs on the back of my neck stood on end, and I clenched my hands into fists at my side. He had to be fucking kidding, right?

I took a step toward him, steadily holding his gaze as I asked, "Or what?"

A small scream of frustration erupted from Alina as she pushed herself to stand between us. "Stop it! Just fucking stop, please!"

Like it was divine intervention, three trill alarm beeps blared, causing us all to stop. Concern slammed into me as my brows furrowed. What now?

Estrid's voice floated through the air, and I quickly realized she was having a witch project her voice through all the sectors. My stomach dropped. Nothing about this could be good.

"Attention all students: please make your way to the pavilion for a mandatory emergency meeting. We expect you to all be prompt, and we will be gathering in thirty minutes. Professors will be at your gates to take attendance before you cross over, and if you are not listed on the roll, you will be immediately expelled from the Academy. No exceptions."

I hated my job with a burning passion at this moment. I didn't want to leave this room until we settled the shit brewing between us, but I had no other choice. At the end of the day, I swore to protect this academy and all the students within it and that had to take precedence right now.

"We have to go, Alina," I gently instructed, knowing she wouldn't respond well if I sounded forceful, despite having heard Estrid's words for herself.

She let out a heavy sigh before nodding at me in understanding. Swinging her gaze to Dracula, she kept her tone soft with him as she asked, "Would it make you feel better to hang around today until we have to go tonight?"

I spluttered before he could even answer her. "What's going on tonight?"

That was not the agreement they made. Weekdays were *mine*.

Balan's voice called out from the hallway, "Let's go Aldea, students are heading toward the gate."

My eyes rolled toward the ceiling as I tried to take a steady, calming breath despite wanting to scream at him to fuck off.

"Yes," Dracula stated, dragging my attention back to him as he spoke to Alina, steadfastly ignoring the fuck out of me. "If you wouldn't mind, I'd like to remain here. I won't intervene with your day."

She offered him a quick nod. "Okay, that's fine. It will be good to have your strength here to add to our forces if something happens."

I couldn't argue with her logic, but that didn't mean I had to like it.

As she walked toward the door, she looked over her shoulder at me. "Let's go, Lincoln. I'll explain what's going on after the meeting at the pavilion, okay?"

With a grunt of acknowledgement, I shoved past Dracula, bumping his shoulder hard as I walked after her. His answering chuckle only served to piss me off further.

After finding the other professors and students waiting outside for us, I gave Balan and Levia instructions to stand at the gate and take attendance while Trillio and I watched over the students in the pavilion.

I started moving but quickly realized none of them were following. I turned to find them staring at Dracula expectantly, like they were waiting for his orders. I lost my shit, shouting, "Move! Now!"

I would not have my authority questioned here in my own territory.

My blood boiled as I heard a silky laugh. Craning my head in the direction it came from, I found Andrei and Alina glued together at the front of the grouping of students.

Was I losing my ever-loving mind?

With a growl, I turned and prowled through the gate, thankfully hearing the shuffling of feet behind me this time.

How I longed for that brief moment of time where I was Alina's only mate and no one had the gall to fucking undermine my every move.

As all the sectors gathered in our respective areas, filling the pavilion, I offered tight, cordial nods to the other lead professors of the academy. I turned in a circle to scan the area as our students slowly trickled in after being accounted for at their gates.

Dracula took quick steps toward me as Alina popped through the gate with Andrei in tow. As he reached me, I spread my feet, holding my wrist and lifting my chin.

"I'm not here to try to take over," he admitted, coming to a halt at my side. He didn't deign to make eye contact with me, facing forward in the direction of the academic building while I remained facing back.

"What are your intentions?"

We both knew what my question was about: Alina.

He heaved a deep, heavy sigh before turning to look at the side of my face. "I'm sure they're the same as yours. To claim my mate and protect her until my dying breath."

"You know the dangers you're putting her in by claiming her and bringing her into your world," I responded, my tone short and clipped as I seethed. "And in doing so, you're cutting off my ability to protect her in the same manner you wish to do."

As our students began to fill in, I watched Alina exchange words with a small blonde girl that was a part of the shifter sector of students. It was interesting that she hadn't made friends in her own sector but seemed to have one from both the demon and shifter ones. We had rules in place to keep them as separate as possible, but I didn't press it with Alina. The small bouts of happiness that filled her eyes while talking to her friends for these brief moments wasn't worth upholding the rules that I found to be ridiculous anyways.

Shouldn't we be urging them to build ties here that would translate to better relations in the territories outside of the academy?

We remained quiet for a moment before Dracula finally said, "Your parents risked everything to ensure you never stepped foot into my castle again. Is that something you're willing to go against now?"

I ground my teeth together. If he was more

capable of keeping his fucking goons in line, my family wouldn't have had to leave in the first place.

"For Alina, I'd do anything," I answered easily, letting my eyes run over her slender frame, smiling as soon as I spotted one of her own brightening her features. It was interesting how her joy brought me happiness in return.

She continued to chat but must have felt my eyes on her as she turned to look at me, gracing me with another beautiful smile.

Fates, she was everything to me.

Dracula turned at my side to face the students, eyes drifting to Alina as well, but she had turned back to the blonde before she could see.

"Are you willing to work together to ensure her safety?" he questioned, making me scoff in response. "We have a vested interest, but our feud is only hurting that goal."

Glancing at him from my peripheral, I asked, "What did you have in mind?"

I wasn't going to concede Alina to him—ever—but I would hear what he had to say because there was truth to his words. I didn't want him here in my domain, and he didn't want me in his, but if we gave our stubbornness up, she would have extra protection. Both places were proving to be dangerous in their own ways now.

"If Alina agrees to it, I want to be able to visit here whenever she wants without you throwing a fit." I rolled my eyes. As if he wouldn't act the exact same way if I showed up unannounced in his space during his time with her. "And in turn, you will have access to my castle, to accompany her if she wants you there."

"So, we can't enter each other's space unless Alina is the one to invite us there?"

"Yes."

If the exchange in my room was any indication, it was clear that she was over the feud between us, so perhaps this would kill two birds with one stone. We would have the understanding that we were doing this for her happiness and safety, but neither of us would have to concede our underlying desire to have her to ourselves.

"Fine."

"I'm having a ball tonight to officially introduce her to the board members and their families."

My body went rigid at the admission. I hated the idea of her becoming the center of their attention, but I knew my girl would never have agreed to it if it wasn't something she wanted. I just couldn't figure out for the life of me *why* she would want to be the center of attention to the most powerful, ruthless vampires in Sanguis.

I didn't have a chance to respond, noticing the student's gazes turning toward the academic building.

Turning to look over my shoulder, I spotted Estrid exiting the academic building. She stepped to the edge of the steps just outside the door, pausing to observe each professor. Estrid offered nods as her gaze tracked from each sector to the next before nodding one final time, as if reassuring herself that everyone was present and accounted for.

The chatter around us died down as she began to speak, projecting her voice with magic. "Thank you for coming, students. I know this is not how any of us wanted to spend our Monday morning, but we would be remiss in keeping you in the dark of what is going on at the academy. Recently, we have had several security breaches across multiple sectors."

Immediately, gasps and hushed whispers began to fill the air. The amount of people milling in one place soon multiplied the whispers to a loud buzz, easily overwhelming Estrid.

"Silence!" she yelled, with a bite to her tone that was reserved for very specific occasions. Turning around, I glared at our sector in warning to add to her command. Instantly, the crowd ceased speaking, and she continued as I turned to face her once more, "I know this is alarming—it's the first time our academy has ever faced security breaches, much less multiple. Please know that all the staff is working relentlessly to ensure your safety, and we will not rest until we can, without a doubt, say there is no longer a threat."

During our brief call yesterday, she'd mentioned that all professors were required at a meeting tonight to discuss all the information we had gathered about the various threats. She hoped that we might be able to determine a course of action before deciding to take our collective knowledge to leaders of the territories in Praeditus for assistance. I hoped that it led to meaningful discussion and not fingers being pointed with dumb accusations behind them.

My eyes drifted to Professor Helen, the biggest pot stirrer of the damn staff. I still couldn't figure out why she lashed out at Alexandra during the testing meeting we'd had to determine which sector the girl should be in, but I had a bad feeling about her.

The meeting was called to a close after Estrid dropped the bomb that students who didn't feel safe enough to continue this semester would be allowed to go home with no repercussions and could return next year to start fresh.

I completely agreed with the offer, though I could see that some of the other lead professors were whispering furtively with the others. It would be hard for the other sectors to accommodate a new wave of students in addition to whoever returned from this year, but thankfully we didn't have to deal with that in ours. We had a high dropout rate due to how ruthless the classes and students were with each other, so I always had enough room.

Professor Trillio's voice boomed from the back of our group. "Back to your dorms! Classes are canceled, so get to your room and stay there. Let's go!"

Using the opportunity to not have to direct the students, I called out for Alina as her and Andrei turned to head toward the gate. "Spitfire, a moment of your time please."

She approached Dracula and me with Andrei in tow, even though I did *not* call for him. I resisted the urge to roll my eyes at him trailing after her like a lost puppy. "Dracula told me about what's happening tonight, and I will have to remain here for a mandatory meeting with the staff pertaining to the security breaches. In the future, though, if you wish to have me with you, I will be there to help you."

Her head reared back in shock before her eyes danced between my face and Dracula's, silently questioning if that was true.

"And if you wish to have me here at any point, Lincoln has agreed not to get in the way of that either," he added.

Her mouth popped open as her brow furrowed, "Uh, okay. That's nice of you both. Weird, but nice, I guess."

I felt Dracula's gaze on me as he spoke. "With classes being canceled, I'd like to bring Alina and Andrei to my castle early, if it's okay?"

I knew his question wasn't really to ask permission, but I wouldn't spit in his face and call him out for it.

"If Estrid needs any explanation for their whereabouts, I'll be sure to convey it to her," I answered, hating that I had to stay behind while she faced this night.

My eyes darted to Andrei's stoic face and when he met my gaze, I jerked my head, indicating I wanted him to come talk to me. As he approached, I walked a bit away from Alina, not wanting her to hear this conversation. Her feathers would *definitely* be ruffled, and as much as I normally loved her sass, I simply did not have time for it today.

"Yes?" he asked, his tone defensive, like he expected me to talk shit.

He was in for quite the surprise.

Crossing my arms over my chest, I stared him in the eyes as I quirked a challenging eyebrow. "I'm entrusting her safety to you tonight. We both know what these gatherings can be like. They're going to be circling the new blood, looking for any signs of weakness. Can you handle it?"

He didn't hesitate for an instance before nodding. "Absolutely. I know we have our own issues but know that I would never allow her to be harmed."

That's exactly what I wanted to hear, and for the first time, I realized I was relieved that she had him so loyally at her side. What the hell had my life become? Sharing my woman with two other men, and gladly at that? Fuck, what a mess.

"I'm trusting you," I warned before walking back to say goodbye to my spitfire.

Fates, let Andrei and Dracula be enough to get her through this night.

CHAPTER TWENTY
ALINA

"There's a carriage waiting for you out front," Drake informed Andrei the second we crossed through the portal, like he couldn't wait for him to be out of our space. "They'll take you to your family's estate."

Anger churned in my gut at his blatant dismissal not even two seconds into us being here. I knew Drake said that he was going to try to forget what he'd seen after Andrei and I had kissed before he brought me to his castle the first time, but I knew it wasn't that easy for him. He *knew* Andrei meant something to me and was clearly trying to separate us.

Glaring at Drake for his rudeness, I tightened my grip on Andrei's hand I'd taken to go through the portal, hating the thought of him having to be around his family for a second longer than he had to. "No," I responded firmly, feeling guilty for even having been part of the planning for an event that forced Andrei to see them.

Without my and Drake's plan, he wouldn't have been here, and with classes canceled, we had so much extra time today. He wasn't supposed to be with his father for more than a couple hours, and he most definitely wasn't supposed to leave the castle and go spend time with them where I couldn't watch over him. The entire situation made my body erupt, pinpricks of fear and uncertainty stabbing through me at the plan suddenly changing

Drake looked at me with his typical, stoic expression. Stepping forward with the intention of arguing with him until he gave in, I was stopped, yanked back by Andrei pulling at my hand.

"It's okay, Alina," he breathed out before stepping up and giving Drake a nod. "Thank you, that's very kind of you. I will return tonight with my family for the ball."

My mouth dropped open at how easily he rolled over and accepted this. I would have fought for him, and he should have known that! He didn't need to be the one to piss off Drake. I'd take up that mantle willingly if it meant keeping him safe and having nothing that Andrei did make it back to his father's ears.

With a final squeeze to my hand, he gave me a pleading look to not fight him on this. Slamming my mouth shut, I ran my tongue along my teeth as I silently seethed. Every part of my body was coiled tightly, anxiety tensed within me and ready to snap, but I couldn't make decisions for him.

Andrei dropped my hand and turned to open the front door, leaving without looking back at me. As soon as the door clicked close, I turned my fury on Drake, not giving a shit about Lo hearing what I had to say to him if she was around.

Whirling on him, I marched up to him and slammed my palm against his chest. "What the fuck was that? You are such an asshole. You can play nice with Lincoln out of nowhere, but you treat Andrei like garbage you can kick to the road?"

His head pulled back in shock, his mask falling away as he reached out to grab my shoulders lightly. "Alina, what are you talking about? I know he doesn't get to see his family often while he's at the academy, so I figured it would be nice for him to be able to spend time with them before the ball."

My chest heaved as fury stoked the fire to my

core, unsure whether to believe Drake's words or not. Was he seriously *that* clueless about the type of people he had on his board? Ones who clearly abused their families and traumatized them.

I opened my mouth to ask him those very questions, but just like when I'd come close to talking about Lo and Drake's kind personalities, it felt wrong to divulge such personal information without Andrei's consent. Closing my eyes, I took a steadying, deep inhale of breath and held it for a long moment before slowly letting it out.

"You are so fucking clueless," I whispered, opening my eyes to stare up at him and finding his blue ones gazing back at me in question. "Or purposefully ignorant. I'm not sure which yet."

I didn't want to admit that I felt hurt by his actions. A part of my heart had shifted to a place where I wasn't purposefully seeking reasons to be upset with him anymore. No, now I wanted him to give me reasons to believe that he wasn't the tyrant I first thought him to be. Because if it turned out he was...Well, I thought it might actually devastate me now.

Realizing that truth had me mentally sprinting toward my cemetery of bullshit I wasn't ready to sit with. This was yet another thing that I wasn't sure how to come to terms with, so I dug up a fresh, deep hole and tossed it all the way to the bottom.

Ripping my arms out of his grip, I moved to walk past him. Drake didn't let me go far, grabbing my bicep to hold me in place. "Alina! Can you please explain to me what I did this time to make you so upset? I thought I was doing something nice for them. Jeoffrey talks often about how hard it is to send Andrei away for those long semesters. Him and Serena love their son so much. Why would you be mad at me for offering them this time?"

I shook my head as I stared into his searching eyes, biting back the urge to huff and shout about how horrible Jeoffrey likely was to his family based on what I had seen from his son. "It's not my place to open your eyes to the truth of the people you've chosen to surround yourself with, but maybe you should have a closer look. There are reasons people have risked their lives to get away, Drake."

For once, the man seemed too stunned to speak. Once again, I yanked myself out of his grip and continued up the left side of the stairs toward my room. Alone time was exactly what I needed.

I was still feeling rattled about the attack on the students and the one dead body I'd seen, struggling to not think about how easily it could have been

Alexandra. To add to that stress, Lincoln and Drake had come to some weird understanding, and then Lincoln had sternly talked to Andrei after purposefully pulling him away from me. It felt like the men all had their own shit changing that I wasn't privy to, despite absolutely being a part of it.

I wanted to know their thoughts on the situation involving all four of us, even if it wasn't something I liked. It was important to me that I knew their boundaries within this, so I could *just fucking respect them*. They were making it impossible with the way they were acting, though. I wasn't a child, they didn't need to coddle me and make decisions without any of my own input.

As soon as I ascended the top step of the stairs, Drake's voice called out in a chilling tone, halting me. "Alina. At the ball tonight, you cannot challenge me like that in front of them. Do you understand me?"

It took me a moment to process that he was allowing the dark, domineering side of himself to come back to the surface. Did he really think he could show me the kind, softer side of himself for a few days and then expect me to roll over and take his commands now? If so, he was in for one hell of a rude awakening.

Dropping my hand on my hip, I clicked my tongue against my teeth as I turned over my shoulder to stare down. I countered, "If you think that I'm going to keep my mouth shut if I see you doing something I don't condone, then you might have to have a talk with Fate and tell her to give you a new mate. I will never be that woman. Do *you* understand me?"

Did I seriously just spit out my acceptance of being his mate?

I didn't give him a chance to respond, not wanting to feed into the argument since I was pretty fucking certain I had made my point crystal clear. Speeding down the hall, I heaved a sigh of relief after closing the door behind me, laying my forehead against the door as exhaustion hit me full force. I truly didn't know how anyone handled having so many men in their lives.

"Alina?"

On instinct, I whipped around at the sound of Lo's gentle voice. My hand fluttered to my chest, heart pounding in my chest at the shock of finding someone in my room. She sat on the edge of the bed with the red satin dress Drake bought for me in her lap.

Empathy shone in her sweet brown eyes as she

stood and held the dress out. "Drake was going to have a team sent up here to help you get ready and pamper you, but I had a feeling that wasn't something you would like and told him not to do that. But I wanted to see if you wanted to get ready together?"

The offer was so unexpected, and it hit me right in the fucking feels after feeling so distraught getting ready alone for the last party I'd attended. My knee-jerk reaction was to tell her that I wanted time alone. When she sensed my hesitation, she placed the dress on the bed and moved to leave. I held my hand out, shaking my head as I grimaced.

"Wait, I'm sorry," I rushed to say. "I've had a very exhausting past twenty-four hours, and Drake just pissed me the hell off before I stormed up here."

It wasn't fair of me to take my shit out on her, and I truly appreciated that she'd known I wouldn't want a team of people in here with me but would likely still want to spend time together. From our time together Saturday night, I knew that she wasn't someone to fill the space with unnecessary chatter. We could exist in pleasant silence if one of us wasn't in a talkative mood. She reminded me a lot of the petite, blonde shifter, Bex, in that manner.

Our companionship felt easy and companionable without being forced.

Her lips thinned as she blinked at me, "What did he do now? I swear he can't go a single day without sticking his foot in his mouth. Love him to death, but he's an idiot sometimes."

And just like that, we fell into an easy camaraderie as I caught her up on what happened at the academy and with Drake at the stairs. While I did understand her explanation of why he was so adamant we look united to show no weakness to these people, we both agreed his delivery left much to be desired.

After taking a long shower to relax and take care of all the necessities, she'd quickly offered to curl my hair for me, swearing she had the best products to help get the volume and hold I needed without weighing it down. Excitement bubbled within me as she got started. We were interrupted a few times by some of the event coordinators popping in for last minute choices that needed to be made, but Lo handled it quickly, barely pausing to blink before answering them.

"How do you do it?" I asked in awe, feeling like I would have made an absolute nightmare of this event if I hadn't had her help.

Glancing in the mirror at her as she stood behind me, twining a strand of my hair around another roller before pinning it in, I saw her face fall for the first time since meeting her. A sadness radiated from her, but I didn't push to ask where her mind had gone.

After putting a few more rollers in place, her warm eyes met mine in the reflection of the mirror, offering me a small smile before breathing out softly, "It's a harsh world for a woman, no matter where you're from, Alina. I've learned that if you don't make decisions, someone will make them for you, and I'm not willing to ever give up that control ever again after I was turned against my will."

My stomach soured at her quiet admission. I *knew* exactly how it felt to lose my agency, and I remembered clearly how hard I'd struggled to come to terms with the loss of control in my life.

Lo settled on top of the vanity, selecting a variety of products to start on my makeup. With a brush in her hand, she continued, "So, maybe it seems trivial when it's things like planning an event, but I'll never again give up the power and control I've fought for and claimed."

After closing my eyes at her instruction, she started to apply the eyeshadow, continuing to open tc me as she painted my eyelids with gentle strokes. "When Drake found me, I was completely rabid. I would have been one of the out-of-control vampires that your family was called in to kill if it wasn't for him."

The impact of her words hit like a punch to the gut, and I sucked in a sharp breath, feeling winded. She was probably right, and I didn't like the way that made me feel.

"While he does fuck up occasionally, it's never out of malicious intent," she explained, her breath puffing over my cheeks in soft, warm waves as she leaned closer to smudge the crease of my lid. "He has a kind heart that has been taken advantage of by many wanting to use him for his power and wealth. It's made him cold and hard to everyone besides me, and even now, I hardly see the same spark within him, except for fleeting moments. He's been alone for a long time, carrying around the burden of his position and the solitude it has forced him into."

"Why doesn't he give it up?" After all, what was the point of staying in a position if all it brought you was strife?

Her hands stalled their motions on my face for a moment before she sighed. "Because of his heart. He knows what it takes to lead this territory, and he also knows how easily the power could go to someone's head. He doesn't give it up because he doesn't trust anyone to take care of his people like he would."

My mind whirled at that. He cared about all of those within Sanguis so much that he would sacrifice his own happiness for them? It would take someone with an incredibly selfless heart to do that for as long as he had.

Now I felt like an absolute jerk for my words to him earlier about Andrei. Maybe he really did try to see good in people and thought he was doing something kind by giving their family time together.

"I'm struggling to understand who he is on the inside versus the persona he allows everyone else to see outside of these castle walls," I admitted softly, body sagging with the exhaustion seeping through me as I struggled to puzzle all of this out.

"He is quite the conundrum to crack," she agreed with a chuckle, though her voice turned serious when she spoke again. "It's worth it when you do finally break through, Alina. I don't know a better man than Drake."

Opening my eyes when her hands fell away, I looked at myself in the mirror to admire the smokey eye she'd created as she admitted with a wistful sigh, "Just remember that you have an eternity together to learn from each other. You're both individuals with your own histories full of moments that shaped you into who you are, for better or worse. It will take time for you to learn what's true to each of your hearts and to establish trust on top of it."

"Wise words," I mumbled back, nodding as I chewed them over.

Comfortable silence took over as she finished my makeup and moved on to my hair. Gently, she took out the rollers before using three different products on the curls, giving them a beautiful soft, wavy pattern, versus the tight curls I'd always tried and failed to make. The soft, wavy curls were so much more flattering, and I found myself sitting up and inspecting my look with awe.

"Wow, Lo," I breathed out, shock clear in the way my mouth gaped back at me in the mirror. There was no way this was me. "I look ready for war."

Her hand fell to my shoulder, gently squeezing as our eyes met. "Good, because our titles might be given based off a game, but it's anything but that. Every step you make and each word you utter will be scrutinized. Without fail, all the details of tonight will make their way to the masses by tomorrow night. There's no more hiding after this. You will be known as the Queen of Sanguis to all."

She left me then, and I sat there, reeling as I stared at myself in the mirror for a long damn time. I couldn't bring myself to move from the chair to put on my dress as her words truly hit me.

I'd been so focused on how this event could help me start the process of getting the answers I desperately needed that I hadn't thought of the finality of this move.

You will be known as the Queen of Sanguis to all.

This ball, the announcement that came along with it, would be the final nail in the coffin to my name with the slayers. Any forgiveness I could have begged for would go out the window as I willingly claimed this.

Was I ready to say goodbye to that part of my life, forever?

CHAPTER TWENTY-ONE
ALINA

A knock sounded at my door, rousing me from the empty place I found my mind floating in as I sat on the edge of my bed. I was still in my robe and had stared at the dress laid out on the center of it for who knows how long. Each time I'd tried to reach for it, I'd snatched my shaking hand back before I could actually touch it.

It should have been easy. This was the last step I had to take to achieve everything I'd set my mind to since leaving the slayers behind. Drake was handing me the opportunity to achieve everything I wanted on a silver platter, so why did this feel like a monumental moment that I couldn't ever turn back from?

If this didn't work out, where would I escape to? Even if I ran to Ordinarius, I would be tracked by the very people I grew up around if I ever slipped up. I would never be able to bring myself to fight them, and it would all be over for me. A few days ago, I would have welcomed the thought, but now...Now I had a few reasons to want to keep going.

Knuckles rapping against wood sounded once more before the door opened slightly. Drake called out, "Alina?"

I didn't respond as he walked in, shutting the door behind him. Instead, I pulled my knees to my chest, wrapping my arms around them and relishing in the shield they created for my aching chest. He was here to force me into the dress, force my arm in his, and present me to everyone I heard talking in the distance. Music floated through the air and chattering was plentiful. The party was in full swing, and here I was, the woman of the night, hiding away. Lo's words echoed in my mind once more.

There's no more hiding after this.

Fear of my decision pressed heavily upon my chest, and Drake's larger-than-life presence left me feeling boxed in and overwhelmed. Short, jagged breaths puffed from my lips, and I just *knew* he was going to rip the choice away from me. I couldn't embarrass him or make him look weak—he'd made that perfectly clear.

"Darling," he breathed out softly, eyes running over me before crossing the room to sit next to me. "I came here to apologize for what I said earlier..." He trailed off, reaching a hand to comfort me before seeming to think better of it and dropping it in his lap. "What's bothering you?"

"They'll want my head," I whispered, the truth of my words slamming into me like a bag of bricks as I stared at the far wall. "All of the slayers I grew up with, every single one of them. This will only further cement me as a traitor in their eyes, especially after the way I escaped...after I killed my friend."

Skye's big grey eyes swam in my mind's eye, and all I could think about was the way she'd trembled as she tried to push me away, too weak to do anything to fight me off.

My breathing grew erratic as everything piled up —the memories, the emotions, feeling like I couldn't ever possibly be good enough. Shoving my head between my knees, I tried to get a grip on myself but found myself falling apart instead. Big, heaving gasps escaped me as I struggled to center myself. Tears sprang to my eyes, falling down my cheeks in a steady trickle.

"I...I can't do this," I gasped, squeezing my legs as I trembled. "Please, don't make me."

I hated how weak I sounded, but this was me. I couldn't be the stoic, strong Van Helsing I'd been trained to be my whole life right now. I'd spent so much of my life distancing myself from my emotions to fulfill that role that I found myself completely without the necessary skills to cope through the big emotions right now when it mattered the most.

As his arm wrapped around me, I pleaded again, "Please, no. Don't make me."

"Darling, shhh," he cooed, gently pulling me into his embrace.

I all but fell into his lap, but as soon as I was there, the tears fully took over. With gentle hands, he caressed my back, consoling me.

"I was wrong to tell you that you would make me look weak if you questioned me," he muttered, confusing me with the sudden change of topic. My thoughts were already scrambled, there was no way I was going to be able to follow his logic right now. "You make me better—stronger, even—by calling me out. Every time I asked the Fates for a mate, I asked them to give me a woman who would challenge me. I got everything I asked for and more in you."

His kindness was not what I expected—not after

the way we parted. Not with how much emphasis he'd placed on this ball needing to go perfectly.

I hiccupped and swallowed thickly around the hard, insistent lump in my throat. Drake's hand moved from my back to stroke my hair as he continued, "If you don't want to do this tonight, I will send everyone home right now, Alina."

I swore I heard my heart shattering at the ease of his offer, one that went against everything he'd planned for with this ball.

His voice turned into a snarl as if reading my thoughts. "I don't give a damn what they think about us anymore. Let them think we're weak for it. Let them underestimate us because I know for a fact we make each other stronger than all of them combined. Let them come for us."

My throat tightened with an entirely different emotion as his conviction bled through. He was willing to throw everything he'd stressed to me out the fucking window all because I was a sobbing mess, experiencing cold feet like a runaway bride on her wedding day.

Sniffling back the snot clogging my nose, I pushed from his lap. Brushing at my tears and finding my hand came away with mascara, I couldn't help but let out a sobbing laugh. I couldn't imagine how much of a fucking wreck I looked like.

"You mean it?" I asked with a wobbly voice, hating the vulnerability and weakness I was showing to the vampire who a week ago I staked my entire reason for existence on killing. "You'll cancel it?"

A part of me wanted to think that he was just putting on a show, furthering the impressive facade he'd constructed since luring me to this castle. It would have been so much more comfortable for me to handle than the way my heart swelled as he moved to lay me on the bed, pushing onto his feet.

"Consider it done," he growled, walking briskly to the door. "Fuck all of them. It's you and me now, Alina."

He meant it. I felt it in the depths of my soul. He'd meant every word he'd uttered since I tried to kill him in that combat room.

He wasn't perfect, but fuck, neither was I. Despite my raw fury being unleashed upon him and my insistence that he was the villain in my story, he'd remained by my side even when I didn't want him there. He'd worked in the background when I refused to accept his words or help at face value, even at risk to his own position in Sanguis.

All my reservations crumbled with his actions at that moment. I was on my feet and grabbing his hand before he could turn the doorknob, pulling him around and pressing him against the door to stop him from going.

My hands threaded into his slicked back hair, pulling on it lightly as I pressed onto my tiptoes. He wasted no time in finding the soft curve of my waist and lifting me onto him, giving me exactly what I needed. Slamming my mouth against his, my tongue delved between his soft lips, tangling with his in a flurry as pent-up emotion came pouring out of us.

An appreciative growl rumbled from his chest as he devoured me, moving his hands to grip my half-exposed ass, the short robe riding up with my spread legs that were wrapped around him.

Everything about this felt right. How had I fought our connection for so damn long?

One of his hands moved to the back of my neck, using a small amount of pressure to pull me back just enough to stare into his eyes. His chest heaved as he growled, "I'm never going to let you go if you don't walk away right now. Tell me to stop if you don't want this."

I couldn't tell him that. I wanted this so fucking

badly that I felt like I was on fire with need after letting all my barriers drop with him. I accepted this, one hundred percent.

"I want this," I answered, staring back at him with unwavering certainty. "I want you, Drake."

His lips surged back toward mine as his hand moved from my neck to my collarbone, trailing his fingers toward my breasts as I leaned back to give him easier access. He tugged the side open, exposing my breast before cupping it and squeezing. Rolling my nipple between his fingers, he varied the pressure until I moaned into his mouth.

A trail of fire followed his every touch, leaving me burning for him as I leaned into him, desperate for contact. Before I could process the movement, he had us flipped with my back against the wall. My head fell back, and my eyelids fluttered shut as he worked his mouth down my jaw and over my neck, lavishing my skin with soft bites followed by soothing licks of his tongue.

His hot mouth trailed further down until he sucked my nipple into it, swirling his tongue around my peaked, aching bud. He was driving me crazy with need, my clit throbbing for attention.

"More," I panted, attempting to push him back so I could force him to his knees for me.

He was an unmovable mountain of a vampire, though. The only response I pulled from him was a bite on my nipple that pulled a hiss from my lips at the pained pleasure it filled me with as I felt the warmth of my blood trailing down my skin.

My back arched as a moan crossed my lips, spurring him into action. His arm hooked under my leg, spreading me as he shoved a knee beneath my ass to hold me up against the wall.

"Yes," I moaned as his free hand worked its way to my wet pussy, parting my folds and finding my throbbing clit.

He applied the faintest amount of pressure with his thumb against the swollen bud, and already I was crying out as he sucked on my nipple hard before biting down again. My orgasm built within me swiftly, and as his thumb began to rub circles over me, my hips began to rock to their own rhythm.

Moving his attention to my other nipple, he sank his fingers into me. He grunted as I rocked against him, fucking his hand as much as I could in this position. Still I needed more.

Reaching down between us, I tried to grab his belt to gain access to his cock.

"Not like this, darling," he murmured, halting my hand before whirling us off the wall and walking us back toward the bed. "Let me taste you. Let me bring you pleasure. It's all I've fucking dreamed about since laying eyes on you."

What was I supposed to say to that? No?

"Okay."

He wasted no time in laying my ass down close to the edge of the bed before dropping to his knees and spreading my legs.

I leaned onto my elbows, keeping my eyes on his face as he ran his tongue across his lips and purred, "Such a pretty pussy, wet and waiting for me to fuck with my mouth."

He surged forward, mouth closing around my clit as we groaned in pleasure together. Watching him feast on my pussy was a new level of erotic torture I'd never experienced before. He was making the sounds of a man devouring the best meal of his life. His blue eyes rose to meet mine as he moved his tongue from my clit to stroke inside of my heat.

"Shit," I hissed, fucking lost in the intensity of passion in his eyes.

When he slipped two fingers into me and curled them up, I knew I was a goner. He was going to drive me straight off this cliff, and there was no damn way I could hold my sounds in. I didn't give a shit if all his board members heard us.

His tongue flicked back and forth between my clit and inside my pussy, driving me into a frenzied, needy mess. Drake grinned like a mad man as my mouth fell open and my release crashed through me, squeezing his fingers tightly. He continued to lap at my clit, riding out my orgasm until my head finally fell back, breaking our eye contact as tingles spread through my limp body.

As I laid back fully and stared at the ceiling, I realized I needed to make one more big decision after the one I'd just made with Drake.

Was I going to go out there and become the Queen of the board?

CHAPTER TWENTY-TWO
ANDREI

Agony tore through me as I took in the green-yellow bruise around my mother's eye, proof of my father's vitriol and outbursts. She used to heal as rapidly as any healthy vampire would, but over the years, I'd noticed it was taking her much longer to do so. I often had to plead with her to keep up with her blood intake, but she was wasting away, and I couldn't help but think that it was getting worse without me here.

My heart beat erratically at the thought. He'd done this to her. He'd lured her into this marriage under the same upstanding, honorable, and kind guise he put on for everyone else. And then ever so slowly, he'd shown her his true self after she gave birth to me, trapping her by using me as a tool to control her.

As soon as I was old enough to become a threat, long after she'd lost all the fire of rebellion, he'd flipped the tables. Now she was the tool he used to control me.

Fucking bastard.

We had a goddamn deal. I'd mind my p's and q's and be at the top of my class, and he'd leave her alone. He clearly hadn't upheld his end of that bargain, and I planned to make it a fucking problem for him. I didn't care if he had hundreds of years of fighting experience on me, I'd risk my life to put an end to this now.

We had lived in fear of him for far too long.

My mother's hand cradled my cheek, staring up at me with such adoration in her soft green eyes that it almost brought me to my knees. "I love you, Andrei," she murmured quietly, brushing her thumb across my cheek gently. "You shouldn't have come here. Your father has been..."

She trailed off, not needing to speak the words into existence for me to understand. He'd taken out his anger on her for whatever the hell had upset him this time. It was un-fucking-acceptable, and it had to *end*.

Placing my hand over hers, I squeezed lightly, heart lurching at the feeling of her frail, bony hand beneath mine. "I didn't have a choice. Dracula had a carriage prepared for me and thought I would want to come visit with the extra time I have today. It was either explaining why I didn't want to come home or take the carriage. You know I didn't have a real choice."

With an exhausted sigh, one that whispered of the last twenty-three years of the life she had to endure by my father's side, she nodded in understanding. "He's in his office, so just try to—"

"Try to what, Serena?" My father's voice boomed from behind me. The fight or flight instinct within me caused my body to tense. Flight was what my body begged for, but I wasn't going to run. Around the ripe age of seven, I'd learned what happened to my mother when I ran.

It still took everything in me to not flee as my first instinct, though. Even to this day. *That* was the control this fucker had terrorized into me and my mother.

"Nothing, Jeoffrey," she murmured despondently, dropping her hand from my face and backing away.

Turning to face him, I glared as my heart beat

against my ribcage. He was already in his formal suit for the ball, with his dark hair combed over and gelled into place. Those damn beady eyes bore into me, daring me to face him as they always did. I always submitted eventually, dropping my own eyes to the floor in subservience.

I hated how my voice shook as I maintained eye contact and said, "We had a deal, Father. I'd keep my top spot at the academy to be eligible for you to submit my name for the board at the end of the year, and you'd leave Mom alone."

I never gave a shit about qualifying for an empty spot on the board, but my father seemed to think it would be a direct reflection of his failure as a man if I didn't. In the end, I fought for my spot on the board because it would allow me the power to go against him one day as well as staying near my mother. I needed that spot, and I'd worked my ass off to ensure that I would be in a position for this final year to be as qualified as I could.

Graduating in the top spot was the final piece of the puzzle I needed to ensure I wouldn't be passed over for serious consideration by Dracula. Once your name was denied for a position on the board, it could never be submitted again.

"And you didn't uphold your end of that

bargain," he spat, storming toward me with red flaring over his tanned skin.

To the outside world, he looked like a classically handsome, clean-cut man. To us, he just looked like the fucking devil.

Stand your ground, Andrei. Don't show him your fear.

Standing nose to nose, we glared at each other. His spittle splashed onto my face as he taunted me, "You're a weak, pathetic little boy. I gave you everything, Andrei, *everything*!"

My mind whirled in confusion at his words, and I fought the urge to look to my mother for confirmation. What could I possibly have done to raise his ire like this?

"Did the first week rankings come out?" I asked, hands clenched into fists at my side, in a more subdued tone.

How could anyone have beat me? Even Maya wasn't a threat with her tactics anymore, having been expelled by Dracula.

A lifeless laugh came from him as he shoved a finger into my chest hard enough to make me wince despite my attempt not to. "You're second, Andrei."

No...how? Dracula or Lincoln had to have done something to rig the score. The cunning motherfuckers. The lingering bruise around my mother's eye made my stomach churn, and I swallowed down the need to vomit my hatred at my father's feet. Neither of those idiots knew what was at stake for me if I wasn't in that top spot, and I was powerless to make them understand.

He bared his teeth at me as his fangs lengthened. It took everything I had to keep my face stony as he roared, "To a fucking Van Helsing of all people. How could you embarrass me like this, letting a slayer of all people top you?"

"No, that's impossible," I countered as my mind spun. There's no fucking way she could have beat me when she'd only been at the academy a week and missed classes during that time. "It has to be a mistake."

Suddenly, his hand was around my throat, and I couldn't breathe. The hand wrapped around my throat and shot forward, slamming my back into the wall. I grasped at his wrist with both of my hands, fighting to loosen it just enough to take a breath. I'd honed my fighting skills over my years at the academy with the hopes of meeting his level, but there was a reason he was a Knight on the board. He was damn strong and agile.

As vampires, our strength grew the longer we

lived. Despite my attempts to do everything imaginable to be able to stand my ground with him, I couldn't help but feel like my efforts was futile as I stood here, mouth open and eyes bulging as he seethed, "You're going to go with us to this ball tonight, and you're going to sweet-talk Dracula. Maybe if he takes a liking to you, he'll overlook your failure and consider you still."

"Jeoffrey," my mother's soft voice called out, trembling as she pleaded, "stop hurting him. Please."

I didn't have to see her, hearing the barely restrained tears in her voice, and the helpless hatred and rage that had made itself a home in my heart over the years reared its useless head. If there was one thing my father hated more than anything, it was the weakness he related to tears.

As his attention turned to her, panic swelled within me, and I stopped trying to pry his hand off, cocking back before letting my fist smash into his face. It must have taken him by complete surprise because his ironclad grip loosened as he stumbled away from me. I swallowed deep, gasping breaths.

"You think you can stand up to me, boy?" he roared before launching himself at me.

I tried to evade him, but he was still fucking

faster than me, and he easily grabbed me around the throat once more. With an ugly sneer coloring his features, he used the grip on my throat to slam me down into the floor. White hot pain seared through me as the familiar feeling of breaking ribs stabbed through me. Breathing became that much more difficult from the pressure the broken bones put on my lungs.

Crouching down to my side, he grabbed my cheeks so hard that blood spilled into my mouth from digging into my fangs. It was useless trying to put them away as my bloodhaze took over.

I hated this man.

I hated the way I had to slowly watch my mother inch closer to death each day.

I hated the way he controlled my life.

I hated the way I still feared him.

"You haven't had enough, huh?" he taunted with a chuckle before letting his fist wail on my face.

Pain blossomed *everywhere,* and though I threw my hands up and tried to stop his attacks, my resistance was futile. The bones in my wrist shattered as I tried to block my face from his next punch. I barely grunted with the pain, the wound an old, familiar friend.

"Stop!" my mother screamed, and the pain I

heard in her voice hurt more than anything he could do to me. I knew I would heal from this, but she never would. She told me over and over how she blamed herself for never being strong enough to leave with me.

Knowing that fighting back would only prolong the fight, I stopped trying to fend him off, letting him get a few more hits in for free as my hands dropped to my side. She'd never stop trying to defend me in her own way, but all it would do was add fuel to his fire.

I was certain there was some sick, depraved part of him that got off on hearing pain in the voices of the people around him.

After standing to his full height, I watched his knuckles drip with a mixture of his split skin and the blood from my wounds. I flinched as he hocked up spit, sneering as he dropped it onto my face.

"Pathetic," he rumbled before pulling his leg back and giving me one last swift kick to the ribs.

Blood sprayed from my mouth as I curled onto my side and coughed from the impact.

"You're going to get that spot back, do you hear me, Andrei?" he demanded, anger dripping from each damned syllable he spat at me. "I don't care if you have to kill her to get it back. Do what needs to be done. I'll clean up the mess with my connections."

Through the haze of pain I mumbled, "But she's Dracula's mate."

There was no way he'd want me to risk drawing his wrath, right?

Fuck, please let that be true.

"You believe that bullshit?" he asked in a dry, humorless tone. "No fucking way. I don't know what his move is, but I don't believe it."

Fuck it. I might as well rip the bandage off while I was already down and out.

Gasping around the pain spearing through me, I rasped, "She's my mate. I can't hurt her."

My mother's gasp echoed through the room as my father bent down. He wrapped his fingers tightly around my chin before yanking my head to the side, looking at the back of my neck before asking softly, "You care about her?"

I should have known the question, the soft tone, was a fucking ploy. I should have kept my damn mouth shut, but the genuine curiosity in his tone had the little boy in me hoping that this would be the one thing that he could understand.

"Yes, more than anything," I admitted.

White spots blossomed in my vision when he

stood and kicked me, compounding the pain already searing in my ribs. Spit flew from his mouth as he bent and yelled, "Wrong! That whore is nothing! She is a useless fucking distraction that will ruin all my plans."

Pain seared in my scalp when he worked his hands through my hair and yanked my head up to face him as he crouched in front of me once more. A twisted smile pulled his lips up as he said, "It seems that you're at a crossroads, my boy. Either remember what the fuck I raised you to do, or I'll kill your distraction."

Cold chills broke over my skin at the thought of him harming Alina. Panic clawed at my gut as the devastation of the truth set in. He would do it if he felt pushed to it. *No.* Absolutely fucking not. I would take a million more beatings if it meant keeping her from being touched.

"We're going to run the board together one day, son," he said, cackling with a manic glee to his eyes. "No one will ever be able to stop us. I already have some of the members on my side. I just need you to take one empty seat to have majority, and you *will not* fuck up all my carefully laid plans."

It was on the tip of my tongue to tell him I'd never give up Alina, but as if he sensed my rage, he was gone and back in the blink of an eye. He held my mother in front of me, his hands wrapped around her neck as his eyes gleamed maliciously.

"Did you not realize that offering me control over you with your mate's life made your mother's life expendable?" he taunted, squeezing her neck until her face turned red and she scratched at his hands.

I tried to push up, to get to her, but black dots danced in my eyes when I tried to lurch forward, the pain seconds away from pulling me under.

"Tell me, son," he demanded with a cruel laugh, "which one will you choose? Focus on your task at hand, get the seat on the board, and your mother is safe. Choose your mate, and your mother dies."

How had my life turned to this? Bile rose in my throat at the implications of my careless actions. I was to blame.

I had known I couldn't let him find out about Alina, yet for some reason, I still wanted to believe that there was even an ounce of compassion in the man who should have taught me what it meant to be a man. To be a father. To be a husband. I took a calculated risk. And I fucking lost.

No one was safe because of *me*.

There was no real choice here. My mother had

no one except me to look out for her. Alina had Lincoln and Dracula. They'd watch over her.

They *had* to watch over her. Because I'd failed her as spectacularly as I'd failed my mother.

"I'll fall in line," I muttered, heart numbing as the words fell from my lips. "Don't hurt Mom."

The twisted, shit-eating grin that spread over his face twisted my gut with nausea. He released his hands from my mother's throat and let her fall to the floor. She landed on her hands and knees, wobbling as he turned on his heel and walked away. She was quick to crawl over to me, pulling my head into her lap after I let my body collapse to the floor to wait for my healing to begin.

As her fingers ran through my hair, I felt the heat of her tears falling onto my face as she whispered, "I'm sorry, baby boy. I'm so sorry. You should never have to give up the one that is fated for you."

Alina.

The thought of seeing her tonight and having to dismiss her from my life was a pain unlike any I'd felt before. Broken ribs, cracked wrists, and blacked eyes would never compare to the grief that slammed into me then, stealing my breath as I grappled with the truth.

The truth was I knew that even if I distanced

myself from her, she'd fight for me. She'd fight for *us*. I had to truly make her think I didn't want our bond anymore to keep her away.

I was going to break her heart.

I was going to break my promise to Lincoln.

I was going to lose the woman that I fucking *loved*.

All I could do was fall into the dark place in my mind that I reverted to in these moments when it all felt like too much. Too many emotions. Too much pain.

I just wanted it to stop.

Resigned to the fate I thought I'd accepted long ago but lost sight of as Alina brightened my life, I built a barricade in my mind as thick as I could. I didn't want even the faintest whisper of her voice to get in, or I'd crack. And that was something I could no longer afford.

Knowing she wouldn't be able to hear me now, I said my goodbyes.

I'm sorry, baby girl. One day I hope you can understand and forgive me.

CHAPTER TWENTY-THREE
ALINA

Fastening the tie of my robe, nervous energy fluttered in my stomach. Drake's eyes felt like they were burning a hole into the side of my face from where he'd leaned against the door to watch me once more. I was thankful he'd given me a bit of space after...all that.

The passion had been electric between us, and in the wake of my orgasm, I'd felt so at peace with my choice to accept Drake. But as the fuzzy euphoria faded away, the reality of what had happened set in.

Swallowing my anxiety, I finally forced myself to look over at him as I puzzled through what this meant for us moving forward. There was no hiding the look of satisfaction on his face with that little fucking dimple of his on full display as he smirked at me. I wanted to be mad at the smug expression, but I found myself chuckling instead, turning the devilish smirk into a full-fledged grin.

"Are you going to tell me that was a mistake?" he questioned, pushing off the wall to stand in front of me.

As he grabbed my hand, I looked down and watched as he twined our fingers together, mulling over his words. He'd bit me hard enough to draw blood, so I had to assume he'd gotten enough in his mouth to swallow, which meant all I needed to do was drink his to complete our bond.

The thought of it made my chest tighten, bringing my panic rushing back to the surface. As my heart tried to beat its way out of my chest, I took a deep breath in through my nose and let it, and my anxiety, go slowly through my lips. I didn't need to complete the bond now. All I had to do was take this one step at a time.

With a deep breath, I glanced back up at him, reveling in the blue gaze staring back at me, and shook my head. "I don't regret it, nor do I think it was a mistake, but I need to know that you will let me take this at my pace, okay? I'm not ready to complete the bond yet."

The way he answered would be a good indicator

of whether I would ever complete the bond. His answer was I needed to know that he wouldn't force me into such a permanent and deep connection until I was truly ready. There was something almost too intimate about having the ability to connect telepathically, and I had already realized with my current bonds that I wished I could let the walls down completely with them. But I couldn't, and I wasn't sure that I was ready to add a third connection to the jumble in my mind just yet.

There were so many things I needed to work through and accept before I would feel comfortable doing so, and it was clear Andrei and Lincoln still needed to do the same.

The bond should have represented the joining of two souls and minds into one, with no limitations. It was a beautiful concept, to know someone so openly and thoroughly that you could let them have access to every part of you, unfettered. I only hoped that I could give them all what they deserved one day.

With Lincoln, I'd had no idea what we were doing before the bond snapped into place, and with Andrei exchanging blood had been a purely emotional choice, but with Drake...I wanted us to commit to our bond when we could truly open ourselves completely to each other. I was nowhere near being able to do that with him yet.

His hand lifted to grip my chin lightly, insisting on the intense eye contact that made me feel so fucking vulnerable every time. Each time he did it, it felt as if he was peering into my soul, and my instinct was to glance away, to hide from him.

"Look at me, darling," he softly demanded.

Dragging my eyes up from where they had landed on his chest, I tried my best not to fidget under the weight of his gaze.

"I have waited so long to find you. I would wait just as long to ensure you felt comfortable before taking that step," he answered, and the knot in my chest loosened in relief, and I drew in a shaky breath. "What matters to me is that I have you at all, in whatever way you're willing to share with me right now, okay?"

"Okay," I breathed out before a smile toyed at my lips. "Does that mean you're going to accept that you have to actually share me with my other mates?"

I knew I was testing him, and it was truly okay if we needed to take baby steps to work up toward sharing our time. But as Drake's brow furrowed and his eyes narrowed, it hit me that he didn't know Andrei was my mate as well.

Shit.

His eyes flickered with the black threatening to consume them completely, and his nostrils flared with the deep breaths he seemed to be forcing himself to take. "Andrei?"

I nodded the best I could with the grip on my chin holding me in place. My heart stuttered in my chest, and I'm pretty goddamn sure I stopped breathing for a moment.

I didn't want to ruin this moment for us, but it was only fair that he knew exactly what he was getting into with me.

"Are there *any* more?"

I couldn't help the scoff that came from me as I responded, "Fates, I hope not. You three are more than enough for me."

We stood there for a few tense moments, my stomach rolling as my chest tightened in anticipation of what he would say. It hit me then, that I couldn't accept any of the three vampires walking away from me.

"Okay," he whispered, barely audible even with my enhanced hearing before he leaned in to press his lips to my forehead

"Okay," I said, equally as quiet, as he pulled back to peer at me with creased brows.

I pressed up onto my toes as he leaned down, pressing our lips together in a tender, chaste kiss as his arms encircled me, holding me tightly to him. My feet lifted off the ground as he pulled me up, peppering kisses on the edge of my lips before moving to my cheeks and then to my neck, making me giggle at this affectionate side of him.

When he stopped showering me with kisses, the mood sobered as he looked at me and asked, "Am I canceling this ball, darling?"

Something had clicked into place within me at this acceptance of our bond.

This was my life now, no matter how hard I initially tried to fight it. I had to say goodbye to the life I'd always known, closing that chapter with certainty and acceptance.

It felt like a betrayal to my family when I'd been staring at the dress with the thought that he was going to force me into the choice when he came into the room.

How could I possibly become the Queen of the very creatures we'd sworn our opposition to?

Drake didn't press me into answering, and I took a minute to think back on all the little moments of confusion and doubt that had swarmed within me since being turned. I'd been forced to open my eyes and see this feud from the vampire's point of view, and without a doubt, there was wrong done by the slayers. I was willing to accept that now.

If things remained the way they were, no one would ever feel vindicated, and we would be destined to continue this vicious cycle. I didn't want to sit by and watch it spiraling out of control.

Wetting my lip as nerves bubbled up within me, I voiced all the thoughts swirling within me as clarity washed over me. "If I accept this role, I don't want to just be the woman who stands at your side and has no voice. I want to bridge the tremendous chasm between slayers and vampires. I want to have a purpose in this role."

I could accept that my previous chapter was over, but I wanted to know that I was in charge of writing my next one. I wouldn't give up on the slayers despite knowing I wasn't welcomed with them anymore. In my heart, they would always be my family, even if they didn't feel the same about me. I wouldn't turn my back on them, but I knew there was no changing what I was now: a vampire.

I couldn't spend the rest of my life hating who I was now. Nor did I want to.

"It will be a hard road to travel," he responded, warning coloring his tone. "How do you know the slayers wish to change anything? You cannot project your wants onto them if they are not willing to change."

I shrugged my shoulders as the truth of the matter flowed through me. "I don't know, but I don't want to give up before I've even tried. Is that something you will support?"

There was no hesitation from him as his lips curved into a smile once more. I'm certain my insides melted when he answered, "Let's change Sanguis, my Queen."

Warmth pooled in my chest, and for the first time, I felt like I'd found my true purpose in life. Maybe Lincoln was correct in his assumption that Devorare never had a previous owner because she was always meant to be with a hybrid. Maybe *our* history book, the book where a Van Helsing took three vampire mates, would be the one that wrote the story of unity between the two species.

"Then let's show them a united front at this ball," I finally answered before laughing and adding, "but I think I need Lo's help to fix the mess you made of my face first."

Pressing a quick kiss to my lips, he muttered in jest, "You do look a bit scary, killer."

Swatting his chest as he put me down on my feet, I warned, "Be careful, I could try to kill you again."

His warm laugh filled the room as he turned for the door. "Try is the operative word there, darling. I'll go find Lo and send her up."

For once, the warm, fuzzy feelings flowing through me didn't bring a wave of guilt along with them. Even as I sat back down at the vanity and laughed at the disaster I'd made of my makeup, I found myself looking more confident than I ever had before.

Lo appeared in the doorway, sticking her head in before her eyes settled on my reflection in the mirror. Her mouth dropped open as she rushed in, shutting the door behind her before she ran to me with concern etched into her face.

"Alina, are you okay?" she questioned, dropping to her knees at my side as she reached for my hand.

"Lo, for the first time since being turned," I started, but paused as I thought back to everything that had happened since. A gentle smile pressed onto my lips as I continued, "For the first time, I can actually say that yes, I'm okay now."

Pride shone in her eyes as I squeezed her hand and looked back at the mirror.

"I'm ready now," I told her and myself.

She set to work cleaning off my face before reapplying the makeup in silence, letting me soak up this new found confidence and energy I knew was required to take on the crowd out there.

My thoughts drifted to what Lincoln and Andrei were doing, and I decided to test out whether they could hear me through the bond. Letting my walls down, I felt my tie to Lincoln and tried his first, though the distance made me feel like easily contacting him probably wouldn't be possible.

Linc?

I waited a few moments before focusing all my energy into it and trying one more time.

Linc?

I gave up and switched to my connection with Andrei. I fully thought I'd be able to connect to him since the ball was in full swing and we should have been in the same building again. But as I called out for him, I was met with not only silence, but what felt like a stone-cold barrier I'd never felt through the bond.

Andrei? Can you hear me? What's going on?

Something was wrong, and rage boiled through

me. If his father was behind whatever the hell it was, I didn't give a shit what his position on the Board was—I'd kill him.

CHAPTER TWENTY-FOUR
ALINA

Staring in the mirror, I took in my full look, awed by the magic Lo had seemed to work on me. More than ever before, I found myself believing that makeup was *armor*. I looked stunning yet fierce with a bright red lip that matched my dress. The smokey eye Lo had done made me look dramatic in a way that I'd never been able to achieve when doing my own makeup.

If I was someone else and saw me, I'd think *that's a bad bitch who has her shit together*. Crazy how makeup could help obscure not only physical blemishes, but emotional ones as well.

"Are you ready, dar—" Drake started as he entered my room, stopping abruptly as I turned to face him.

His mouth was parted as his eyes ran the length of me, and I could feel a blush rising up my neck and onto my cheeks. It wasn't every day you could make someone like Drake completely lose themself in you. The way each of my men made me feel like I was the most beautiful woman in the world was something I would never get over.

Shaking his head, he seemed to come out of his stupor as I walked to him, and he extended his arm to me. "Would you do me the honor of being on my arm, darling?"

Placing my hand into the crook of his elbow, I offered a nod. Drake exuded a calming presence, but I couldn't shake the feeling that something was amiss—my stomach wouldn't settle, and my chest felt tight, leaving me feeling off-kilter. "Yes, let's do this."

Beautiful music filled the air as we made our way toward the staircase off the main entryway to the castle. The doors were wide open, allowing guests to either gather outside where the entertainment was set up—including everything from fire breathers, to acrobats, and even psychics—or mill in the cavernous foyer and rooms to the left and right of the entrance.

Lo had decided on a carnival theme, and she'd

gone all out, something I hadn't thought possible with the castle being tucked into a mountainside. Surprisingly, there was plenty of room just off the front of the castle that she'd ordered the planners to lay down fake grass to make it look like a lawn and less sterile. Her words, not mine. I personally found the castle to be incredibly warm and inviting, but maybe that was more because of its occupants.

Turning the corner, I took in the decor for the first time. "Wow," I breathed out quietly.

The inside was more subdued, with a pianist and violinist playing a song that was as dark and haunting as it was beautiful. The lights had been dimmed to add to the enchantment of the theme, with black candles scattered throughout as the main source of light.

"Look up," Drake murmured as we descended the steps and stood beneath the vaulted ceilings.

I gasped as I saw two acrobats suspended in the air—by what, I wasn't sure. I watched in silence, completely in awe as they flipped recklessly, seemingly defying gravity and the laws of physics.

Lo appeared from the hallway leading to the kitchen with glasses of champagne in her hands. "Hi!" she greeted cheerfully before placing a flute in each of our free hands. "You make such a dashing pair, if I do say so myself."

"Thank you, Lo, for everything," I said, pulling away from Drake as Lo moved to hug me.

We held each other for a moment, and she settled my frazzled energy a bit as she murmured in my ear, "We've got your back. You're a part of the family now."

She pulled away, offering me one last warm smile before I watched her cold mask slip into place in the seconds before she walked out the front doors.

"She's pretty special," I said, glancing at Drake. He nodded and held up his glass in response.

Clinking them together, he murmured, "Cheers, darling. To our future."

We drained the half-filled flutes quickly, depositing them on a passing staff member's empty tray before he offered his elbow to me once more. Settling my hand back into the crook of his elbow, he steered us forward and out the doors.

I had to resist the urge to squirm as all chatter died and a man dressed as a jester rushed over and called out, "Presenting for the first time, King Dracula and Queen Alina!"

Thunderous applause erupted as people began

approaching us, splitting into two lines on either side of the red carpet that had been rolled out from the front door.

As we descended the steps, I kept my chin held high, squeezing Drake's elbow as nerves flowed relentlessly through me. His hand moved to rest on my shaking one, rubbing the tops of my fingers that very well might have been cutting off his arm's circulation with my ironclad grip.

Walking through the line of people, we separated to shake hands and exchange hellos with the gathered board members and their families. Some seemed genuinely kind and happy to meet me, extending best wishes upon Drake and I as if we'd gotten married, while others were guarded, offering polite handshakes and tight smiles.

By the time we made it to the end of the carpet, I drew to a slow stop. Andrei was there, eyes fixed studiously on the ground. His shoulders were stiff with hands fisted tightly at his side. I rushed to him but was stopped as a hand shot out to wrap around my bicep.

"Hello, Ms. Van Helsing," a slimy voice greeted cheerfully from next to him, making me turn to glare at whoever had stopped me from reaching Andrei.

As I stared at the man, I took in the sharp angle

of his clean-shaven jaw and cheekbones and realized this had to be Andrei's dad. Except for their eyes, they shared the same complexion and several other features.

Every move we made here was purposeful, not to mention being carefully watched, so I dropped my eyes to his hand on my arm before demanding in an icy tone, "Remove your hand from me. Now."

I wanted everyone who was watching the exchange to see that I wouldn't tolerate such harassment or manhandling.

His jaw ticked and the way the corner of his eyes pinched as he removed his hand. The annoyed expression was on his face for all of a second before he forced a jovial smile to his face and held his hands up. "I'm sorry, I meant no offense. I just wanted to ensure I had the pleasure of meeting you."

He wasn't fooling me, but as Drake made his way over and offered a cold, polite greeting, I took the distraction of the music swelling as an opportunity to turn to Andrei. Wanting a moment to check on him in private, I glanced around for a quiet, more secluded area. A large red and white striped tent sat in the near distance, and I could easily spot a dance floor lit up on the inside.

Maybe I just needed to take him where his father couldn't observe us. I turned to Drake, grabbing his hand and squeezing it gently before saying, "I need to talk with Andrei about an assignment I missed last week, honey. I'll be right back if that's okay?"

That made it look normal and platonic, right?

Despite having pulled the black back into his eyes, I felt the confusion and alarm radiating from him at my words. Perhaps he could pick up on my anxiety.

"Of course, darling," he answered easily, not relaying the emotions I sensed in him. "I'll come find you in a few minutes in order to properly introduce you, and then we'll spend time with each board member."

"Walk with me to the dance floor?" I asked Andrei as I placed my hand on his arm, gently prodding him in that direction.

He didn't answer, but nodded once, still refusing to meet my eyes. Keeping pace with him, I glanced up at him and murmured quietly, "I tried to speak to you through the bond, but I couldn't get through. Is everything okay?"

He let out a heavy sigh as we reached the dance floor, and as I reached to put my arms around his neck to dance, he backed away.

"Andrei?" I asked softly, confused at his behavior.

Why wasn't he speaking to me?

Finally, he lifted his eyes to meet mine, but I almost wished they hadn't. The malice I saw radiating in them stunned me into taking a step back, confusion swimming in my head as I tried to make heads or tails of the sudden change in his demeanor.

"You acted like you hated Maya for cheating her way to the top, but how the fuck can you say that and turn around and do it the exact same way?" He hissed with ice in his eyes. "You slept your way to the top of the leaderboard and knocked me off after just one week of being here. I've been here for *years* adding points to my score."

Recoiling at the insult, I glanced around to make sure we were still alone.

"What the hell has gotten into you?" I hissed. "Why would you say such a thing? Did your father do something when you went home?"

"I'm simply stating the truth, Alina," he responded in a clipped, short manner, crossing his arms across his chest. "I knew you were just a slut who would bend over for me after I found you fingering yourself in that window."

My blood boiled, rage simmering just beneath the surface at the barrage of insults. No one was around for him to put on a front with, so what the actual fuck?

"Stop this right now, Andrei," I demanded, letting my own fire burn in my eyes. "I will not stand here and let you talk out of your ass to me in such a disrespectful and cruel way."

A cold laugh fell from his lips before he said, "It's pathetic, the way you crumbled at the first crumb of kindness I showed you. It was so damn easy. *You* are so damn easy."

My teeth ground together, and I struggled with the urge to lash out and blow the teeth out of his mouth with my fist. How fucking dare he? Here I'd been concerned about Drake being a wonderful actor and playing me, but maybe I'd been an idiot all along with the wrong guy.

I waited to see a flicker of confusion, or fear, or *something* to show me that he wasn't acting this way of his own accord, but all I saw in his eyes was cold disinterest. My stomach roiled with anger when I spotted pity swirling in his hateful gaze.

"You're so full of shit right now," I huffed back, not willing to believe that he pulled the wool over my eyes like this. I hated that I could hear the lack of confidence in my voice because that meant he could hear the exact same thing.

Already, I could feel my heart shutting down, hardening until a protective barrier formed around it. I'd never left myself so vulnerable and open with anyone, and everything in me screamed and raged to shut him out—to protect myself from whatever else malicious shit he managed to spew. For a second, I almost gave into that voice, but then my brain whizzed through all our moments together.

When he'd pulled me between his legs at the party and showed me the first glimpse of his heart.

"The party is okay. But I'd rather sit out here under the light of the moon with you than go back."

"Is that what you tell all the girls you want to get on their knees for you? It's suave, I'll give you that."

"No, baby girl. I've never said anything like that in my life, and I'm pretty sure my reputation would be ruined if you told anyone I said it, so I'm placing a lot of trust in you."

Then when he'd shown up at my door after we'd already agreed to go our separate ways. How we'd consumed each other the second we broke and gave into our desire.

"Exchange blood with me, Alina. I know it's damn

near impossible to find one mate in this life—let alone three—but I know you're mine, baby girl."

That was my Andrei. That was the guy who was my mate. This asshole was the version of him that I'd run into that first day—that asshole, alpha facade that he put on for everyone else to keep them away from or beneath him.

My lips thinned, and I used the anger burning in my chest to melt away the ice that began to consume me at his callous words.

I wasn't going to believe his horseshit.

I wasn't going to let my fear of rejection and abandonment win this time.

"Tell me if something is going on, Andrei," I pleaded, staring at his stoic face and hating how desperate I sounded, but fuck I *was*. I was desperate to have the man I...fuck. The truth of my feelings hit me like a tidal wave crashing through me relentlessly. I couldn't hold them back for fear that I would drown beneath their truth.

"I love you," I breathed out as I closed the short distance between us. Placing my hands on his crossed forearms, I stared up into his light green eyes lit up by the swirling multi-colored lights surrounding us. "I love you, Andrei. There's nothing we can't face together if you just let me in."

I believed every single word down to the depths of my soul.

Ripping his arms out of my hands, he took another step back before shaking his head, lip curling in disgust. "It was a mistake to complete the bond with you. I don't want this. I don't want you."

Tears sprung to my eyes at the admission. I *knew* he didn't mean what he was saying, but it fucking hurt after I'd poured my fucking heart out, admitting that I loved someone for the first time in my life.

"I don't believe you," I hissed as a single tear rolled down my cheek, my teeth grinding together. He stared at me blankly in return.

Apparently, the conversation was over because he didn't even bother to respond before turning and walking away. I waited for him to stop. To look over his shoulder. To do anything to break him out of the thrall of whatever the hell was happening here, but he didn't.

Sliding my gaze to his father, I narrowed my eyes when I found him staring back at me. With a wide, fake as fuck smile, he waved at me before reaching out to clap Andrei on the back as he approached.

It was fucking subtle, but it was there. Andrei flinched at the touch from his father, which confirmed my worst fears.

There was no way in hell Andrei would ever make the decision to walk away from me...from our bond. I'd been lucky enough to see the real man lying beneath the persona he wore around everyone else. I held onto that version of him like a life raft as I struggled to not let my heart shatter in the middle of the dance floor, as I watched him walk away. I feared I wouldn't ever see *my* Andrei ever again.

Turning my sadness into a burning rage, I clenched my fists at my side as I realized what needed to be done.

Lo was right when she said this wasn't a game—this was war.

I was the fucking Queen of Sanguis now, and I'd use all my power to ensure I buried Jeoffrey six feet under.

Order book three, Bite of Vengeance, here: mybook.to/bite3

Order the final book, Bite of Justice, here: mybook.to/bite4

Turn the page for chapter one of Monsters Within, which is Alexandra's story!

OTHER BOOKS BY R.L. CAULDER

Curious about Alora's parents who run Hell in this world? Read their series here:

Monarchs of Hell (Completed Series)

Co-write with M Sinclair

Insurrection: mybook.to/Monarchs1

Imbalance: mybook.to/Monarchs2

Inheritance: mybook.to/Monarchs3

The Creatures We Crave

Monsters Within: mybook.to/MonstersWithin

Monsters Below: mybook.to/MonstersBelow

Monsters Above: mybook.to/MonstersAbove

The Vampyres' Source (Completed Series)

Co-write with M. Sinclair

Ruthless Blood: mybook.to/Ruthless1

Ruthless War: mybook.to/Ruthless2

Ruthless Love: mybook.to/Ruthless3

The Pack Prophecy (Completed Series)

Outcast: mybook.to/Outcast

Outlaw: mybook.to/OutlawPP

Oracle: mybook.to/OraclePP

Darkness Rising (Completed Series)

Desolation: mybook.to/Desolation

Detonation: mybook.to/Detonation

Devastation: mybook.to/DevastationDR

Monster's Naughty List (Standalone novella)

mybook.to/Naughtylist

Inferno (Standalone book)

Co-write with M. Sinclair

mybook.to/InfernoMC

Captured by the Monsters (Standalone book)

Co-write with M.J. Marstens

mybook.to/CapturedMonsters

ABOUT R.L. CAULDER

R.L. Caulder is a USA Today bestselling author who lives in her writing cave away from the intense heat of the Florida sun with her husband and furry writing assistants, MeowMeow and Winrey. Life is never boring for R.L., who has hundreds of imaginary friends constantly vying for her attention and begging for their stories to be told.

If you're looking for ways to interact with R.L., you can find her on Facebook in her group:
The Cauldron: R.L. Caulder Reader Group

THE CREATURES WE CRAVE: MONSTERS WITHIN

ALEXANDRA

I knew life wasn't sunshine and rainbows for everyone, but eventually the clouds always broke, revealing the sunlight once more for them. But in my case, the darkness that seemed to follow me never cleared.

I had learned a long time ago, life wasn't fair, and at some point, I just accepted it.

The only bright spot was when I was able to climb into my bed, crack open a spiral notebook, and forget reality even existed while being transported into the world I created when I put my pen to paper.

I poured all of my despair and desire onto those sheets. The ink was my pain, and the pages were my savior.

It's where I found myself now, contemplating

the events of the day and how I would cope with them. I was lounging on my bed in an oversized Aerosmith t-shirt I'd found at the thrift shop and some black sleep shorts.

Shoving the rest of my chocolate chip cookie into my mouth, I grabbed the plastic cup filled with the delicious delicacy known as RumChata. Taking a gulp of the cinnamon alcohol, I swallowed down the lump of cookie that lodged itself in my throat before setting the cup back down on my nightstand.

The alcohol had been given to me as a bribe to not tell on the girl across the hall for smoking a joint. I honestly didn't care what she did—I wouldn't have turned her in anyway, but I wouldn't turn my nose up at alcohol.

Despite not having any friends here, I kept to myself...it was just easier. My life had enough chaos without me creating enemies. I had my own shit to worry about. If the girl wanted to smoke pot to get through her days, who was I to judge? We all had our own ways of coping.

The RumChata left a trail of light heat in its wake as I reached for my black spiral notebook that had seen better days. The edges of the pages curled slightly from being bent a bit when I wrote at odd angles. Flipping to the next blank page near the back of the book, I realized that I would need to grab another one soon and add this full one to the plastic bin beneath my bed. That bin held the only things in the world I cared about, the only things that held any value for me.

As a ward of the state, I hadn't enjoyed many luxuries in life growing up. Even now, being on an academic scholarship for my junior year at a small private college, I wasn't afforded much. *The single dorm room was definitely a plus, though.*

I couldn't dwell on the fact that all the possessions I cared about could fit into one measly bin beneath my bed. One day, things would be different—that day just wasn't today. I was what you could call a "pessimistic optimist."

My scholarship covered my classes, school materials, boarding, and a small stipend for food. I'd be the first to admit I had a pretty shit diet. I wouldn't eat all day, then I'd use my budgeted allowance for the day to order a large pizza and cookies and binge eat as I wrote through the night.

Another terrible habit was my almost non-existent sleep schedule, and I often found myself cursing the first rays of morning light as they streamed in through my small window. They took me away from my fantasy world filled with delicious men I was unhealthily obsessed with, signaling that I'd once again be heading to classes running on fumes.

Often I dreamt of being one of the supernatural creatures of the world instead of an isolated, forgotten human stuck in an endless loop that kept reminding me of my place in life.

But unfortunately, this seemed to be the hand I'd been dealt. I just needed to find a way to make the most of it.

That didn't stop me, though, from checking my teeth to see if they'd elongated to sharp points like a vampire's, trying to conjure fire into existence in my hand like a witch, or wishing I'd grown a pair of demon horns overnight.

Maybe I was just a late bloomer in the supernatural community? At least, that's what I liked to tell myself when I found myself sinking in the bleakness of my life.

Grabbing a pen with a slightly gnawed black cap from my nightstand, I backed into the corner of my bed against the wall, a cozy space where I had my pillows arranged and smashed in a nest of sorts to engulf me. Drawing my knees up, I rested my notebook against them, closed my eyes, and tipped my head back to rest against the wall, thinking of where I would be transported to this time.

It was time to cut myself loose from reality and escape to the world between my pages. A world that inspired awe and forged hope within my soul. Hope that one day the world I lived in would be a better place.

My fantasy world was one in which I righted the wrongs of the world. Where the monsters most people were afraid of helped me hunt down the true bad guys—the humans.

Because I can assure you, my monsters were angels in comparison to the true evil that lurked in my reality. Humans just happened to wear skin suits that were more pleasing to the eye.

Closing my eyes, I allowed my mind to drift to the image of my monsters, sinking into the alternate life I'd created for myself.

At first, when I'd created them, there had been nothing beautiful about my monsters, but they had morphed in my mind over the years. Before I learned how to write, I drew them as faceless shadow creatures draped in the fabric of black cloaks with ripped edges at the bottom. They moved in the darkness, shifting with the shadows, undeniably hidden from the human eye.

Then, as I wrote them in stories instead of drawings, when they weren't traveling in the darkness, the lower halves of their bodies were still mostly swirling shadows, but there was a section in the middle of their chests that thrummed with a steady glow, like a human had their heart.

Each of my three monsters had a different color that emanated from the piece of them I liked to think of as their soul, spreading into their necks and up into their faces like veins beneath the surface.

Lucien was red.

Elwin was green.

Kylo was blue.

Then, to top it all off, they had four arms, two on each side, with razor sharp claws at the tips of their fingers. Some might find them disconcerting, being so devoid of humanoid features, but it's what I loved about them. What you saw was what you got, unlike humans.

I had met too many dark, ugly, twisted humans for me to trust them.

They'd smile to your face to placate you, whispering the words you wanted to hear, all while taking what they wanted before leaving behind a husk of a person.

The ones who stole.

The ones who raped.

The ones who thought they deserved everything simply because they breathed.

In my fantasy world, my monsters and I snuffed the arrogance and entitlement out of every single one of those fuckers. Sometimes discretion was needed, so, in addition to their monster forms, they had a human form so they could blend in with society and be at my side.

Which brought me to the task at hand. Opening my eyes, I thought of where I wanted to begin with this one. Today's chapter was about the Dean of Students who had lifted my skirt this afternoon and told me he'd forget the claims of me cheating on my essay if I *helped* him.

I hadn't cheated.

There was no need to when academics were a natural gift of my mind. The only way I was even able to attend this college was due to the academic scholarship I'd been awarded. Without it, I'd be on the streets without a penny to my name, like most kids after they aged out of the system.

There was definitely no way I'd risk any of that by cheating on a dumb creative writing essay that I could ace without struggling.

The problem was that Chloe Blufount didn't like that I continuously ranked above her for the top spot in the undergraduate class for English majors. Our creative writing professor instituted a public ranking board to encourage excellence, and with my talent for writing, I edged Chloe out every year. But Chloe was a girl who was used to getting her way, especially since her father's money usually got her everything else she wanted. He could buy her lip injections, lash extensions, a constant fake spray tan, and her continuously revolving hair colors, but he'd never be able to buy her top rank in our class.

I was proud of that.

So this was how she got me out of the way instead. Feeding the skeevy dean lies, knowing full well what his reputation was. Chloe was one of the monsters beneath a pretty human skin suit, offering me on a silver platter to a man who took what wasn't freely given, knowing I had no one to help me fight my battles other than myself.

In reality, I had smacked his hand away lightly, told him I'd take the zero on the assignment, and quietly left his office, not wanting to ignite the temper I'd heard about many times.

It finally came to me, how I wanted this scene to go. The specific way I wanted the dean to suffer. I let the ink glide on the page, closing my eyes and summoning my bloodthirsty monster to reenact the scene in the manner I truly wanted.

Lucien.

He'd slaughter for those he loved without blinking. Touch what was his and die a painful death as a result. It was that simple to him.

The scene was finally set. There I was, sitting with my legs crossed in the chair in front of the dean's oak desk, with the dean standing and leaning against the corner of it, eyeing me like a pig.

As Lucien stepped from the shadows in the corner of the office, his fingertips gleamed like freshly sharpened obsidian daggers. His form shifted as he approached slowly and intentionally, like a predator stalking his prey, confidence and danger radiating off of him in waves. His blood-red eyes with black slits were pinned on his target with unwavering intensity.

Truly, he embodied the creature of nightmares kids would fear coming from the shadowed corners of their rooms.

Just as the perv put his hand on my exposed leg and drew it up toward my skirt, as he had in reality, Lucien tutted at him. "That simply won't do. The only person allowed to touch my angel is me."

The dean stood, frozen in fear of my monster,

and I smiled wickedly when his beige dress pants darkened and the scent of urine permeated the air. All it took was Lucien's talons touching his skin in the faintest whisper of a touch.

The dean knew he had just become the prey.

The shadows on Lucien's face parted to reveal his lips as he smiled at the dean, putting his rows of sharp teeth on display. The dean screamed, begging for mercy, in the seconds before his hands were swiftly cleaved from his wrists.

Maybe that act should have scared me—it was what I truly wanted, and craving that type of violence wasn't normal. But instead, it unfurled a sense of justice and satisfaction within me, perhaps even a hint of desire toward Lucien for the vicious move.

Alright, it was more than a hint of desire.

It wouldn't be the first time their possessive and sometimes barbaric actions had turned me on. But it wasn't a surprise because I had written them to be exactly like that.

The thing was—my creations weren't just monsters. They were my soul mates, and I had created them to be extremely protective and territorial over me. Something I'd lacked in my life growing up. They all had distinctively different personalities, but their underlying love and need to keep me safe shone brightly through their shadowy depths.

The dean's screams echoed through the expanse of his office, but no one came to his rescue. No one could save him—he was damned from the start of my story.

He fell to his knees as blood poured in rivulets from his severed wrists, pooling beneath him in an ever-expanding crimson lake. Snot poured from his nose as he sobbed and begged, "Please, spare me. I'm sorry. I'm so sorry."

Narrowing my eyes as I stood from my chair, I planted the bottom of my boot on his chest before kicking him backward. "Too bad you won't be able to say sorry to all of your other victims," I sneered. Then, huffing out a dry laugh, I added, "Though, your death will be enough of an apology."

As the words left my lips, Lucien towered over the dean before ramming the tips of his pointer fingers into his eye sockets. The dean only screamed for a few seconds before the bliss of silence descended through the small office with his death.

I soaked the moment in, smiling smugly at his fate. He wouldn't be able to abuse his position of power again.

Meanwhile, Lucien retracted his talons from the

dean and grabbed a handkerchief from the desk, wiping off his top hands' talons with his lower two before tossing the rag onto the dean's body. Dramatically, he rolled his eyes and murmured, "I hate when they make me get my hands so dirty."

A true laugh burst from me as I called him on his bullshit. "You're such a liar. You get upset when you *don't* get to handle our situations this way," I reminded him as I leaned back onto the desk with my hands on the edge. "Though I'm sure Kylo and Elwin would love to hear if you're changing your ways," I added teasingly. "You'd make their lives so much easier."

It was his turn to laugh, and the sound truly made my heart skip a beat. I lived for their love and joy—it fed my own.

"Don't let Kylo lie to you either, angel," he rebutted. "He'd be bored if he wasn't constantly trying to contain my urges under the blood haze."

As Lucien came to float in front of me, leaning in close, I widened my eyes and fake pouted. "But what about poor Elwin who has to deal with calming Kylo down when you inevitably go against his commands?"

He paused as if truly giving it a thought before chuckling. "Yeah, I feel bad for the bastard, but we all know I'm not going to stop. No one fucks with you or my brothers and gets away with only a slap on the wrist."

The reminder of his wrath had my eyes falling down to the dean, and my body shivered at the memory of his touch on my leg.

Lucien sensed my distress, his voice dropping low as he whispered, "You're okay now, angel. He'll never touch you again. You are ours."

The possessiveness of his words, combined with the deep tones of his voice, made heat pool between my legs. An ache began to build, demanding I find a way to satisfy it.

I had yet to bring myself to cross the line of being intimate with my creatures as I wrote my stories, but today felt like the day that was going to change. I needed a little something extra to cheer me up after having to swallow my outrage at the dean's actions. I'd wanted to punch him in the mouth and tell him where he could shove it with his suggestions, but seeing as I couldn't give in to that desire... I'd give in to this one instead.

Keeping reading here: mybook.to/MonstersWithin